BEHIND THE REDWOOD DOOR
a Guy Mallon Mystery by

John M. Daniel

Oak Tree Press Taylorville, IL

Oak Tree Press

Oak Tree Press books may be purchased for educational, business or sales promotional purposes. Contact Publisher for quantity discounts.

First Edition, October 2011
Cover by Kurt Bredt
Interior Design by Linda Rigsbee

ISBN 978-1-61009-023-0
LCCN 2011932913

For Susan, with love, and
for Warren, our North Coast companion

ALSO BY JOHN M. DANIEL

Play Melancholy Baby
The Woman by the Bridge
One for the Books
Generous Helpings
The Poet's Funeral
Vanity Fire
The Ballad of Toby and Lark

AUTHOR'S NOTE

This is a work of fiction. Although I have borrowed the landscape and scenery of California's redwood coast for this book, all characters, events, and places—including Jefferson City and Jefferson County—are entirely imaginary, and no resemblance to actual characters, events, and places is intended.

As for this imaginary setting, imagine the smallest county in California, just north of Humboldt County and just south of Del Norte County. It is bordered on the west by the Pacific Ocean, and on the east the county line runs along the summit of the Jefferson Alps range. The county's main industries include lumber, fishing, and, of late, Indian gaming and marijuana cultivation.

Jefferson City, the county seat, is the only community of any size; its population is about twelve thousand. It is located on the coast, with a fishing harbor originally built in the eighteen-sixties.

CONTENTS

PART ONE
BOYS WILL BE BOYS

CHAPTER ONE

J ust as the sun was coming up on the morning of Friday, June 18, 1999, there was a break in the clouds, and Carol and I went out for a walk along the nature trail by the ocean, down the road from our house. The rising sun lit up the waves and brightened the snow-white egrets wading in the lagoon. The band-tail pigeons had come back to roost on the skeleton of their wind-whipped tree. And out there, over the ocean, we saw a pair of ospreys mating in the air, doing their circle dance for what seemed like ten minutes, then coming together high in the sky and clasping each other's claws as they went into a downward spiral, breaking their bodies apart just before they hit the water, then flying up and away together, heading for the forest to the south. "God," Carol said. "I want to do that!"

"Why not?" I said. "We don't have to be at the store till ten."

"I was hoping to get some weeding done in the garden this morning."

"Aw c'mon. You'd rather weed than—"

I was interrupted by a giant crack of thunder out over the Pacific. The sun disappeared behind clouds, and the rain began falling again. Hard.

"Well, so much for gardening," Carol said.

We grinned together and held hands as we ran back to the house and up the stairs.

An hour later, we were still in bed, listening to the rain pound our roof and the wind lash the side of our house with a pine tree.

"Well, you can't count on the weather on the redwood coast," I said, "but you can count on one thing: there will be weather."

"You miss the heat, don't you?" she asked. We had lived in Jefferson County for three years. We used to live in Santa Barbara, where it was warm most of the time, especially when the dry Santa Anas would blow out of the mountains. It was Carol's choice to move to the North Coast of California, and my choice to move wherever she went.

"No, I don't need the heat."

"Do you miss the publishing business?" She and I had owned, and been owned by, a small-press publishing business in Santa Barbara. We published poetry in limited editions. A gentle profession, you might think. Think again. In the line of duty as a publisher, I was threatened and chased by thugs in Las Vegas and marched through a tropical jungle at gunpoint by a cocaine smuggler, I had a ton of books dropped on my body by a religious fanatic, and had my warehouse burned down by an arsonist. I've had loud arguments with the police, who seemed to resent my solving murders and other crimes that they didn't want to bother with. Now that was behind us. Carol owned Scarecrow Books in Jefferson City, and I, at the age of fifty-seven, for the first time in my adult life, was largely unemployed. I helped out some in the bookstore, but not for pay.

"No, I don't miss publishing," I said.

"Are you sure?" she asked, taking my hand and holding it to her sweaty breast. "Because if you—"

"I don't need the heat," I said.

We had a good day at the store. The weather was foul outside, which meant we had only a sprinkling of customers throughout the day, and some of them came in only to get out of the rain. But it was a good day nonetheless. Carol spent a lot of time in the gardening section, and I weeded poetry. We closed the shop at six and walked under our umbrella two blocks to the Redwood Door, our favorite tavern on the town square of Jefferson City. We had dinner there every Friday evening.

The place was jammed with the usual noisy mix of laid-off loggers, furry fishermen, assorted North Coast artists, and small-town downtown riffraff. Down at the end of the bar was a mean-looking little man in a black wool watch cap, whom everyone called Nails; I say little, but he looked about five foot four, which made him four inches taller than me. Next to Nails sat his giant sidekick, Louie Luau, who looked as dumb as shoe leather. The two of them were there every Friday night, in the same seats. Maybe every other night too. According to Gloria, they were both fond of boilermakers, a shot of Yukon Jack washed down with a bottle of Anchor Steam. Nice guys, for all I knew, and I was always glad to see them from a distance, even if I would have been nervous if one of them were to ask me for a light.

We walked in and sat down on stools at the bar, and Gloria, the bartender, sauntered over and said, "Guy comes into a bar, and…"

It wasn't the first time Gloria had used this line, and Gloria was not the first bartender to say it every time I sat down on a bar stool. (Hint: never make a pun on a person's name. They've heard it before.)

"…and he and his lady order the usual beverages?" Gloria continued.

"Jim Beam me up," I answered. (I admit I use that one a lot myself.)

She turned to Carol and said, "Bombay?"

Carol smiled and said, "Bombs away." A new one. Carol still surprised me, every day.

Gloria poured with a heavy hand and set our drinks before us. Gloria was a hard-working lady who seemed to like owning a tavern. Her smile made her look thirty-five years old, but the lines around her eyes were more like fifty-five.

Carol and I toasted each other and winked as we sipped, then folded our hands on the bar and relaxed in the warmth of neon and chatter, waiting for our regular Friday-night dinner: oyster shooters, a bleu cheese burger split in two, and a Cobb salad, also split in two.

"Great place for a rainy night," I said.

"Of which we have our share in Jefferson County," Carol answered. "This time of year."

"What time of year is that?"

"The rainy season, January to December."

"You're not sorry you moved here? You miss Santa Barbara?"

Carol laughed. "Are you kidding? In Santa Barbara the sun shines all the time and all the beautiful people grumble, 'Another shitty day in paradise.' Here, there aren't any beautiful people, thank God, and when the sun shines everyone celebrates. Besides, I like rain. Nice weather for egrets, geese, forests, and worms in the garden."

Gloria brought us our oyster shooters and picked up our cocktail glasses for refills. I was just reaching for the Tabasco when I felt a heavy hand on my shoulder and heard a deep, friendly voice say, "Howdy, strangers."

Carol and I swiveled around on our stools and faced Pete Thayer, the lanky, grizzle-bearded editor of the *Jefferson Nickel.* He gave us each a squeeze and a kind smile.

"So where's your honey this evening?" Carol asked, referring to her good friend River Webster. River and her teenaged son, Freddy, were the last remaining members of the Webster family, one of the two families that founded Jefferson City, back in the eighteen-sixties. In addition to being a full-time single parent, River also owned the *Jefferson Nickel,* one of Jefferson City's two newspapers. The *Nickel* was a weekly.

The other newspaper, a daily called the *Jefferson Republican,* was owned by Seamus Connolly. Seamus and his teenaged son, Charles, were the last two remaining members of the Connolly clan, the other founding family of the city and county.

The families had hated each other for generations. The two newspapers were not on speaking terms.

Carol and I didn't take sides in a feud that had run out of gas before we came to town. Except to say that River Webster was a loving, gracious, generous soul, whereas Seamus Connolly was the town bully, a big shark in a small pond.

In addition to editing River's newspaper and writing all its editorial content, Pete Thayer was also River's lover.

"River's in the booth back in the corner. She's pretty upset, and I hope you two will come and have dinner with us. She needs some cheering up, and we need help finishing a bottle of Jefferson Red."

"That sounds great," Carol said, and I called Gloria over to let her know we were relocating.

When we reached the booth in back, River stood up, gave us both a shaky smile, and hugged Carol. She was a tall, handsome woman with a halo of brown curls surrounding a strong, kind face, but this evening that face had become fragile. "I'm so sorry, you guys. I'm not good company tonight, a real mess!" She did a mea culpa with her fist against her tie-dyed T-shirt.

Carol said, "River, what's wrong? Sit down, sit down."

We all sat, Pete and River on one side, Carol and I on the other. River wiped her eyes and tried to smile. "I'll be okay," she promised.

"Oh bullshit," Pete sputtered. "She's upset, and she should be. Goddammit. Freddy got attacked."

"Attacked?" Carol and I said it together.

"I'm probably over-reacting," River said. "Have some wine."

Carol asked, "What happened?"

River shook her head. "It's okay. Really."

"Come on, tell us. What happened?"

River downed her glass and poured herself another, while Pete waved to Gloria to have her bring another bottle. "Tell them, honey," he said.

River nodded.

"Last night," she began, "after midnight, so it was really early this morning, Sheriff Blue Heron pulled up in front of my house out on Bear Gulch Road, with the spinning red light flashing on top of his car. I was watching through my front window, because I was worried about Freddy, who hadn't come home from the movies. I wondered where he was, because that's what mothers do is worry, especially when the kid's fifteen and out with friends who have only been driving for a month. But I was too cool to call the sheriff about a teenager out late at night, and now here the sheriff was, getting out of his car and letting his passenger out of the back seat, and the passenger was dressed in an orange jump suit like a prisoner at the county jail, and the prisoner was Freddy. My crazy kid. Blue left the red light on and walked him to the front door. I let them both into the house and I'm like, 'What's going on? What's this all about?'

"The sheriff said, 'He won't tell me what happened. I expect you to get it out of him, and I want you to come to my office Monday morning so we can file a report. And I want that jump suit back. Now if you'll excuse me—'

"'Just a damn minute,' I said. 'Jesus, you can't just bring my kid home in a cop car and not tell me what this is all about.'

"He says, 'River, I have no idea. I could have booked your son here for indecent exposure, but I know it wasn't his fault. Now you get him to tell you what the hell happened, and we'll take it from there. I have to get back to the town square. They're doing a Solstice thing. It's a zoo down there. Bunch of total loonies.'

"So I mellowed out a bit. I offered Blue a joint for the road, he said he couldn't possibly do that, and I knew it. I reminded him it was legal. 'I have a grower's permit,' I said. He reminded me it wasn't legal for me to give it away, but of course he had a smile on his face and his hand held out, so I slipped him a little present from my bathrobe pocket.

"When the sheriff's car was out of sight I turned to my son and said, 'Okay, mister, what's going on? What's this about indecent exposure?'

"You know teenage boys. 'Nothing,' he says, says he wants to go to bed, and I'm all, 'Not till you tell me what happened,' and he goes, 'Can I at least change out of these stupid clothes?' I say no he cannot. 'Sit down at the kitchen table,' I told him. I said, 'Spill, kid.'

"He gave me a look like 'aw, Mom,' but he sat down, and I put on the kettle. Thing is, he wanted to tell me all right. It just took a little time; it's like once the ketchup starts coming out of a bottle? You know? Blood all over the plate.

"Anyway I guess Freddy and his best friend Mickey Chan were just getting out of the movie and they went to the food court of the Mall, which shouldn't even be there, and Freddy had a cheeseburger and fries because I don't serve garbage at home, and then they went out into the parking lot where Mickey had parked his car. But as they were about to get into Mickey's car, these three other kids, the biggest kids in Freddy's school, grabbed Freddy and carried him off with them and stuffed him in their own car."

"A certain new Jeep Cherokee I'm willing to bet," Pete said. "Because I am sure who was behind all this."

"Honey, don't make accusations," River said. "It doesn't really matter who did it. That's not the point."

"The hell it's not." Pete looked up and smiled at Gloria, who was advancing with a tray over her head. "Here comes our food."

Dinner was delicious, if you like greasy burgers and fries, and we were all hungry, so the four of us ate without talking for a while, until Carol could wait no longer. "Who?"

"Charles Connolly, right?" I said.

"Never mind who did it," River said.

Pete said, "You're right, Guy. Chunky Connolly."

"Nobody calls him Chunky anymore," River said. "He's Charles. He hasn't been called Chunky since kindergarten."

"When he used to rub Freddy's face in the sandbox. So it was Chunky. Charles, whatever. Chunky."

"Let it go, Pete."

"Then what happened?" I asked. "How did Freddy end up in a jumpsuit?"

Pete took over. "So these three big kids, who shall be nameless but whose initials are Chunky and his goons, stuff River's son in the back seat of Chunky's Cherokee and they take him to the Jefferson Marsh Wildlife Preserve, also known as the waste water reclamation plant. Here it is the middle of the damn night and they march Freddy out on the end a long trail between two holding ponds. When they get to the end of the trail, where the water reclamation plant meets Jefferson Bay, they start ragging on him because he's always preaching tolerance for the homeless who hang out on Jefferson Square, downtown. Freddy's like that. He's a kind human being, and he's always leading clothing drives, getting kids to give up half their lunches to be delivered to the homeless, trying to get the high school to interact in a meaningful way, because that kid is a saint. I'm sorry, but that's what he is, a saint.

"So these bastards, pardon me, but these teenage assholes strip Freddy stark naked, telling him it's time for him to give his clothes to the homeless on the square. Laughing at him. Calling him names I wouldn't dare print in the paper."

River slapped the table, then touched the back of his hand with her forefinger. "Pete, we've been through this. This story is not going in the paper. Forget it. I don't want to embarrass Freddy any more than he's already been."

Pete nodded. "Okay, not in the paper. Anyway. Left him there without a stitch on except for his Adidas. Ran back to Chunky's Cherokee and tore out of the parking lot, horn blasting like a big ugly laugh."

Pete Thayer was a born agitator, a muckraker, a rabble-rouser, a believer in moral outrage, and most of all: a writer.

"At least it wasn't raining," Carol said. "At least it was June, not February."

"But it was cold, colder than you'd want to be out naked in," River said. "Poor kid could have frozen to death. But Freddy did the sensible thing: he ran to keep warm. He ran right to the police station, which was over a mile, but head. "I want to go home. I left Freddy alone. He practically kicked me out of the house, but it's time for me to get back there." She put a hand on my cheek. "Thanks for listening to me babble."

"Are you going to be okay?" Carol asked.

River smiled at her and said, "Sweetie, I think it's time to get over this incident. I'll support Freddy whenever he needs me, but he doesn't seem to need me much anymore. Good night, you two."

CHAPTER TWO

T rue to his word, Pete Thayer did not name names. But true to his nature, he did not kill the story, either. The following Thursday, June 24, the *Jefferson Nickel* had a two-page spread feature on the subject of hazing. It was incendiary. He had interviewed Police Chief Wayne Marvin, Sheriff Blue Heron, and Principal Bud Bailey of Thomas Jefferson High and forced each of them to admit that there had been several reported incidents of hazing the previous academic year, starting with some traditional Halloween pranks and building to a pattern of malicious mischief that went on almost every weekend, weather permitting.

This juvenile crime wave could not be pinned on any one individual or gang; all that could be said was that some students found it disgusting, some found it frightening, and some found it hilarious fun. Nobody admitted to knowing any perpetrators.

As for the kidnapping incident, Principal Bailey reminded Thayer that since it had happened during summer vacation and not during the school year, the boys were not subject to school discipline. Pete reminded the principal that the school administration had looked the other way throughout the school year whenever hazing incidents happened, an accusation the principal denied.

Pete closed his piece with an impassioned plea for a full investigation:

I was a geeky dweeb in high school in the San Fernando Valley in the days of Ozzie and Harriet. I always hated Ricky Nelson because he was cool. But that wasn't his fault, and I knew that. The real kids to hate weren't even cool, they were so hostile.

I didn't have many friends, but every friend I had got pushed around by bullies. It wasn't just a matter of some big kid giving a small kid a wedgie or noogies in the hallway. It was gangs of big kids, doing their elephantine best to make individual smaller kids hurt—physically and emotionally. Sometimes it was vandalism, like slashed car seats or notebooks soaked in urine. More often it was verbal abuse and harsh laughter about a classmate's acne, his weight problem, his divorced parents, his inability to play team sports, or his hobbies from chess to cooking. One friend of mine was held down and his head was shaved because he had said in class how much he enjoyed The Catcher in the Rye. Another was bound naked to a bench in the boys' gym with adhesive tape and left there for the rest of the day until he was found by the custodian, who was a bully himself. Now and then the hostility would bloom into full violence, and a child would get bruised, cut, bloodied, sprained, even broken. One boy was shot with a BB gun while he was riding his bike through a suburban park; he was being targeted for still riding a bicycle at the age of fifteen. He fell off the bike, broke his neck, and was rushed to the hospital where he died the next day.

And nobody did anything about it. About any of it.

Some of those same bullies are still down in the San Fernando Valley, working in banks, real estate companies, insurance businesses, auto dealerships. They belong to the Rotarians (as I do) and go to church (as I don't), they have families now, and they watch sports like the rest of us. And they're still bullies. They're the reason I moved to Jefferson County, to get away from the bullies who made my life difficult in high school and made it utterly miserable for many of my friends.

So don't blame me if I am appalled and infuriated to hear about the rash of criminal hazing going on at the high school in my adopted home.

Something has to be done about this atrocity before another child is killed.

The following Monday I finally got to meet the famous Seamus Connolly in person. It was Monday afternoon, so I was working alone at the bookstore. I was up on the second floor, looking through books in the local history shelf in the California history section. I was enjoying the smell of old paper and dust—used bookstores smell entirely different from new bookstores—when I heard the sleigh bells on the front door jingle, telling me we had a drop-in. I trotted down the stairs and took my place behind the front counter.

No question who he was. His smiling face filled four column inches every day on the editorial page of the *Jefferson Republican*. I didn't read the *Republican* often, but Connolly's image was memorable: beefy, balding, and all-business. Now here he was in the flesh, smiling down at me, his arms folded across a stack of newspapers on the counter.

"Help you?" I offered.

"I'm delivering your papers," he said. "Where do you want me to put them?"

"Uh, we don't carry the *Republican*," I told him.

"I'll get you signed up. I got the distribution agreement out in my car. Where should I put these papers?"

"I don't think we want to carry the paper," I told him. "I'm sorry, but—"

"What the hell you talking about?" He was still smiling, one of those smiles you can buy at Wal-Mart. He pointed to a stack of last week's *Jefferson Nickel* on the end of the counter. "You carry that piece-of-shit rag."

"Yeah, so—"

"Don't your customers deserve a balanced diet when it comes to news in this town?"

"Well, it's not really—"

"Listen my little friend." I looked up into his face and wondered what had happened to that smile. "You're a businessman, right?"

"Not particularly."

"Yeah. Well I can give you a lesson in business. Listen up. Every copy you sell of my paper, you're going to earn twenty-five cents. You'll probably sell a dozen copies a day. Three bucks a day, enough for your latte or your yogurt or your wheat germ or whatever, and the *Republican* is a daily. How much income does the *Nickel* bring you in a week?"

I shook the coffee mug next to the *Nickels*. "Feels like about seventy-five cents, but that all goes to charity."

The smile was back. "Can I talk man-to-man with you?" he asked.

"I'm a man," I answered. "Talk."

"That paper's all bullshit. Pete Thayer's an idiot. Now you may say my paper's bullshit and I'm an idiot, but that's what's good about America. Every idiot gets to say what he wants, am I right? Don't bother to answer. I know we agree about that. All I want is equal space. How about we put my paper right here, next to Pete's." He shoved his stack over until it abutted and towered over what was left of the *Jefferson Nickel.*

"It's not up to me," I said. "I've been trying to tell you that. I don't own the store."

"Who does?"

"My wife. Carol Mallon."

"Where is she?"

"Gardening. I'm minding the store today."

"And you can't make a simple business decision like this? I thought you said you were a man. I was hoping we could see eye to eye."

"To do that I'd have to climb on a stool."

Seamus Connolly laughed out loud. "How short are you anyway?"

"I'm not short," I answered. "I'm five feet. Tall."

He chuckled again. "Okay, kid," he said. "I'm going to leave this stack of papers here, gratis, and your boss-lady can make the decision. If she doesn't want to carry a real newspaper for a change, that's her funeral, and she can throw them away. Oh. Excuse me. I mean she can recycle them. But not till she reads this morning's editorial. I'm trying to get my word out. I'm entitled to equal time. Good day, my friend."

He jingled his way back out the door, and I opened up a copy of the *Republican* to the lead editorial, right under the smiling face of the tall publisher I'd just talked man-to-man to.

BOYS WILL BE BOYS, SO THEY CAN BE MEN

I don't usually indulge in debating through newspaper editorials. I know there are two sides to every issue, and even when I'm dead sure I'm right I think another person—specifically another newspaper publisher—has every right to be wrong. I also want you to know I happen to like Peter Thayer. He's a good guy. We're fellow Rotarians, we both root for the Giants, and we both depend on a successful, growing business climate in our wonderful county, even if he doesn't know it or won't admit it.

But I really must take issue with his namby-pamby doe-eyed discourse on teenage high jinks. Hazing? What hazing? I've heard a few rumors, and to me it all sounds like teasing, practical jokes made in the spirit of fun.

Pete, come on. It may not be politically correct for me to say this, but boys will be boys. And it's a good thing. Boys should be boys. (Consider the alternative.)

It may surprise you, Pete, as it will surprise a lot of my readers, I'm sure, to learn I was a nerd in high school too. I warmed the bench for the football team, the Jefferson Sharks, four years in a row, never got to play unless Jefferson was at least thirty points ahead of the competition. And I got razzed for it. I got thrown into the school fountain every year on my birthday. There were times I wanted to cry.

But I didn't cry, and now I'm glad it happened.

Why? Because that's what made me tough, able to stand up tall and p—— with the big boys. It's all about stronger boys helping weaker boys get stronger, so that when they get to be men, they'll be real men. Real red-meat (sorry, there I go being politically incorrect again), six-pack (oops!), hair-on-your-chest (sorry, ladies), grownups. The kind of grownups it takes to make this city, this county, this state, and (though you'd never know it judging by the present administration) this nation great.

At the heart of it all is competition. If we pamper the sissies, they'll always be sissies, and I doubt if any sissy is happy about being that way. I started off as a sissy, an over-privileged rich kid who had never even been in a fistfight, but that all changed when got to high school. I took my lumps, I learned to compete, and by the time I graduated I wasn't a sissy in any man's book. If it took a little "hazing" to kick the sissy in me out the door, so be it and thanks, fellas.

So come on, Pete Thayer. Give it a rest, give me a break, give us a wink and a smile, and let's allow boyhood competition do its part to make America great.

I had just finished reading the editorial and was folding the newspaper when the author of the piece stormed back through the jingling door. "I gotta use your phone," he said, louder than necessary. "I got two flat tires out there."

"Bad luck," I said. "You want to call Triple A?"

"Triple A my ass. Bad luck my ass. I'm calling the police. Give me your damn phone."

"The police don't change tires," I pointed out. I handed him the receiver and turned the phone around so he could dial 911.

When he was done talking to the police, I walked out with him to the curb to inspect the damage. Sure enough, somebody must have let the air out of the two back tires of his BMW. "Fuckin bums," he muttered.

"Bums?" I looked at the bumper sticker midway between the two flat tires: "IMPEACH PRESIDENT CLINTON—AND HER HUSBAND TOO."

"On the town square, two blocks away. My family built that square for the people of Jefferson City, over a hundred years ago. Now look at it. Bums. They know whose car this is. They knew what they were doing."

I was teased a lot when I was in school, too. The biggest kids used to pick me up and hurl me between them as if I were a medicine ball. It didn't teach me to be any bigger.

"God damn bums," Seamus repeated.

"Boys will be boys," I said.

Only a few other customers came into the store during the rest of the afternoon, so I had plenty of time to browse and poke around in the local history books. Most people already know about our rocky coast, our redwood forests, our towering Jefferson Alps. The history's just as wild.

On the top shelf of our local history section, back in the part of the room where the light is poor, I found four copies of a book called *A Long, Long Crime Ago: A History of Jefferson County,* by one Donald Webster, published in 1927. I stood on a stool and pulled a copy off the shelf, blew a cloud of dust off the top, and carried the stool out into a better-lit aisle, where I sat down and began to read and look at old photos and maps.

On Thursday, July 1, the *Jefferson Nickel* hit back. Pete wrote an editorial for that issue, all about the phrase "politically correct." I quote:

Whenever I hear someone apologize for not being "politically correct," I know two things. First, I know the apology is not sincere. Second, I know that the speaker is assuming a license to deliver an unacceptable and insensitive remark about someone else's race, gender, faith, appearance, age, profession, politics, nationality, sexual preference or another target of prejudice. "Forgive me for being politically incorrect" means, in effect, "I'm rude and proud of it." Well, forgive me for being politically correct, but that sucks.

So the following day, of course, there was a letter to the editor of the *Jefferson Republican*:

My little boy, Fieldmouse, has zits on his butt, okay? Well, some of the other boys in his high school class saw him in the shower and they laughed at the zits on his butt, okay? Well that's really, really not very nice. How would you like to have zits on your butt? Fieldmouse can't help it. Those boys deserve to be in San Quentin, and I'd be happy to drive them there in my Volkswagen bus.
(signed) Rabbit Webfoot

"Aw Jesus," Carol said, when she read that over lunch. "These people really need to get a life."

"Well, I suppose this is just what they call high jinks. Teasing, right?"

"That's fine," Carol said. "Until somebody gets killed."

CHAPTER THREE

"Happy Friday the thirteenth," River Webster said, holding her tequila glass up and clinking it against Carol's gin, then my bourbon.

"Another hot August night," I said. "As Neil Diamond once said."

"It's hardly hot out there," Carol said. "It's really chilly out there."

"Hardly happy, either," River added. She downed the shot and waved her fingers at Gloria, who was washing glasses at the other end of the bar. "And here's to Pete Thayer, darn him. Damn him. God damn him." River smiled sadly into the mirror behind the bottles.

Gloria brought the Cuervo bottle and filled River's glass. "That's number three, honey," she said. "I'm keeping count."

"I love you," River told Gloria. "You take good care of me." She took off her purple hat and placed it on her lap. The hat slipped off her lap and fell to the floor.

We were seated at the end closest to the front door. The bar makes a right-angle turn there, and River was on the corner, with Carol and me on either side of her. That way Carol and I could have eye contact with each other and with River without twisting our necks off. From where I sat I could also watch the other drinkers all along the bar.

"What's going on with you and Pete?" Carol asked. "You two are having some trouble?"

"Irreconcilable differences. We just think differently is all. Which is okay, God knows, I mean it's a great big world with room for all kinds of people, but a relationship isn't a great big world, and neither is a newspaper, and I think I need another shot, just one more. Yeah. Bottom line. We broke up." River put fingers to her eyes, then smiled sadly, first to Carol on her left, then to me on her right. She put her hand on the side of my face and gave my cheek a little squeeze.

"Too bad," I said. "Breaking up is the pits."

"That too," River agreed. "I mean I love the man dearly, and he makes me laugh, but the problem's mostly about business. Okay, double whammy, business and pleasure. I don't know whether to fire him or kill him. Just kidding." Seeing Gloria at the cash register, River tapped her shot glass on the bar and called, "Little help here, Gloria?"

Carol and I didn't ask any more questions, but that didn't stop River Webster from answering them. "He's doing this big exposé of the fishing industry. He won't tell me what it's really about, is the problem, because for crying out loud I own the paper and I don't want him using it as his own personal murder weapon. Gloria!"

Gloria sauntered over and wiped the bar in front of River while she filled her shot glass with Jose Cuervo. "Last one, honey," she said.

"Okay. After this one I'll switch to beer."

"O'Doul's," Gloria said.

"Whatever. I can't tell the difference at this point." Tears began to leak from River's eyes and crawl over her cheeks. "Shit."

Carol put an arm around River's shoulders.

"He won't tell me what he's writing about. Says it's for my own protection," River said. "Then he goes and tells me he's going to stick it to the Connollys once and for all, like he's doing me a favor by opening up old wounds. He doesn't get it. He just doesn't get it."

"I've been reading up on the Webster-Connolly feud," I said. "The Connollys sound like scoundrels, but that's all in the past."

"Not that Seamus is any prince of a fellow," Carol remarked.

River nodded. "Or Chunky either, but that's not the point. The point is, it's a small town and a small county and we have to get along with our neighbors. Right? Even if our neighbors don't have any interest in getting along with us? Right? Peace has to start somewhere, right?"

"You're a saint, River," Carol said. "Now what's all this about the fishing industry, and what's that got to do with the Connollys?"

River shrugged and shook her head. "Pete seems dead set on putting the fishing fleet out of business. Mister big-shot muckraker." She finished her shot and licked the inside of the glass, then laid it on its side on the bar and rolled it back and forth between her hands.

"Pete has something against fishermen?" Carol asked.

"Some fishermen," River answered. "Certain fishermen who shall remain nameless." She turned her head and nodded to the far end of the bar, at the back of the room, where Nails and Louie Luau were knocking back boilermakers. "Pete doesn't approve of the way they fish, like he knows anything about it."

"I assume you're talking about his catch-and-release issue?" Until I'd read what Pete Thayer had to say about catch-and-release, I'd never given it any thought. But the more I thought about it, the more I agreed with him. Still. "I don't get the connection. What's it got to do with the Connollys?"

"I have no idea, and I don't want to know," River said. "Either he kills the story, or I will. I'm going to shut down the paper before this gets out of hand, if I have to."

"I can't imagine this town without the *Jefferson Nickel*," Carol said.

"Me neither," River said. "Or the *Jefferson Nickel* without Pete Thayer. Or me without Pete Thayer. But that's enough whining. You two have another drink, and I'll get Gloria to bring me that beer. Time to put on our happy face." She gave us each a mock smile, then a real one. "Don't worry about me. I've been through worse, than this, and Pete was a joy to love while he lasted. Twelve years. Not bad." She reached into her straw bag and pulled out a change purse. She emptied it onto the bar and slid a heap of quarters in my direction. "How about some tunes?"

I spun my stool around and dropped to the floor. I walked over to the jukebox, fed it all the quarters, and punched a bunch of buttons. "Harbor Lights" by the Platters was the first up; I picked that one for the gentlemen in the back of the room, but I doubt if they knew the song or liked it or even heard it. I returned to the bar, retrieved River's hat from the floor, and handed it to her. She threw it back on the floor. I climbed back up onto my stool. Gloria had refreshed my drink.

I felt a hand on my shoulder and heard the words, "Hey, folks." I turned my head and saw Pete Thayer standing behind our threesome, one hand on my shoulder, one on Carol's shoulder, and his bearded chin nuzzling the top of River's head. River waved his chin away as if it were an insect. She did not look up from the bar, where she was playing table hockey with her shot glass.

"Friday night at the Redwood Door," Pete observed. "Quite a routine you guys have."

I didn't know whether or not to invite him to join us, but I caught a coded message from Carol's face that told me it wasn't a good idea. (Mental telepathy comes in handy, as long as you don't want to keep secrets from the one you love. Carol and I don't keep secrets from each other; I tried once, and it doesn't work.)

Pete shrugged and agreed with himself. "Yep, quite a routine. Well, I see some fellows I've got to say howdy to, so—"

"You do that, Pete," River muttered. "You do that."

Pete Thayer gave my shoulder a squeeze and he winked at me. What an ancient, wise face that man had: understanding eyes, a smile that carried both joy and sorrow, an untrimmed hedge of gray beard, and thick eyebrows arched in constant surprise. He ambled off, patting the backs of friends as he made his way to the far end of the bar.

The smell of burgers and grilled onions gave me a nudge, and I said, "Well, I guess we ought to think about ordering something to eat?"

"I'm not hungry," River said, "but you two go ahead. I'll just mooch a few of your fries. Gloria!"

Down at the other end, Pete was sitting next to Nails, and they appeared to be in a conversation, except from what I could tell, Pete was doing all the talking. Figures. So far I had never heard Nails say a word, or Louie Luau either, for that matter. Nails was nodding, though, or maybe just bobbing his head like a toy turtle.

Gloria appeared before us, and Carol said, "Guy and I want to order some dinner."

"The usual?"

"Yeah. Start us off with the oysters. Bring the burgers with our next drink."

"You got it," Gloria said.

River said, "And my beer. Not O'Doul's. A real beer."

"Honey, I can't serve you any more alcohol. I know you're driving."

"Gloria, I know my way home like the back of my hand." She held up her hand, palm up.

Gloria smiled and pinched River's cheek. "You know I love you, baby. I'll bring you a cup of coffee."

"Okay."

Gloria picked up River's shot glass and sashayed away, then returned with a cup of black coffee. We all stopped talking for a while. I was the first to notice that Pete and Nails had both left their places at the bar. Carol saw me looking that way, and she turned around to see what had caught my attention. Then River looked. "Hmmm," she said. Louie Luau was by himself, stealing French fries from Nails's plate and sticking them one by one into the neck of the ketchup bottle before popping them into his mouth. When the French fries were all gone, he stood up and walked toward the back of the tavern.

"Twelve years," River Webster repeated. "Twelve beautiful years, sort of."

"How did you get to know him?" Carol asked.

"He came up from Berkeley back in nineteen-eighty-seven," River said. "I need some cream for this coffee. He came up to do an article about the Steelhead Rancheria for *In These Times,* just in time to see the shit hit the fan. That's a whole nother story, and I don't want to get into it. Seems like just yesterday, seems like a million years ago." She drummed her fingers on the bar. "God damn it, where's Gloria? So Pete decided to stick around after we lost the

Steelhead Rancheria to Seamus Connolly, and I got him involved with all the local lefties, and pretty soon we had a paper. Well, I had a paper, okay, but I wouldn't have started the paper without him as the editor. And writer. And ad salesman. Oh the hell with it, I'll drink it black."

Gloria brought the oyster shooters and we all stopped talking for a while. River sipped her coffee, then glanced to the far end of the bar. "I wonder what happened to Pete and those guys. It's been like twenty minutes. What the hell's going on, other than it being none of my business. I'm going to go find out."

She stood up, stumbled, grabbed the stool and steadied herself, then weaved her way to the back of the room.

"Do you think she'll be all right?" I asked Carol.

"She'll have a hangover and a heartbreak," Carol answered. "Poor lady. Here comes our dinner."

I was finished with my half of our bleu cheeseburger when I looked down the bar again. Louie Luau and Nails were still gone, and Gloria had cleaned up their corner. Carol turned and looked. "Where did everybody go?" she asked.

"Beats me. It's like the Bermuda Triangle back there. Do you think the four of them are in the back room playing pool?"

"Not likely, for several reasons, chief among them being that the Redwood Door doesn't have a back room. Kitchen, bathrooms, and that's it. Maybe they're out in the parking lot behind? Smoking cigarettes? Getting stoned? I'm done with the salad. Let's trade plates."

The scream was so loud I bobbled the salad plate and dropped oily lettuce all over my lap.

"Jesus Christ, he's been murdered!"

The room stopped chattering. Suddenly you could hear the basketball game on the television competing with "Shrimp Boats" on the jukebox. Gloria picked up a couple of remote controls and silenced them both. The Redwood Door was filled with a very loud hush. From where I was sitting, all I could see was the backs of people's heads. Everyone was staring, watching the woman at the back of the tavern. Waiting.

River Webster appeared frightened, furious, wild, and very sober. She opened her trembling mouth and shouted, "Gloria, call nine-one-one. *Now!*"

Then she turned and disappeared into the dark corridor that led to the back door of the tavern.

The chatter returned to the room, sounding like a garbage disposal going full blast. I put my hand on Carol's arm, to ask her: *Was that for real? Who was murdered? And most of all…*

Carol turned her face to me and answered with a nod: *You'd better get on back there.*

I nodded and got down off my stool.

I shoved open the back door and walked out into the mist. The tiny three-car parking lot and the alley behind it were lit by a dim yellow floodlight. River rushed into my arms and hugged me around the neck, sobbing and snuffling. I held her gently, stroked her hair, hummed to calm her down, and finally she let me breathe. She backed away enough for me to see her anguished face hiccupping and gasping in the mist, then pointed at the body slumped against the brick back wall of the Redwood Door.

Pete Thayer sat on the wet asphalt, his back against the bricks, his head and shoulders propped up by the side of a Dumpster. The expression frozen on his face was one of shock and disbelief. His throat was gashed wide open, with the bloody handle of a large kitchen knife still protruding from the wound. His sequoia-green sweater was soaked with black blood.

"Guy, what are we going to do?" River stammered. "What the fuck are we going to do?"

"Gloria called. The police will be here soon. They'll know what to do," I said.

"No they won't. The police don't work after dark in this town."

"The sheriff, then."

"No he won't."

"Where are the others? Those fishermen?"

"Gone," River said. "Poof. Gone."

"Did you see them leave?"

"I didn't see anything or anyone. I came out the door, and that's what I saw. Oh God, Guy, what, what what what—"

She was in my arms again, bawling like a baby. "My sweet Pete! Guy, is it okay for me to take that horrible knife out of his throat, maybe clean him up a little? Poor Peter!"

"No, River. Sorry. Let Sheriff Heron take care of that. He'll be here soon."

River broke out of my arms and started pacing around the parking lot. She came to rest leaning against the only car in the lot, a midnight blue BMW.

The door opened behind me and I turned to see Carol emerge. She nodded to me, then glanced at the body, then crossed the lot to embrace the woman who was trembling with fury and fear. With no words, she led River back into the bar and left me alone to wait for the sheriff.

The heavy mist had turned into a light rain, which was gently washing the victim's face and wound. I shivered in the chill, but I couldn't leave the scene, so I paced in a circle to keep warm. At the end of my third lap I found myself staring at the back end of the midnight blue BMW, reading the bumper sticker: "IMPEACH PRESIDENT CLINTON—AND HER HUSBAND TOO."

The back end of the car was lower than it should have been, and I checked, knowing what I'd find: two flat tires in the rear.

It felt like forever, but it was probably only a couple of minutes more before I heard the sheriff's car barreling down the alley behind the Redwood Door. It turned into the lot and came to rest beside the BMW, and Sheriff Blue Heron got out without shutting off his engine.

Blue Heron was a tall, fat Steelhead Indian with a gentle, intelligent face. I was predisposed to like the man because he was a reader; he bought at least a book a week from Carol's store, and they weren't all westerns. Well, most of them were westerns, I guess, but good westerns.

He held out his hand and said, "Hi there, Guy. What are you doing out in all this weather?"

I shook his hand, then pointed at Pete Thayer's body.

"You do this? Just kidding. Aw, Jesus. Aw, Jesus." Blue walked over to the dead man and squatted down for a closer look, shining a spotlight on the anguished face and the gory mess below. "Aw, Jesus."

He stood back up and walked back to where I was standing. "You're shivering," he observed. "Here." He opened the passenger side of his car. "Get in the vehicle," he said.

I did as I was told and he walked around and got in behind the steering wheel. He lifted the car phone and punched a couple of buttons. "Yeah," he said. "I'm in the parking lot behind the Redwood Door. We have a unique-type situation here. You're going to have to wake up the police department. We need an ambulance, we need a coroner, and we need somebody who can act like a detective....Now...No, now...I don't care, now...Never mind that. We need a dusting kit, crime scene tape, all that shit. Oh, and save me some of that pizza." He hung up the phone.

Blue Heron let out a giant sigh. "So, Guy, tell me what's going on here. Everything you know. Your turn. Go."

"The dead man, that's Pete Thayer, publisher of the *Jefferson Nickel*."

"Tell me something I don't know. Who killed him?"

"I don't know that."

"Any ideas?"

"No good ones."

"Tell me some bad ones."

"I really don't know," I said. "I mean, I don't want to say something stupid."

"Say something, anything. When did you last see Pete Thayer alive?"

"By now I don't know how long ago that was, but it was inside the bar."

"And what was he doing at the time? Who was he with?"

Blue Heron fired questions at me, and I started answering, first in short sentences and then building up to paragraphs about this horrid Friday night. I told him everything I knew, including what River said about Pete's plans to expose the fishing industry for catch-and-release cruelty, River's distress over losing her lover and maybe firing her editor and maybe shutting down her newspaper, and the strange disappearance of Nails and Louie Luau.

Blue Heron did not take notes. "That's it?" he asked when I was done.

"That's whatever it is," I said. "Except to say I'm going to miss that man a lot."

"Me too, I guess. Now, do you carry a cell phone?"

"Hell no."

The sheriff opened up a compartment on the dash and gave me a quarter. "I want you to go inside and use the pay phone in the back hall. Call Seamus Connolly up. I don't know the number. He's in the book, okay? Tell him his vehicle is parked behind the Redwood Door, and the two rear tires are flat. Ask him what he wants you to do about it. Don't tell him anything else. You got that? Don't tell him anything else. Then report back to me."

I stepped out of the car. It was raining harder now, so I ran to the back door of the tavern and ducked inside. I found the Connolly phone number in the book that was hanging by a chain from the pay phone. I called. It rang eleven times.

I hung up and went back out into the rain, where I found an ambulance and a police car clogging the alley behind the lot. The sheriff was standing beside a uniformed officer, and they were both shining their flashlights on the corpse.

"Excuse me," I said.

The policeman said, "Sir, please go back inside. We're very busy here."

The sheriff chuckled and said, "What did you find out?"

"No answer," I said.

"Shit. I was afraid of that. Okay, listen, Guy. I want you to go back in there and make sure River Webster gets home safely. Can you do that for me?"

"You don't want to talk to her?"

"I'll be talking to her in the next couple of days. And you too. And your wife. Don't leave the area till I say it's okay. We all have a lot of talking to do. Now get out of here so I can talk to this officer and take care of a few details."

The tavern was nearly empty when I got inside. Nothing like the word "murder" to clear the room. I didn't see River Webster at the bar or in any of the booths.

I didn't see Carol, either.

I asked Gloria if she knew where River and Carol were, and she poured me a Jim Beam on the rocks. "They left," she told me. "River was in no shape to drive. She was sober, but she was a complete train wreck. So Carol drove her home, in River's pickup truck. She told me to tell you you're on your own, and she'll call you tomorrow morning so you can go out to River's place and pick her up. So. How are you doing, Guy?"

"I'm okay."

"You sure?"

"No."

"What happened out there, Guy? Out back? Can you tell me?" Gloria's face was twitchy, and she was strangling her dishtowel.

"Pete Thayer was stabbed in the throat with a kitchen knife. He's dead. The sheriff and some cops and an ambulance are cleaning up the mess. Pour me another."

As I drove home it occurred to me that if somebody wanted to kill Pete Thayer (and somebody did), would that person want to kill River Webster, too? Because if somebody wanted to kill River Webster, they'd know exactly where to find her. They might even be there waiting for her to arrive. Her and Carol.

But when I reached home, I found the lights were on and River's truck was parked out front. I walked into the house, and there in the living room sat two beautiful women, very much alive and very much drunk, a bottle of gin and a bottle of tequila on the coffee table between them. They were both crying, and I was so happy to see them alive that I felt like crying, too.

The next morning, River wept her way through a breakfast that consisted of four cups of coffee and a banana. Her hand shook, her lower lip trembled, and she rubbed her eyes with the heels of her hands, whimpering, "Shit, shit, shit shit shit!"

We didn't talk about Pete Thayer.

We didn't talk about the Connollys or about Blue Heron or about Nails or Louie Luau. River only talked about her ferocious hangover, and Carol and I said nothing. But I knew that River's mind, like mine, was full of the bloody body of that firebrand friend of ours, slumped like a gunny sack next to the

Dumpster, on the wet asphalt of the dimly lit parking lot behind the Redwood Door. The knife.

After breakfast she went into the downstairs bathroom, where she stayed long enough to worry Carol and me; but when she emerged, she wore a fragile smile and fresh lipstick. "I'm okay," she said. She went into our living room and put on her floppy purple hat. She repeated, "I'm okay. I have to go home. Thanks, you two."

Carol hugged her and asked, "Are you okay to drive?"

River thought a moment. "I guess," she said.

"Not good enough," Carol said. "Guy, you should follow her home."

"Okay," I said.

River said, "You don't have to."

"I want to."

"Thank you. Thank you both, so much. Aw shit." But she controlled her face, forced the smile back on, and led the way out our front door.

I followed River Webster's pickup truck north on Highway 101 until she took the exit for Bear Gulch Road. She led me twenty miles up the curvy road into the foothills of the Jefferson Alps. This far inland there was no trace of coastal fog, and it was a sunny, late-summer day. The road took us in and out of the deep shadows of redwood forest pockets, alternating with sunlit meadows full of golden grass, where sheep grazed. Just before the road began to climb steeply into the mountains, River turned right and led me down a narrow paved lane bordered by redwoods and thick ferns.

When we emerged from the copse we drove through a white gate and onto a gravel driveway in front of a faded Victorian house that appeared to lean slightly to the left. It was a three-story mansion with a front porch, a tower, a bay window on the right side, and gables galore. Parked in front of the walkway to the front porch was a black Jeep Cherokee.

River parked her pickup behind the Cherokee, and I parked behind her. We both got out and stretched.

"Is that your Jeep?" I asked.

She gave me a frown. "No way. I need you to come inside with me. I'm not sure I can handle this by myself."

"Handle what?"

"Come on. Please."

She led me up the walk and onto the porch, then through a dark paneled front hall and into a parlor. The parlor was a lovely room, or had been and perhaps could be again: a stone fireplace, redwood wainscoting, flower-print wallpaper, glass-fronted bookcases, overstuffed chairs, oak tables, a grand piano, and an Oriental carpet full of a busy, rich, dark design.

At the far end of the room, on the window-seat of the bay window, sat two teenage boys, a bong sitting between them. One boy was slender as a ballerina, the other built like a side of beef. The slender kid looked up and said the minimum. "Mom."

River did not answer him and instead addressed the beefy boy, who wore a dopy, arrogant grin. "Chunky, what are you doing here?" she asked.

"Me? I'm just kickin' with my main man here. Hi, River."

"You may call me Miss Webster," River said.

The big kid turned to his main man and asked, "That okay with you?"

The other boy shrugged and giggled.

The beefy boy stood up and hooked his thumbs in his jeans. "See, I figured it might be kind of a sensitive issue type-thing," he said. "Having a mother called 'miss.'"

River took off her hat and threw it on the sofa. "Chunky, you have to go now. There's something I need to talk to Freddy about."

"His name is Charles, Mom," Freddy said. "Jesus."

Charles strode across the carpet and offered me his hand. "Hi," he said. "Charles Connolly."

I shook his hand. It was massive and hot. "Guy Mallon," I said.

"Oh, yeah. I figured that was you. The bookstore guy?"

"Chunky, Charles, whoever you are, I want you to leave," River said, a tremble in her voice. "Now."

Charles nodded, as if to a reggae beat, and said, "That's cool." He turned to Freddy. "Later on, Frito." Then to me. "Nice to meet you." Then, "Bye, Miss Webster. Enjoyed talking with you." He sauntered out of the room, and then we heard the front door close and his Cherokee kick in with a series of explosions. Through the front window we watched him spray gravel as he pulled a U-ey and sped away.

"God, Mom," Freddy asked, standing up, "what the fuck was that all about?"

"Sit down, Freddy."

The boy sat down. He picked up the bong and said, "You want a hit?"

"Not just now. Freddy, this is Carol's husband, Guy Mallon."

Holding the bong in his left hand, Freddy stood up and offered me his right. He looked over my head as we shook, and his fingers felt like a handful of cold French fries.

"Let's all sit down," River said. "Please. I have something important to tell you."

Freddy sighed and sat back down on the window-seat. He picked up a pack of matches.

"Not now, Freddy."

He placed the bong on the seat next to him and threw the matchbook across the parlor. "What?"

"Let's go in the kitchen," River said.

"What?" Freddy repeated.

"In the kitchen. We can talk better there."

So we followed River into the kitchen and we sat at the kitchen table.

"What."

She took a deep breath and held it, then let it out. "Darling, I have some awful news." The heels of her hands were back on her eyes.

"What."

"Pete died last night."

"Pete who? You mean our Pete?"

River nodded into her cupped hands.

Freddy looked at me with huge eyes. "This true?"

"Fraid so," I said.

"How? I mean, shit, I mean—"

River lifted her fragile face. "He was murdered. Stabbed to death, downtown. He's gone, Freddy. Our Pete is dead. Murdered."

"Jesus Christ!" the boy cried. Suddenly he looked no more than twelve years old. "He was right!"

"Who was right?" I asked.

But Freddy didn't stay around to answer. He stood up and rushed to the kitchen door, which he opened with a yank, then slammed his way outside.

River wept. I put my hand on her shoulder and said, "Do you know who he's talking about?"

"Pete, probably," she said between hiccups. "Peter Thayer was like a father figure. He's the one who got Freddy interested in the homeless. Would you go out there and talk to him, Guy? He won't talk to me, poor kid."

"Why do you think he'll talk to me?"

"He'll like you. You kind of look like a kid yourself."

Bullshit, I thought. *I just look short.* But I did as I was asked and went outside through the kitchen door. I walked across the lawn to the other side of the backyard, where I found Freddy sitting on a stone bench with his fists tucked underneath his black T-shirt. His right knee was bouncing like a jackhammer.

I sat down next to him. The sun was hot on my head, and the air smelled as if a skunk had died nearby. "I guess this must be pretty rough on you."

"Mmm." He didn't look at me. I don't think he was looking at anything, even if his eyes were wide open.

"I mean I never knew my own father, but still...." Then I ran out of gas. I was talking bullshit, and I had no idea what to say next. So I winged it. "You said, 'He was right.' You mean Pete? Did Pete tell you he was in danger?"

Freddy shook his head slowly. "My best friend, supposedly." The knee stopped pumping. He pulled his hands out from under his shirt and rubbed his face. "Shit."

"Best friend," I repeated. "As in Pete?"

Freddy stood up and finally looked me in the face. "You don't know shit," he said. "And you're better off that way. Don't open a can of worms."

He turned his back on me and walked into what I realized was a thicket of tall, lush marijuana plants lining the back of the yard. The skunky smell came into focus for me. I watched the slender teenager disappear into the redwood forest behind the crop of pot.

As I walked back across the lawn I saw the enormous climbing rose covering the whole south side of the house, except for where it had been clipped away from windows.

River came out of the kitchen and met me in the yard.

"How is he?" she asked.

"I can't tell, but it doesn't look good."

"It's so unfair. He's just a child."

"I've seen this house before," I said. "I mean I've seen a picture. In that book by Donald Webster."

"My great-grandfather," she said. "His father built this house. That rose is over a hundred years old. I think that's what's holding the house up."

"You have some other plants too," I mentioned, pointing my thumb at the cash crop at the back of the yard.

"Thirty-four plants. That's all I'm allowed."

"I see."

"Don't judge me, Guy Mallon. I have a grower's permit and I need to make a living. Come on back in the house. We have to talk."

"I'm talked out."

"No, you're not. Come on."

We went back into the kitchen, which smelled like fresh coffee. River poured us each a cup. We sat on either side of the kitchen table, facing each other across a plate of cookies.

"What?" I asked.

"Guy, I don't want to shut the paper down."

"The *Jefferson Nickel*?"

"The paper, yes, and all it stood for. Pete went too far sometimes, but it's a good paper, and there has to be something in town besides the *Jefferson Republican.*"

"But you were ready to close it down anyway, River. Or fire Pete. Or both. Now it seems to me—"

"I've changed my mind," she answered. "I need that newspaper. It's what I stand for. But I also need someone to edit it. Write it. It's a money-maker, believe me. And it's vital to the community. You see what I'm saying? Guy, don't look away. *This is important to me.*"

"God damn it, I hate it when somebody says that," I told Carol over cocktails that evening. "'This is important to me.' It means if I don't do exactly what they want me to do, I'm a bad person, I'm responsible for their misery. It's ridiculous. It's rude. It's emotional blackmail. I don't have to put up with crap like this."

"You have to do it," Carol said.

"Do what?"

"Write and edit the *Jefferson Nickel.*"

"Why? Just so River Webster can have a—"

"Because you want to, Guy. I can read your mind better than you can."

I snorted. "I'm not in the publishing business anymore."

"Yes you are. It's in your blood. I'm married to a publisher, and I always will be."

I thought about it for a while. True. I loved publishing, and I missed it. "But I'm a book publisher. I don't know the first thing about editing a newspaper."

"Leave the business end to me. You edit the paper. Write columns. I'll take care of the business end—payroll, accounts payable and receivable, taxes, whatever. It's going to work, Guy."

"But the *Jefferson Nickel* has this political agenda. I'm easy-going. I don't make waves in my home town. I'm a poetry publisher, for Christ's sake. Or was. And God knows I don't want to end up like Pete Thayer."

"Of course not. But the *Nickel* doesn't have to stay political. All River really cares about is having a voice in the community. She's a lot saner than Pete was. She's a loving person, which makes her a better person than Seamus Connolly. The paper will have a new focus: it will be historical, not political. The news from the past! Just think of the stories. Just think!"

"But Pete Thayer was a businessman," I said. "I don't know the first thing about business."

"Fortunately, I do."

"You? You don't want to be a publisher. You tried it and hated it."

Carol smiled. "It might be fun. Scarecrow Books practically runs itself nowadays, and it barely pays the rent. We could use some cash flow, come to think of it. The *Nickel* runs in the black. It's successful. And River wants us on board. On salary."

I went out into the kitchen and poured us more drinks. I came back to the living room and set Carol's martini on the table by her left arm. I said, "You seem to have given this a lot of thought."

Carol looked up from her *New Yorker* and gave me her wicked Irish grin. "River and I planned the whole thing last night, before you got home. It started as a game to keep her from going out of her mind. I admit we were both pretty smashed, but I've been thinking about it all day today, and I still think it's a good idea."

She held up her glass, and I brought my glass to hers for a kiss.

What would I do without this woman?

Editor.

Here I go again.

"But no politics," I insisted. "No controversy. No enemies."

She gave me the face that says relax. "You'll be fine if you stick to local history, Guy. Everybody loves local history. You'll have fun writing it, and the research will be a snap. We have a whole section devoted to the subject in our bookstore.

"Right." I thought about that book I'd looked at, *A Long, Long Crime Ago: A History of Jefferson County,* by Donald Webster.

"No politics. Right. Just history." And I thought:

Here I go again.

INTERLUDE
The Connollys and the Websters

I

In the early afternoon on the fifth of March, 1867, the *Golden Harp* sailed into a sheltered cove on the wild, rocky coast of far northern California. It was a clear, sunny day, the first pleasant weather these Irish sailors had seen in weeks. They had been at sea for five days, sailing from their last port through choppy waters and a cold, drizzly wind; but now, as the ship sailed into the bay, the air felt warm on their faces and the clear, green water was calm as a lake in summer. Tall stones rose out of the bay and stood like ancient, weathered statues, and curious otters and seals swam to the sides of the ship as if to welcome the sailors home.

One young man reached for a rifle, but the captain stopped him. "We're going ashore, and we're going in unannounced," the captain told his brother. "Right, then, lads. Tie up to that big stone there and we'll go have us a look around."

The Irish sailors and the sailor's wives and young ones all cheered. There were fifty-four of them, and every one of them was named Connolly. Captain Brian Boru Connolly and his five brothers, Patrick, Dennis, Kevin, and the twins, Bill and Bob. And their half-wit sister, Katie, who could haul a rope as hard as any of them. Three of the brothers had wives, and all three of the wives had little ones. And there were Connolly cousins, too, with wives and children, and the whole lot of them worshipped Brian Connolly and obeyed his command to the letter.

"Quiet down, you dogsbodies!" Brian shouted. "I said we're going in quietly. Unannounced. Now every heathen savage in California is going to know we're here."

"I hope they're friendly," one of the women said.

"Oh, they'll be friendly, all right," Patrick said. He shouldered his rifle and pointed at the shore. "They'd bleeding well better be. Oh Jaysus, there they are."

Brian pulled out his spyglass and looked over his brother's shoulder at the crowd of brown-skinned pagans gathering on the stony shore. Their expressions revealed nothing. "Put down the gun, Paddy," he said. "We don't want to frighten the bastards."

"Why not? They need to know we mean business, don't they?"

"Pull your head out of your arse, lad. We want to be able to use these sods." Brian turned to Dennis and Kevin, who were standing behind him. "Get four cases of whiskey out of the hold. We're going ashore. With whisky. And guns," he added.

The whole boatload of Connollys let out a cheer that echoed off the cliffs on either side of the cove. And still the benighted savages stood stone-faced and waited.

The Irish, all fifty-four of them, stood on the sand, inland from the rocks, and faced the natives, who were dressed in furs and leather, their clothing and hair adorned with strings of nuts, pebbles, shells, feathers, and bits of sand-polished wood. There were at least as many Indians as there were Irish, and they too had brought their families. Men, women, and children young and old, the little ones peeking around their mothers' legs, the whole lot of them with black eyes wide open, and not a one of them smiling or blinking.

"They stink," Dennis observed.

"Not as bad as you, mate," Kevin said, and the twins giggled.

"They're not naked," Bill observed. "We should have stayed in the bleeding Caribbean, like I said."

"The Caribbeans didn't have what we sailed all the way from Dublin for," Brian snapped.

"The women were naked there," Bob grumbled.

"It's cold here," Brian explained. "In any case, you wouldn't want to see one of these greasy sows naked, you can take my word for that." He addressed the Indians with a loud, commanding voice. "Do any one of you filthy, disgusting blighters speak English?"

The Indians broke their stare and looked at one another. A few of them nodded to the tallest, fattest of the lot, and the big Indian stepped forward. He opened his mouth and spoke. In flawless English, he said, "In the beginning God created the heaven and the earth. And the earth was without form, and void; and darkness was upon the face of the deep. And the Spirit of God moved upon the face of the waters. And God said, Let there be light, and there was light. And God said—"

"That's enough!" Brian shouted. "Jaysus Christ."

The tall Indian smiled and spread his arms out. "For God so loved the world, that he gave his only begotten Son, that whosoever believeth in him should not perish, but have everlasting life!"

Brian put two fingers into his mouth and whistled, and the Bible lesson was over. "Christ," he repeated. "The God damned missionaries beat us to this place." He grinned at the Indian and said, "So you aren't a bunch of ignorant heathens after all?"

The Indian smiled back. "Neither," he answered.

"Where are those missionaries now?"

The Indian dropped his smile on the sand. "Died of fever."

Then Brian noticed the blob of yellow metal the size and shape of a sardine, which hung from a thong around the brown man's neck. It shone in the afternoon sun. He approached the Indian, his finger stretched out to touch, but the Indian stepped back.

"What is that?" the Irishman asked.

"Fish."

"Where did it come from?"

"River."

"I know fish come from the river, you sod. I mean where did you find that thing?"

The Indian turned his back on the Irish and pointed. Brian gazed at the hills and at the forested mountains that rose high, high into the eastern sky. "From the river," the Indian insisted.

Brian nodded. He turned and faced his countrymen, feeling a grin in full bloom on his face. "Ladies and gentlemen, we have found it! This is what we sailed all the way from Dublin for! Now break out that whisky, boys. We're going to have a party with our new neighbors."

The next day, Brian, Patrick, and Kevin Connolly hiked off across the fields toward the mountains, accompanied by the big Indian and two of his young men. The brothers tried to converse with their Indian guides, but whereas the Irishmen had a gift for gab, the Indians had a gift for silence. They may have been taught English by the missionaries, but the big one, whose name was something like Tchlkmsh, was the only one who spoke English aloud, and he was stingy about it.

They followed the big river through the springtime fields spotted with gay flowers. The morning was chilly with fog, but the afternoon sun, when they were a few miles inland, was warm, then beastly hot. Brian asked Tchlkmsh the name of the river, and the Indian answered, *"Tchlkmsh."*

"But that's your name, if you can call that a name."

"It means 'fish.' The missionaries called me Fish. They called this river Steelhead."

"Steelhead? What does that mean?"

"Kind of *Tchlkmsh.*"

It took them all day to cross the flatlands, climb the foothills, then make a camp for the night at the base of a mountain, before a vast curtain of forest. They built a fire, ate nuts and cheese and bread, and drank whisky, which made both the Irish and the Indians grin and guffaw. They had found a common language.

While Brian, Patrick, and Kevin were off mountain-climbing, the rest of the Irishmen stayed behind to build shacks, with the help of their new Indian friends, in a meadow overlooking the mouth of the big river. The women and children slept on the ship at night and explored the beach in the daytime. The Irish women washed clothes in the river and cooked with the Indian women. The Irish children made friends, played games, and picked fights with Indians their own age. Every evening the two peoples met on the stony shore around a driftwood fire, where they ate fish from the river, shellfish from the sea, acorn mush, and greens. They drank whisky until there was no whisky left, and then they drank a dark Indian tea made from bitter bark and roots. The Irish pretended not to like the acrid tea, but they drank their fair share and more, because it made them feel as if they could sing sentimental ballads all night long.

It took Brian and his brothers two more days to reach their goal. The Indians led them up through a forest the likes of which they'd never even imagined. Red-barked trees whose girth was that of a house reached into a crowded sky, higher than the Irishmen could see. Vast thickets of ferns as big as horses. Surrounding the enormous trees were carpets of shamrock-shaped vegetation, green on the topside, purple underneath. Birds of all description filled the silence, from hawks overhead to ravens and jays in the trees, to sparrows scurrying in the brush, all scolding with joy. Animals furry and scaly slithered and skittered about the forest floor and through the branches of the giants.

On their second morning in the forest, the men followed the river until it split in two. Fish pointed to the smaller fork, the steeper and faster of the two, which led to the left. The men stopped to drink water from the icy river, then continued their uphill climb. Brian asked Fish the name of the tributary they were following.

Fish said a word that sounded like an iron gong ending in shattered crystal. "It means Yellow Stones. But the Russians called it Sticks."

"Sticks? Russians?"

"Miners. They were here when I was a boy."

"Where are these Russians now?"

"Dead," Fish said.

"Fever, like the missionaries?"

Fish looked Brian in the face and did not answer.

That afternoon, Fish stopped them and had them sit on a large, flat stone that overlooked the Sticks River and faced a tall, sheer cliff on the other side. A hole scarred the cliff, as if a monstrous vixen had dug herself a home to whelp in.

"Is that the Russian gold mine?" Brian asked.

"They built cabins on the bluff."

"Whatever happened to those bleeding Russians?" Patrick wanted to know.

"They harmed the earth," Fish explained, and he would say no more.

Brian looked to the other two Indians to see if they had any information to add, but they both looked straight ahead, either indifferent to the question or deaf to the English language. Giving up for now, Brian asked Fish, "So how do we cross this infernal river?"

"This time of year, we don't."

Brian respected this idiot, but he wasn't going to be deterred by savage superstition. "Kevin," he ordered, "go down to the water and have a look."

The young Irishman clambered down the rocks to the roaring river's edge. Brian and Patrick watched their brother from above. Suddenly Kevin pulled off his boots, shed his outer jacket, and dove head-first into the current. He disappeared.

"Jesus, Mary, and Joseph!" Patrick cried. "What is the damned fool doing?"

The lad stood up now in the midst of the river, which was as high as his chest. He grinned up at his brothers, holding one fist high above his head and shouting words they could not hear over the water's rage. Then, as quickly as he had emerged, he lost his footing and was swept downstream, his head below the surface.

"Jesus, Mary, and Joseph! Kevin!"

One of the younger Indians scrambled down to the river and ran along the bank. About a hundred yards downstream, he waded in just in time to catch Kevin's tumbling body. Brian and Patrick watched the Indian pull their brother from certain death and back to the river's edge. The two young men, drenched as water rats, crawled onto the dry rocks and stood up. When the Irishman was finished puking, the Indian put an arm around his waist and helped him stumble back to where his brothers waited in fearful anger.

Kevin stood before them on the flat rock. His teeth were clattering and his body shook like a willow in the wind, but he wore a wide grin. He held out a wet hand and opened up his fist. There in the palm of his ice-blue hand was a chunk of gold the size of a whisky cork.

The Indian who had rescued him patted Kevin's shoulder with the back of his hand. Kevin and his brothers looked at the sopping wet savage. Brian said, "My brother seems to have lost his manners along with his good sense. Thank you, sir, for saving my brother."

But the Indian paid no attention to Brian. He held out his hand, palm up and raised his eyebrows.

"What?"

Fish said, "He wants the stone."

Kevin slammed his fist shut and shouted, "No!"

"Give him the stone, Kevin," Brian said.

"I risked my life for this stone!"

"And you would have lost it, too, you hot-headed twit. That bugger earned the stone. Give it to him." Brian used the voice that was not to be disobeyed.

Kevin's face twisted with fear, cold, rage, and greed. "Bugger all!" He flung the gold stone back into the swift river, where it plopped without a sound and sank out of sight. "Damned fool river," he muttered.

The young Indian nodded and smiled.

Fish and the other Indian built a fire on the flat rock. The two wet young men stripped off their clothes to dry and warmed their puckered bodies. Darkness rose from the black water below them, crept out of the bushes, and climbed the granite cliff on the other side of the river.

"I tell you, Fish, my good friend," Brian Connolly said that night, when the last of the whisky was gone, "we need to figure out a way to cross that river. Upstream from here? Downstream somewhere? We need to be on the other side. The Russians did it, didn't they?"

"That river is here for a reason," Fish replied.

Brian laughed out loud. "Yah. And so am I, Fish my friend. So am I."

One week after they had left for the mountains, Brian, Patrick, and Kevin and their Indian guides returned to the village on the shore. They walked out of the soggy meadow, their beard-stubbled faces dripping with sleet. Two Indian men ushered them into a large lodge, where they stripped off their clothes, wrapped their bodies in blankets, and warmed their faces in front of a smoky fire.

Late that afternoon, the heavens dried and opened up in the west, and a sunset lit their supper on the beach. They ate roasted salmon and baked squash and drank buckets of Indian tea. When they were finished with their meal and the Indian women were tending to the children, Brian stood on a log and spoke, his face glowing in the firelight.

"Here's what we're going to do," he thundered to his family, waving a gourd of foul tea in his hand. "We're going back up there tomorrow morning. Half the men. The other half of the men will stay here with the women and young ones, and they'll build us a proper Irish village. We'll be taking turns being up there in the mountain. Trading places every two weeks. We'll be toiling our arses off in both locations, boys, so get ready to toil. Do you hear me?"

"What are we going to be doing up there, Brian?" asked Bob, or perhaps it was Bill.

"Two things, boyo. Two things. We're going to build a bridge, and we're going to get rich!"

The Connolly men built all through the spring and summer. They built houses on the flatlands, next to the Steelhead River, and up in the mountains they built a bridge over the Damfool River, which Brian had renamed in honor of young Kevin. High on the other side, overlooking the cliff, they repaired and rebuilt the decaying cabins of the mining camp left behind by the dead Russians. They added a bunkhouse to eat and sleep in, and storage sheds for their tools—axes and saws, shovels and picks, hammers and nails, lanterns, tongs, and pans—a vast weight they had trudged up the mountain trail, spurred on by their leader's insults and their own lust for gold.

When they weren't building, they were digging like badgers into the mountainside. They reopened the scar the Russians had left and chipped away at its walls, shoveling refuse into a chute that carried it down to the torrent below, where pebbles of gold sank to the river bed to be plucked and panned from the icy water, while lighter rock was washed downstream.

They worked through the soggy spring and into the warm, buggy summer. They swatted flies and fleas and mosquitoes as big as moths. Bears and coons raided their camp and stole their food and had to be shot. Snakes rattled their tails and had to be shot. Ravens and jays laughed at them and had to be shot. As the summer months wore on, the Irishmen sweated and swore, waiting their turn to spend two weeks in the foggy flatlands with wives and young ones.

The Damfool River grew tame, and in July and August the Irishmen enjoyed sitting in its pools to cool off. But by September, the hottest month so far, the river had no force at all, and placer mining ceased. The miners left their tools locked up in the shed and trudged down the trail to the village, four men carrying a potato sack full of golden nuggets, and two carrying another potato sack full of gold-veined chunks.

Brian had the boys put the sacks in his cabin on board the *Golden Harp*, and he stayed in the cabin for two days, running his fingers through the priceless pebbles, finishing the last bottle of whisky, the one no one else knew about, and making a list. *Clothing, potatoes, whisky, two mules, ammunition, explosives....*

II

The first Monday in October, Brian Connolly, dressed in his best, walked into the San Francisco office of Howard Moffat, Assayer, followed by his brothers Kevin and Dennis, each of them lugging a potato sack on a small wagon built for a child. Mr. Moffat took their sacks, stowed their wagons, gave Brian a receipt, and told him to come back the next day, after noon, for the results.

Brian told Denny and Kevin to join the rest of the crew down at the docks, while he spent the afternoon locating the proper office, standing in long, slow lines, and registering the claim to his land in the uncharted coastal mountains to the north. He was given a receipt and told to return in one week for the deed.

He rejoined his brothers and cousins, and the lot of them spent the balance of the afternoon spending most of the rest of their American dollars, what was left of the eleven-hundred-dollar-fortune they had made by selling an entire shipload of Irish linen to dealers in Los Angeles. They bought everything on Brian's list except for the mules. They went out drinking, brawling, and whoring that evening, then returned to the ship and slept like the drunken sailors they were until morning.

"Congratulations, Mister Connolly," Howard Moffat said. "Take that bag of nuggets to the United States Mint, along with this certificate, and they'll give you seven hundred and forty-two dollars for it."

Brian gaped at the assayer, gave him a steely stare. "That's all?" he shouted.

Mr. Moffat raised his eyebrows. "That's what this bag is worth, sir."

Brian shook his head. "Nah. My family, twenty-three men, including myself, worked seven days a week for six months pulling those gold stones out of a hard rock mountain. Why, the labor alone—"

"My fee is thirty-five dollars," Mister Moffat said.

"What about the other sack? The one with the rocks. What's it worth?"

Mr. Moffat produced another certificate. "It would not be worth the expense of extracting the gold from the granite," he said. "But this certificate shows that you have gold in your mine, and if the sample you've given me is typical, you might be able to extract it yourself, with the proper machinery and chemicals. Once you get properly set up, you could earn a small profit."

"How am I going to afford that?"

"You'll need investors, I suppose," Mr. Moffat said. "Or you could sell your claim. I understand Ezekiel Webster is buying claims. But I doubt—"

"I'm not selling my claim."

"Very good, sir."

"Where do I find this Ezekiel Webster?"

"Mister Connolly, your informant is full of manure," Ezekiel Webster said, staring across the giant, cluttered desk in his office on the second floor of the Webster-Shorp Building, a monstrous edifice occupying a full block of Market Street. Mister Webster was a man in his late sixties, with mutton-chop whiskers that more than made up for his bald head. His eyes were glittering blue, like the sapphire that fastened his collar. "Gold mining simply doesn't pay." He handed the certificate back across the desk.

"I don't understand this," Brian said. "My family and I sold our business in Dublin and traveled all this way 'round the Horn because we were told there was money to be made in California. To be plucked out of the festering ground."

"You're too late," Mr. Webster said. "And the truth is, there never was that much money to be made mining gold."

"But people got rich!"

"Not miners. The people who got rich were the ones selling trousers to the miners. The ones selling wine to the trouser merchants. The men who operated the stages and built the railroads so the trouser merchants could take their wares to market. How did I make my money? Building and selling houses to the men who run the stages and railroads. Simple, really, taking wood from the forests and turning it into mansions and neighborhoods. I'm rich, yes, and I thank the Gold Rush for that, but my wealth has nothing to do with gold itself. Now tell me a bit about this land you've claimed. Northern California, up there above Port Silva, up close to Oregon is it?"

"Yes, sir."

"Pretty country."

"I suppose it is," Brian answered. "I've been so busy working—"

"Forests? Redwood trees?"

"Is that what those buggers are called?"

Ezekiel Webster leaned back in his chair and laughed out loud. "Mister

Connolly, I hope you have the rest of the afternoon to spend with me. We have papers to sign. And I want you to come to my house for dinner this evening and meet my family. We have much to talk about, you and I."

Brian Connolly felt a bubbling in his chest, part anger, part wild hope. "You'll excuse my asking, Mister Webster, sir, but what is this all about?"

The old man rapped his knuckles on the cherry wood desktop. "Brian Connolly, I'm going to make you and your family rich, under one condition."

"Yes, sir?"

"You must promise me never to mine gold again. Shall we begin?"

"Very well, sir," Brian babbled. "But I'm going to need an hour off and you'll have to advance me fifty dollars."

"What for?"

"So I can buy clothing suitable for dining with your family, sir."

Webster laughed again. "Come. I'll take you shopping. And then we'll go to my club. Are you a drinking man, Mister Connolly?"

Brian entered the foyer of the Webster mansion and handed his new silk hat to a black butler. The servant led him up the stairs, opened the parlor door, and announced, "Mister Connolly, Madam."

Stepping into the room, Brian found himself surrounded by elegance the likes of which he'd never seen before: rich carpets and sturdy, graceful furniture with velvet cushions, all arranged as if by an artist. A crystal vase held a fountain of long-stemmed red roses. Busts and statuettes stood on marble pedestals. Dark portraits glowered from the walls.

"Ah, Mister Connolly, thank you so much for coming," said Ezekiel Webster, rising from his armchair by the hearth. He held out his hand, and Brian shook it. "Allow me to introduce you to my family."

Brian had no idea what to say, and so he said just that.

"My wife, Julia."

Mrs. Webster offered her hand without standing up, and a smile to go with it. "I'm so pleased you could come, Mister Connolly."

"My son, Jonathan."

A tall, slim man strode across the parlor, a grin on his face and his hand outstretched. "Mister Connolly, I'm pleased to know you," the young man said. "Father's been telling us about you. I understand that you and I are to be business partners, and I'm here to tell you I couldn't be more pleased!"

Brian shook Jonathan Webster's delicate hand and returned the smile.

"May I introduce you to my wife, Esther."

The woman rose and glided across the room to him, as if she were riding a cloud. She wore a dark green satin skirt that swished and kissed the carpet as she walked. Around her neck she wore a choker of garnets with a matching garnet clasp for the collar of her ivory silk blouse. Her auburn hair was piled artfully on her head and held with a bone comb. She nodded her head politely, opened her green eyes wide, and smiled. Those teeth! "Mister Connolly," she murmured.

Brian returned the smile and said, "Enchanted." It was the first thing he'd said all evening, and he meant every word.

"What will the name of this new lumber enterprise be?" Esther Webster asked Brian, when the oyster shells had been cleared from the table and the ancient butler, now sporting a white jacket, was pouring claret into the goblets.

"My company name has always been Connolly Brothers," Brian said. "There are six of us, you see."

"My husband has always worked for Webster and Shorp. I suppose the new company could be Webster and Connolly? The Webster and Connolly Lumber Company?" The young woman sipped her wine, the slight tease of a smile in her eyes.

"I'd have to ask my brothers about that."

"All six of them?"

"Five."

"The name isn't important right now," Jonathan said.

His mother added, "I feel it's so much more pleasant to have business matters settled at my husband's office. Oh, how lovely. Here comes our lamb."

The butler placed the platter before Ezekiel Webster. The tycoon stood and began carving the roast. The first plate went to Mrs. Webster, who clasped her hands and glowed. "Arthur, do tell Cook this looks superb," she said.

"Yes, Madam. Thank you, Madam."

"How about the Jefferson Company?" Esther asked through the candlelight. "Or Jefferson Lumber? Or the Jefferson Lumber Company?"

"Jefferson? Who's he?"

Jonathan chuckled. "My wife is terribly taken with Thomas Jefferson, you see."

"I haven't met the man," Brian said, feeling annoyed and a trace jealous. "Is he in the lumber business?"

"The American president," the young woman explained. "My hero. He declared our independence from England. I hope that doesn't offend you."

"Why should it offend me?" This young woman was trying her best to be a burr under his saddle. He just knew it. He gave a grateful nod to the butler as a plate of lamb appeared on the tablecloth before him.

"Well, since you're an Englishman—"

"Hah!" Brian Connolly roared. "I abominate the bloody English!" He lifted his wine glass. "I drink to your Mister Jefferson. Yes, by all means, the Jefferson Lumber Company it shall be!" He gulped his wine, then sawed off a generous bite of lamb and stuffed it into his mouth before the hostess had raised her fork.

After the last taste of sherbet, the three men stepped out onto the terrace to smoke cigars and drink brandy, and to discuss concerns that would change their fortunes forever. Lamplight from houses below the hill twinkled up through the fog, but the air was unseasonably warm. They discussed a list of plans: a short railway to haul timber from the forest to the harbor. The harbor to be built. What to do about the damned Indians. All right, then, a Protestant church and school for the damned Indians. The fleet of ships to carry logs from the Jefferson City harbor to the City of San Francisco. The lumber mill that would eventually turn those logs into boards before they left the harbor. Housing. Chinese labor. Sawyers. A doctor, a barber, a butcher, a bank. A cookhouse. A whorehouse. A town full of taverns.

"By God, that sounds splendid," old Ezekiel exclaimed, chortling and clapping his hands. "I wish I were going with you young fellows!"

"Gentlemen?" The voice came from the shadow of a potted ficus that stood next to the French doors. Esther Webster stepped out from the shadow and said, "Mother asked me to tell you that coffee is being served in the parlor."

Jonathan said, "Thank you, darling." He turned to the other gentlemen and rubbed his hands together. "Shall we?"

As they were filing into the house, Esther said, "One moment, Mister Connolly, if you please. I'd like to have a brief word with you."

Jonathan chuckled. "Don't let her talk you out of the taverns, Brian. My wife can be most persuasive!" He clapped his father on the back and followed him into the parlor.

"Yes, Missus Webster? Do you object to taverns?"

"I do not object to taverns, Mister Connolly. Nor do I object to whorehouses. But I'm telling you this. I expect you to treat my husband with gentility and respect."

"Missus—"

"He's not a rough-and-tumble businessman like you, sir. Jonathan is a kind and generous man, and I don't want you taking advantage of that. Hear me out. As soon as that new town of yours, Jefferson City, is built and habitable, I'm moving up there, and I'm bringing our son, Donald. I shall be keeping an eye on you, Mister Connolly. If I discover you've treated my husband unfairly in any way, you'll have me to deal with, and you'll find I'm more like my father-in-law than I am like my husband."

Brian could not answer. He ached to grab her by the shoulders, and then what might happen? This evening, on the verge of untold wealth, was no time to be hot-headed. He swallowed and nodded.

Esther Webster smiled in the foggy dew and said, "Very good, then." She placed her hand on his upper arm and gave it a strong squeeze. "We understand each other. Shall we go inside?"

"I don't like it one bit," Patrick Connolly grumbled, as the six brothers settled in for their last night in the mining camp. "We worked our bleeding arses off, our fingers to the bone, digging out that bleeding hole, and now you're telling us to destroy it? That's where the frigging gold comes from, Brian!"

"I made a promise. And my promise is going to make you rich. And you won't have to dig holes in the rock."

"No," Kevin said. "Instead we'll be sawing big trees down, and that's even harder work. I say we keep the hole open."

"I say you'll do as I say," Brian thundered. "First thing in the morning. Now go to sleep before I push you off the porch."

The next morning, all six Connolly brothers crawled down the face of the cliff, as they had done so often, and this time they brought the explosives they'd been yearning for all during the spring and summer. But the explosives this time had a different purpose.

"I don't like it one bit," Patrick grumbled again. "It's an outrageous waste, that's what it is."

"Finish setting those sticks, gentlemen," Brian Boru ordered.

When the dynamite was in place, the brothers crawled to a safe distance, and Brian did the honors. The explosion that echoed through the forest was the loudest sound that any of the brothers had ever heard, and almost as loud was the cascade of granite that blew out of that hole as it collapsed. The rocks tumbled fiercely to the river below, where they piled up in a massive heap of gray trash, a heavy cloud of dust swirling over it.

Kevin was the first to reach the refuse.

"Stay away!" Brian shouted at his brother. "More rocks are sure to fall!"

But Kevin was already clambering all over the pile, bloodying his knuckles in search of broken treasure. Then, from the top of the heap, he shouted his victory, pointing to the pool beyond the pile. "Gold!" he cried. "Gold stones as big as eggs!"

He scrambled down the shifting stones until he was five feet above water's edge. He dove into the pool without removing his boots, smashed, and lay there floating face-down in the shallow water.

When his brothers were able to pull Kevin's broken body from the water, they saw what they had been expecting to see. No gold, just boulders, only two or three feet below the dusty, bloody surface of still water.

The twins bawled, and Dennis and Patrick both sniveled. But Brian shook his head and said, "That boy always was a hot-headed fool."

He looked up at the scarred cliff and saw that the job was done. The mine was closed, and his future was sealed.

III

Ezekiel Webster was pleased. The Jefferson Lumber Company was a success from the outset. Mr. Webster grinned with pleasure several times a week, year after year, as he watched ships from the North Coast sailing and chugging into San Francisco Bay, riding low in the water, laden with logs and lumber. He now had all the redwood he could use to build all the houses he could build, in neighborhoods around the bay—throughout the City, down the wooded Peninsula, back up again to Oakland, and across the Golden Gate to tiny towns dotting the Marin hills. More than enough lumber, and what he had left over, he sold at a huge profit. The rich man became twice as rich. But that wasn't the only reason Ezekiel Webster was happy.

In those first eight years, Mr. Webster had never once traveled north to visit Jefferson City, his boomtown brainchild, home of the Jefferson Lumber Company. He knew the company was in good hands. That Brian Connolly was a fine fellow. A rough-and-tumble manager of lumberjacks and lumberyards, shipyards and sailors, and that's what it took. There was no need to meddle with success.

Best of all, that company and that town and the frontier life that went with them had made a man—a businessman—of Ezekiel's son, Jonathan. The boy, now approaching forty years old, made frequent trips to San Francisco to meet with his father and present him with reports, facts and figures. Taller, he seemed, and confident, both serious and self-satisfied, and still a smiler. It was the figures that mattered most to the son, even if he didn't really understand them, and the son who mattered most to the father, who didn't really understand the son, either.

"That likable and useless child of ours has become a man at last," he said to his wife at dinner one August evening in 1875. That proud and happy thought may still have been dancing in his dreams when he died later that night of a sudden stroke, at the age of seventy-eight.

When the news of Mr. Webster's death reached Jefferson City two days later, the person most concerned by the news was Esther Webster, Jonathan's wife.

The two of them traveled to San Francisco on the next ship, taking with them their fifteen-year-old son, Donald. They arrived at the church one hour before the funeral, during which Jonathan wept; Donald glowered; Julia, the widow, wore a confused smile; and Esther discreetly peered around the nave of the church to locate and catch the eye of Simeon Shorp, Ezekiel Webster's business partner. After a service that seemed to last a week, Esther approached Mr. Shorp at the graveside, exchanged greetings and condolences, and arranged for a meeting at the Webster-Shorp Building the following afternoon.

The three-hour meeting in Simeon Shorp's office was cordial and cutthroat. Wide-eyed Jonathan Webster watched it like a tennis match: his wife and his father's business partner faced off across the vast green leather surface of Mr. Shorp's desk, trading shots, volleying with nods, winks, fierce smiles, raised eyebrows, knuckles tapping lightly on the desktop. The two of them reached an agreement, Mr. Shorp lit a cigar, and Jonathan agreed to return the following day to sign the papers.

After the meeting, Jonathan and Esther went to the ladies' bar in the new Palace Hotel on Montgomery Street, so that they could catch their breaths before returning to Julia's house on the hill.

Jonathan swished a mouthful of brandy through his teeth, gulped it down and whistled. "I hope we're doing the right thing," he said.

Esther sipped her sarsaparilla. "We are."

"But I worry—"

"Don't."

"We've just let go of my interest in Webster and Shorp. That was my inheritance, Esther."

"You now have independence, my dear. You no longer have to sell the redwood to only one customer. You and Brian Connolly will own the Jefferson Lumber company outright, and it will continue to grow. You'll own the ships and the mill, the trees and the land. And together we can build a real city. Think of it as your kingdom, Jonathan Webster. Jefferson City! With schools and parks, beautiful houses—"

"For whom?"

"Build the city, Jonathan. People will come. We'll make sure of that."

"I don't know how to build a city." Jonathan finished his brandy and waved for another.

"I do. You just take care of the business."

Jonathan shook his head. "Esther, I hate to admit this, but all I've ever done is joke with the boys and carry reports to my father. And I'll be lost without

Father's advice. I don't really know a damned thing about running a business."

Esther Webster gave her husband a first-class smile. "Don't worry," she said. "Brian does."

And so he did. Brian had always been a capable businessman, as a linen merchant in Dublin and even more as a lumber man in California. He knew how to manage people and get things done. He commanded a whole growing family of Irish men, women, and children. He supervised a mill, a shipping fleet, a logging crew, and a small railroad, and he kept them all running smoothly. Jonathan was in charge of business affairs—payroll, accounts payable and receivable, and banking—but reported directly to Brian, who often revised his figures. Both partners worked in the Jefferson Lumber Company Building, which was the first building erected on the new town square; but Brian was seldom in his office. His work kept him moving.

As the city grew from infancy to childhood, saloons and emporia sprouted and bloomed on the town square. The town had two schools (one for Whites and one for Indians), three churches (Catholic, Protestant, and Indian), a blacksmith, a brothel, and a grange hall. In the center of the square a bronze statue of President Thomas Jefferson presided over the goings-on, the carts and buggies carrying goods and people, the building blocks of progress. More goods every day. More people every day.

The original people, the Steelhead Indians, were given a choice of felling trees and milling logs for the company or being killed kindly with free whisky; if an Indian misbehaved as a result of the whisky, there were plenty of official and unofficial Irish police waiting for a chance to kill him unkindly.

Chinese laborers came from the gold fields of eastern California to build the railroad for carrying the logs from the forests to the mill. Then they were given the task of building a railroad overland through the forests down to Santa Rosa, in the Sonoma Valley. When they came to collect their wages for this feat, which took them seven years, they were given instead one-way tickets for themselves and their families on the very tracks they had laid.

Esther Webster planned a city, and it was built by the Connollys and by labor imported from San Francisco. All the unmarried Connolly men found wives from various levels of San Francisco society and brought them back to Jefferson City. Several branches of the Webster clan moved north as well. By 1880, Jefferson City had grown to a town of four thousand, boasting a prosperous Victorian elegance of ornately designed houses, with porches, picket fences, rose gardens, Oriental carpets, and grand pianos.

The Connollys and the Websters lived in relative harmony, and both families became wealthy thanks to their joint interest in the Jefferson Company. But over the years the Connollys worked harder, and established other businesses as well, and they made much more money. The Websters didn't mind; they had enough, and they knew they were the cultured, mannered members of society. They were not Irish.

The summer day Donald Webster turned twenty in 1880, he informed his parents that he was in love and intended to marry. Jonathan clapped him on the back. "About time," he said with a proud grin. "Who's the girl?"

"Not so fast," Esther said, no grin on her face. "Who's the girl?"

"You've met her," Donald said. "You like her."

"Darling, please tell me you are not referring to Little Shell."

Jonathan gasped. "Our cleaning girl? Fish's niece?"

"You like her," Donald insisted.

Jonathan scratched his cheek. "Well, liking someone isn't quite the same as…Donald, she's *Fish's niece.*"

"This is nonsense," Esther proclaimed. "I don't want you hurting that poor Indian maiden. You shall not spend any more time in her company. I'll discharge her. Happy birthday, darling."

"Just because she's an Indian—"

"That's not it," his mother snapped. "Little Shell cleans houses."

"And she's an Indian," Jonathan added. "Remember what happened a couple of years ago with young Brendan Connolly? It was quite a scandal."

Donald threw his hands into the air. "Young Brendan Connolly got drunk and raped a half-witted girl named Oyster, and she got pregnant. Fish insisted that they marry, but Brendan disappeared and hasn't been seen since. What on earth does that have to do with me and Little Shell?"

"But Little Shell is also an Indian, isn't she. We're very sorry, son."

"As am I!" Donald answered, his face aflame. "I've enjoyed living with the two of you, but the time has come for us to part." He spun on his heel and trod toward the front door.

"Donald, stop!" both parents cried, but it was too late. Donald was a block from home by the time they reached the front porch.

"Well isn't that just the height of youthful folly," Jonathan said. "Poor lad."

"Nonsense," Esther said. "This won't go any farther."

"But what can we do?" Jonathan asked.

"I doubt if *you* can do anything," his wife replied, "and so I'm going to talk to Brian. He fixes things." She went inside and came back out with her handbag and her parasol. "Step aside, dearest. I'll be back shortly."

When she reached **Brian Connolly's** house, she was as winded as she was furious. She swung through the gate, trotted up the porch steps, and rapped on Brian's front door. Hearing no footsteps from within, she rapped again, this time with the bone handle of her parasol against the etched glass window. Nothing. Well, it was a Sunday in summer, after all. He was probably out for a stroll. She could wait. She sat down on the front porch swing and concocted preliminary schemes. Foolish boy! What on earth could he be thinking? How in the world—

And there he was. There *they* were. Sharing the arrogance of youth, flaunting their inappropriate feelings in broad daylight, right on the avenue, in front of the grandest houses in Jefferson City, for all the whole wide world to see.

They walked through the gate and up onto the porch, *hand in hand.* Grinning. The boy was grinning!

"Really, Donald, you must stop this reckless behavior at once. I insist."

"Hello, Mother," Donald said. "I knew it wouldn't be long before you came here."

"Whatever do you mean by that?"

"We wouldn't want scandal, would we, Mother?"

Esther glared. Her son glared back at her. The Indian girl chewed on her lower lip and fingered the buttons of her blouse. She did not appear to be looking at Esther, but with Indians you never could tell. "Donald, you must tell me what you meant by that remark," Esther insisted.

"Must I? In front of everybody?" Donald raised his eyebrows. "In front of the whole town?"

Oh dear. How tiresome. After a long, thoughtful silence, Esther stood and faced the girl. She sighed. She said, "Little Shell, I will give you my blessing on one condition. One condition for now, that is. I expect there will be other conditions along the way. Let's be honest about that. But for now, one condition."

The girl widened her eyes with nervous hope. She was quite a lovely girl, really, in her own way. She whispered, "Yes, ma'am?"

"There will be a long engagement. I insist on that. In the meantime, I can't have you cleaning people's houses. That's perfectly ridiculous. I shall arrange for you to have a position teaching at the Indian school. Is that understood?"

Little Shell's face brightened into a smile that glowed like a late-summer sunrise. "Oh yes, ma'am!"

Donald Webster put his arm round the shoulders of his beloved. "Thank you, Mother," he said.

"As for you, young man, you clearly have the talent to be a crafty businessman. So no more sitting around the house reading and writing poetry for you. I shall ask Brian Connolly to find you a position working in one of his businesses. Is that understood? I think he will accommodate you."

The boy's grin was back. "I'm sure he will accommodate *you*," he said. "Thank you, Mother."

"And I expect you don't need to be told the other condition. So that's that." Esther turned her attention again to the quite lovely girl and extended her hand. "Little Shell, welcome to our family."

Little Shell, overcome with tears, grasped Esther Webster's hand and held it to her own wet cheek. Kissed her hand. Right there in public, for all the whole wide world to see.

IV

By 1885, the population of Jefferson City had grown to six thousand, and the town now had four schools, seven churches, a lending library, a fire department, a police department, a jail, and a small hospital. It had an ice cream parlor, an ice house, a meat packing plant, a cannery, a fishing fleet and fish market, and a weekly newspaper, the *Jefferson Democrat*. Another dry goods store, another food market, three more taverns, and another brothel. All of the privately owned businesses, including the jail, were owned by various members of the Connolly family. The town also accommodated two doctors, two barbers, two lawyers, a dentist, and a piano teacher, all of whom paid rent to Brian Connolly. Sharecropping farmers lived and worked on Connolly land between the town and the forests, and they brought their goods to market in the town square, which was owned by the Connolly family.

The Jefferson Lumber Company was still owned by the original partners, Brian Connolly and Jonathan Webster, and it was still doing well. The other Websters, however, as well as the other people who came north with Websters to live in this wild new North Coast town, did not fare as well; and by 1885 most of the men were working for various businesses owned by Connollys. Many of them, never having worked so hard in their lives, were pulling up stakes and moving their families back to San Francisco, leaving behind their elegant redwood houses, selling their land back to Brian Connolly for exactly what they had paid for it.

Jonathan and Esther Webster remained the cultural leaders of Jefferson City society, even though the society was not as cultural as they had hoped it would become. Esther chaired the school board, directed the activities of two of the three churches (one White, one Indian, both Presbyterian), and led an unsuccessful campaign to shut down the brothels. Jonathan, who had very little interest in the Jefferson Lumber Company, was given the title of Mayor. He had his office on the top floor of the Jefferson Lumber Company Building, where he received and approved reports from the school board, the police and fire departments, the library, the hospital, and a loose association of Connolly business owners. His desk was never cluttered. Even if Jonathan had had real work to do, his desk would not have been cluttered. He was not a cluttered person.

In September of 1885, Mayor Jonathan Webster finally had something important to do. Early on Monday morning, dressed in his finest summer suit and wearing his black felt derby, he kissed his wife at the depot, shook his son's hand, and smiled kindly at his daughter-in-law, then picked up his portmanteau and boarded the train for Santa Rosa. He stayed overnight at the La Rose Hotel, where he spent the evening drinking brandy in the bar, before retiring to one of the new Carriage House rooms. The following morning, he continued on by rail to Sacramento on highly important business.

On Wednesday morning, Jonathan walked into the Capitol and entered the hall of the state legislature. There he watched, from an honored position on the dais, as the state legislature unanimously established the county of Jefferson. Governor Stoneman himself presented the charter to the mayor of Jefferson City, shook his hand, and congratulated the mayor, the city, the new county, the state legislature, and the state of California. "Our newest county is also our smallest," the Governor thundered. "But today it has every reason to be our proudest. We welcome you, Jefferson County, to the family of California counties!"

The following day Jonathan went by rail and ferry to San Francisco, to pay a visit to his mother, as he did every time he came south on business. Now in her late eighties, Julia Webster was frail and forgetful, but she was always glad to see her boy, especially when he was not accompanied by that wife of his. She made no secret of that, and Jonathan forgave her. She was a dear old woman, worthy of his full attention and devotion.

Jonathan and his mother had always shared the same interest in Ezekiel's business affairs, which is to say that as a young man he had paid as little attention as she did to where all the money came from. Now, to his regret, she seemed just as uninterested in where the money was disappearing to.

"The lumber business is still doing respectably well, I suppose," Jonathan complained. "But really, Mother, my partner is making so much more money from his other businesses around town, that he's let the lumber business slip. He says the real estate market is not as interested as it once was in redwood lumber, you see. And so—"

"And how is that little grandson of mine?" Julia asked, her eyes bright and crinkly.

"Donald? Donald's well, I suppose. He's not so little anymore, of course.

He's the city librarian. It's an honorary position, but his wife makes a small salary as a school teacher."

"His wife?"

"Donald is married, Mother. You know that."

"Oh yes. Yes. Her."

"They were expecting a child earlier this year," Jonathan said. "But unfortunately, Little Shell lost the baby."

Julia raised her eyebrows and rapped her fan against the arm of her chair. "Well, thank Heaven for that," she said. "Wouldn't *that* have been dreadful."

The following Tuesday afternoon, one day later than scheduled, the mayor of Jefferson City sailed into Jefferson Bay on a Jefferson Lumber Company ship. No family was there to greet him, and it was a fine, cool September afternoon, and so Jonathan walked with a spring in his step, carrying his portmanteau from the harbor up to the center of town.

As he crossed the town square he tipped his hat to President Jefferson, then looked up at the tallest building in the county. Looked again. The sign over the door no longer read "Jefferson Lumber Company." In its place was a new sign of chiseled marble, which read "Webster Building." Jonathan was as bewildered as he was proud.

He strode into the building and took the stairs two at a time until he reached his own office on the top floor. He let himself in and found the room stuffy and hot. On a round table in the center of the office stood a crystal vase he recognized as one of Esther's, and in it were a bunch of red and yellow tea roses, wilting and dropping a sprinkling of petals to the lace doily below them. He set down his portmanteau, lifted windows on both sides of the office, then walked to his desk and sat down.

In the center of his uncluttered desktop was an envelope with his name scrawled on it. He opened the envelope with his father's brass letter knife.

My Dear Jonathan,

Welcome home, and on behalf of the City and County of Jefferson, thank you for your recent travels. I am sure you accomplished much to benefit our people.

In your absence, I have finalized a number of business and personal affairs of which I believe you are not aware. Because they affect you and your future, I am describing them and explaining them herewith.

First, I am retiring completely and forever from the lumber business and the Jefferson Lumber Company. I have transferred all of my interest in the

company to my brother, Patrick Connolly, who will be your new partner.
Patrick is an astute businessman, honest, and fair. Perhaps more astute,
honest, and fair than I have been.

Second, as the primary land owner in Jefferson County, by virtue of the
claim dated October 1867, registered with the state of California, I am giving
to you, at no charge, outright and forever, certain land properties: 1) The
home where you now live, in town at the corner of Webster Avenue and
Connolly Boulevard; 2) One hundred acres of farmland and forest, known
as the Bear Gulch, where I have allowed you to build a country home; and
3) fifty acres of farmland on the southern bank of the Steelhead River. It is
my understanding that your son and his wife wish to establish a school there,
along with a collective farm for her people, but of course the decision about
how that land will be used is up to you. I am also giving the land of the town
square (but not the land surrounding it or any of the businesses surrounding
it) to the people of Jefferson City, in gratitude for all they've done for my
prosperity.

Third, I have decided, with the blessing of your new partner, Patrick
Connolly, that my last official act as partner in the Jefferson Lumber
Company firm will be to give the building formerly known as the Jefferson
Lumber Company Building to you, Jonathan Webster, to be known
henceforth as the Webster Building, with the one proviso that the building
will always provide, rent-free, office space for the Jefferson Lumber Company
to use as the company sees fit. Confident that you will accept this token of my
gratitude, I have ordered a sign with your name on it to be made and hung
over the door to the building.

Fourth, and finally, Esther Webster and I are leaving Jefferson City on
Sunday, the day before your return from San Francisco. We are sailing in my
private yacht to Mexico, where she will obtain a legal divorce from you and
she and I shall be married. We shall not return to California ever, but shall
live instead either in Mexico or in Hawaii.

> *Your humble and obedient etc.*
> *(signed) Brian Boru Connolly*

Jonathan rose, whimpering, from his desk and walked to the center of his
office and stared at the roses on his rosewood table. He noticed for the first time
the small envelope leaning against the crystal vase. With trembling fingers he
tore the envelope open and pulled out the note. *"Goodbye, Dearest. Look after*
Donald. Your Esther."
Jonathan picked up the crystal vase—it had been one of his wife's favorite

possessions, an heirloom from her family in Boston—and threw it with all his might at the floor. It did not break, just bounced a bit and poured its water on the hardwood. Weeping aloud now, Jonathan reached down with both hands and grasped all the roses by their stems, then waved them about his head, crying in a shower of red and yellow petals. He threw the dead flowers out the window and returned to his office chair, sat down, and sobbed into his thorn-torn hands, tears and blood dripping onto his uncluttered desk.

As the years passed, it became quite clear that Brian Connolly had been right about his brother. Patrick was more astute, honest, and fair than he himself had been, especially when it came to dealing with his partner, Jonathan Webster. He was astute enough to realize that Jonathan's indolence and ignorance were a drain on the Jefferson Lumber Company. He was honest enough to call Jonathan into his office on the first day of January, 1890, and voice his resentment aloud, to Jonathan's face. "And let's be fair, sir," he concluded after a long list of complaints. "I have to be fair to those in the company who actually lift a finger, don't I? Well, don't I?"

"I suppose you must," Jonathan admitted.

"Yes. I suppose I must. And so I am having the company's lawyers draw up papers to dissolve our partnership. I hope there will be no hard feelings between us."

Jonathan was no fonder of Patrick than Patrick was of him. "Very well," he said. "All I expect is a fair settlement." He regretted that proviso the moment it was out of his mouth.

"I am a fair man," Patrick Connolly said. "I'll give you what I think is fair considering what you have actually contributed to the growth of this business over the years. If you don't agree with my assessment—"

"Just draw up the papers."

Patrick nodded. "I also think it only fair that you return the ownership of this building to Jefferson Lumber, and I in turn will be generous to you in the same way you have been to the company. I will allow you and your family to keep an office here, at a reasonable rent. And as a courtesy I'll let the name of the building remain Webster."

"I gave the company office space rent-free," Jonathan reminded him.

Patrick shrugged. "I'm a businessman, sir. I wasn't born rich like yourself, who never had to work a day in your life."

"And now you wish to turn me out entirely, with no salary whatsoever, and no equity in the company I helped found? How is that fair?"

"I have thought about that," Patrick answered, "and I have decided to give you the Connolly Ice House, free and clear. It's a good business, it earns its way, and as long as it makes money at its current level, you'll be able to draw a salary equal to the one you've been drawing from Jefferson Lumber. Of course you'll have to work for that salary, mind."

"I don't know the first thing about the ice business," Jonathan protested.

"Neither did I when I began," Patrick said. "I learned on the job. But I can't handle that business anymore, so you might as well take it. With my compliments, sir. And no hard feelings?" Patrick stood up, grinned, and held his beefy hand out across his desk.

That was how Jonathan Webster, the former mayor of Jefferson City, California, got into the ice business, a cold, cold business from which he contracted pneumonia the first year. It wasn't the pneumonia that destroyed him, however. Strike two was the competition. The second year, there was a second ice house in Jefferson City. Bill and Bob Connolly, with backing from their brother Patrick, opened an ice business directly between the fish market and the meatpacking plant, which had been Webster's Ice's biggest customers. The citizens of Jefferson City, most of them of Irish descent, mostly preferred Twin Ice, which offered a better price, better service, and free beer for customers on Friday afternoons at Denny's saloon.

Even the loss of his ice business, which he had never cared for, was not enough to destroy Jonathan Webster, who was fifty-eight in 1895. Strike three was the death of his beloved mother, Julia Webster. The morning after he received the news, a rainy May morning, he walked into the Webster Building and climbed the steps to the fourth floor, where he still paid the rent on the most handsomely furnished office in the county. He looked out over the town square from one window, then went to another window and looked down at the harbor, where fishing boats were returning after a night at sea and a lumber ship was leaving for San Francisco, loaded and low in the water. He could see his dilapidated ice house from a third window.

Jonathan shuffled to his desk and sat down. His hands still shook with a palsy that had accompanied the pneumonia he had survived four years before. He stared down at the surface of his desk, now cluttered with memories and regrets. He reached into the bottom left drawer of his desk and pulled out a bottle of brandy, from which he drank until he had the courage to pull open the bottom right drawer where he kept his pistol.

V

By the turn of the twentieth century, there were more businesses named Connolly than people named Connolly left in Jefferson City. The Connollys who remained were the rich and important people in town, owners of the Jefferson Lumber Company, the *Jefferson Democrat,* and all the saloons, stores, and services. But most of the Connollys had sold their businesses to other Connollys and had left for bigger adventures in bigger cities.

By the turn of the century, the only Websters left in Jefferson County were Donald, who turned forty in 1900, and his infant son, Henry. Little Shell had finally given birth, and had died in the process. Donald raised his son with the help of Little Shell's mother, Meadow Fox. They lived in the house on the land out Bear Gulch Road, where Donald wrote poetry and farmed beets, tomatoes, melons, berries, squash, onions, lettuce, corn, and more weeds than he could keep up with. He didn't really need to farm, he just liked pulling weeds. His grandmother Julia had left him a fortune grander than any of the remaining Connollys could even imagine.

Young Henry spent much of his boyhood living with his mother's family, out on the Webster Ranch by the Steelhead River. He went to school in Jefferson City, then on to college at Stanford University, where he met a blond girl named Amanda, who forgave him for being half Indian, or perhaps even loved him for it. They married and he brought his bride back to Jefferson City. They lived in the old Webster House at the corner of Webster Avenue and Connolly Boulevard, and Amanda picked up where Esther Webster had left off, as head of the school board and the ladies' aid society of the Presbyterian church. There were no brothels left to campaign against. Henry occupied his time studying ethnology and wrote several papers about the Steelhead Indians that were published in scholarly and historical journals.

In the early 1920s Donald Webster, now in his sixties, began writing the book that would keep him busy the rest of his life, *A Long, Long Crime Ago: A History of Jefferson County.* He lived to see the book printed in 1927, and to hold his grandson Joseph, who was born that year; and then he died peacefully in the arms of Meadow Fox, his wife's ancient mother.

PART TWO
THE INVESTIGATIVE REPORTER

CHAPTER FOUR

O n August 15, 1999, Pete Thayer's death was all over the front page of the Sunday *Jefferson Republican*. The headline, stretching in block letters from left to right, shouted:

NEWSPAPER EDITOR SLAIN DOWNTOWN
JEFFERSON NICKEL EDITOR AND PUBLISHER PETER THAYER
MURDERED FRIDAY EVENING BEHIND DOWNTOWN BAR

Below the headline, the left-hand column was an obituary of the murder victim, who *was born in 1945, grew up in the San Fernando Valley, studied journalism and political science at the University of California, Berkeley, and came to Jefferson County in 1987 to cover the Steelhead Rancheria controversy for the radical newspaper, In These Times. After the court ruling allowing Seamus Connolly and Jefferson Lumber to proceed with development of the Steelhead Mall, Mr. Thayer resigned from In These Times, remained in Jefferson City, and founded the Jefferson Nickel, in which he offered the community "an alternative view of the events and issues of the day." The Jefferson Nickel was a successful publication, even though it was often at odds with the more traditional Jefferson Republican, the largest newspaper in Jefferson County....*

The right-hand column was a report of the crime, taken for the most part from the police report, which stated *that the murder occurred sometime between 9:30 and 10:00 p.m., according to bartender Gloria Corson. Investigating the scene were Sheriff Blue Heron from the Jefferson County Sheriff's Department and Jefferson City Police Department Chief Inspector Wayne Marvin. "It was grisly,"* Marvin said. *"That was one big knife, and the handle was sticky with the victim's blood.... We'll catch the perpetrator, don't you worry about that. Make no mistake about it. The Police Department of this city does not put up with crimes like this in our home town. We got a quiet, friendly town here, law-abiding, and that's all I have to say at this time." Sheriff Heron declined to comment....*

Between the obituary and the reportage of the crime, occupying the rest of the space and filling three wide columns with oversized type, was an editorial titled "FAREWELL TO MY FRIEND, MY FOE, MY FELLOW JOURNALIST."

It was no secret. I despised everything Pete Thayer stood for and every word he wrote. He was a vestigial hippie, an anti-business, anti-progress knee-jerk radical so-called progressive, a promoter of homelessness and drugs.

It was no secret. Pete Thayer had a lot of friends and fans in this community, the City and County of Jefferson. He spoke for many. The minority, but many.

It was no secret: I loved Pete Thayer. I was one of those friends and one of those fans. Even though I despised his words and his politics, I thought Pete was a great guy. He yelled out loud for the San Francisco Giants, and he had the loudest laugh at Rotary. And I hate to admit it, but Pete Thayer was a damn good writer. His editorials made me spit tacks, but not because they were badly written. They made me spit tacks because they were so damn well written. I read them every week, and I will miss them. I will miss that silly paper of his.

So will the community, even the majority who support growth and progress.

And I want to say this: I pledge my financial and editorial support to the investigation of Pete Thayer's murder. Whoever did this horrible thing didn't just kill a very good person. He (or she?) killed a newspaper in the bargain. And he (or she) struck a cowardly blow at the noble institution called Freedom of the Press. That attack must not go unpunished, and I urge Chief of Police Marvin to do whatever it takes to avenge it.

Goodbye, Pete Thayer. From all of us.

Seamus Connolly, Editor and Publisher

On Monday morning Carol and I got to the bookstore early, before nine. I kissed her goodbye and walked two blocks through a morning mist to the town square. I crossed the square diagonally, until I came to the statue of Thomas Jefferson, who stood on a pedestal and presided over his homeless subjects. River Webster was there waiting for me in the mist. She wore a sad smile, a trench coat, and her floppy purple hat. We touched cheeks, and she said, "Ready?"

"Here goes," I answered.

We walked the rest of the way across the town square, crossed the street at the corner, and entered the Webster Building through heavy doors of redwood and etched glass. The shops on the first floor hadn't opened yet; we climbed the redwood staircase to the mezzanine, where the bar and restaurant were already selling liquor and breakfast, then on up two more flights of stairs to the top floor.

An ornate but solid Victorian structure built entirely of local redwood, the Webster Building was the oldest office building in Jefferson County and a California Historical Landmark; and even though the top floor was only the fourth floor, the Webster Building was the tallest building in the city. It once belonged to the Webster family, until the Websters gave it to the Jefferson Lumber Company in 1890. Over the years the Connolly family turned the first floor into shops serving tourists and locals, the second floor into a restaurant and bar, and the third floor into the accounting department of the Jefferson Lumber Company. By now all that remained of the Webster presence in the building, besides the name (which was carved in marble on the facade), was the top floor, which was leased in perpetuity to the Webster family as long as they could pay their rent. The top floor consisted of a small hallway and a large loft.

By the end of the twentieth century, the only members of the Webster family left in Jefferson were River and Freddy. In 1987, after Seamus Connolly seized the Steelhead Rancheria, River established the *Jefferson Nickel*, which she turned over to Pete Thayer. Pete served as the paper's managing editor and writer; he had a staff of four working for him. River funded the paper, and it did well. The *Nickel* was River's only source of income, but it had brought in enough revenue to sustain itself and pay the rent on the top floor of the building.

Until Friday, the thirteenth of August. Who knew what would happen now? River had me convinced, though. She was not going to give up, the paper would continue without Pete Thayer, and I was on the cusp of a new career.

Scared? Yup. Excited? You bet.

When we reached the *Nickel* office we found the door wide open, and we heard the sound of weeping. What we saw when we walked into the loft looked like the chilly gray morning after a gangland massacre. The windows were wide open. Books, telephones, lamps, pencils, and plants littered the floor. Someone had taken a hammer or a crowbar to the computer monitor on every desk. The contents of the filing cabinets were dumped on the floor and soaked by the water cooler bottle, which lay on its side on top of the soggy pile. At the biggest desk, Pete's, a computer had been pried open and its guts lay all over the surface of the desk. The four staff members of the newspaper were sitting at their desks, their faces filled with shock and traced with tears.

River gasped. "Good God!" she whispered. Then she cried out loud, *"Good God!* What on earth happened? Does anybody know?"

The only response was a chorus of soft weeping from the three women.

"Has anybody called the police?"

"Not yet," Artie Miller answered. Artie was the production manager; he designed the entire paper every week and got it printed.

"The sheriff? Has anybody called Sheriff Heron?"

"We were waiting for you," said Elizabeth Butler, the ad sales department.

River looked around the office, gave me a terror-stricken frown, then walked across the floor, shuffling papers with her feet like fall leaves. She leaned against Pete's desk and said, "Well. Looks like we've got ourselves a lot of work to do here. We probably won't bring out a paper this week. Maybe just a four-pager with ads, entertainment announcements, and a brief story to assure the people of Jefferson County that the *Nickel* is still in business. Meanwhile, we have a mess to clean up."

"River, we've been talking," Elizabeth said. She blew her nose. "I know this is going to hurt, but we can't go on."

"You what?"

"I'm sorry, River."

"You can't do this to me, Elizabeth. You can't do this to Pete! We've worked so hard to make this paper work! Don't give up, just because—"

Elizabeth Butler twisted an imaginary handkerchief in her fingers. "River, you're asking us to put our lives on the line. I've got kids. It's not worth it."

"I've got a kid too," River shot back, "but I feel we owe something to Pete Thayer."

"Pete was murdered, River," Artie Miller said. "Murdered."

"You don't have to tell me that!" She began to weep.

"Frankly, I don't want to get murdered," said Lydia Sweet, who managed circulation. "Not worth it, River. I'm sorry."

River walked across the loft and planted her fists on the edge of Jackie Haas's desk. "And you, Jackie? What does the office manager have to say?"

Jackie was weeping the hardest. "I'm sorry, River. I really am. But it's time to let it go and say goodbye. I was the office manager, and now look at my office. And I loved Pete just as you did, or at least I loved Pete as a boss and all that. That's the thing, River. You can't have a newspaper without a voice. He was our voice. With him gone, there's no editor, no writer. Why go on?"

River nodded. Slowly she turned and walked across the office to where I was standing. She took my arm and brought me into the center of the room. "I think you all know Guy Mallon," she said. "People, sweet people, meet the new editor and chief writer of the *Jefferson Nickel.*"

I looked at them, one by one, and not one of them looked back at me, or at River.

River sighed, a deep groan of a sigh. "Okay. I understand. I love you all.

And Guy and I will bring out the paper anyway." She wiped tears from her eyes. "You're dismissed."

Elizabeth, Lydia, Artie, and Jackie slowly rose from their desks. They hefted their backpacks and briefcases, which apparently they'd already packed, and started toward the open door. Jackie came back to put a comforting hand on River's shoulder, but River shrugged it off, her face in her hands.

When we were alone in the office, River asked me, "What do we do now, Guy?"

I took a deep breath and looked around the room. Cold, damp air was drifting in through the open windows, stirring papers around on the vacant desks. The hardwood floor was littered with shattered glass, along with the rest of the debris. River's face was a wreck of smeared makeup and spastic twitches. "God damn it," she repeated, "what do we do now?"

I said, "Call the sheriff."

"Holy shit," Blue Heron said. "Holy shit." Then he said, "River Webster, you're a walking crime scene."

"Blue, I want you to find out who did this," River told him. "I hate to be a crybaby, but I feel personally violated. You know?"

He smiled at her gently, then turned to me. "What do you know about all this?"

I shook my head. "Just what you see."

"Nobody was in the office between Friday afternoon and this morning," River said. "Supposedly."

"Well, I have to beg to differ," Blue Heron said. "I'm that much of a detective. This damage wasn't done by elves."

"Now what?" River asked. "We have to get this office cleaned up so Guy and I can get to work. We have a paper to get out by Thursday."

Sheriff Heron shook his head. "Not in this office you won't. I'm going to have the whole fourth floor wrapped up in yellow tape for who knows how long. And I'm afraid you can't take anything out of this office, either. This whole room is evidence. You'd better give the paper a rest, River."

River nodded and answered in a firm, quiet voice. "You can have the office. You can have the fourth floor of the Webster Building. But don't try to keep me from publishing my paper, Blue Heron. I'm not afraid of whoever did this."

Palms up, he shrugged and said, "You should be."

"Guy and I are going to keep the *Jefferson Nickel* going, and we're going to use the power of the press to find out who trashed this office and who murdered the editor. And why."

Blue and I looked at each other and exchanged that look that meant we knew we were the two sane ones in the room. Blue frowned at River and said, "Don't go solving crimes, babe. Keep your nose clean. Leave the crime-solving to the police."

"In this town? The police in Jefferson City don't even know how to write a traffic ticket. Besides, they're all in Seamus Connolly's pocket anyway, so what do they care who murdered Pete Thayer?"

"I'm working on it too," Blue said. "You stay out of it. You too, Guy. And be careful with what you publish."

"You can't scare me, Blue, honey."

Blue Heron didn't answer that. He walked over to Pete's desk, where the most damage had been done. "Shame what they did to this old redwood desktop," he said. Then he said, "What's this?" Using a ballpoint pen from his own pocket, he lifted a keychain from the editor's desk. He gave it a jingle and showed it to River. "Recognize this?"

Her face twitched. She reached for it, but he held it out of her reach. "Pete's keychain," she said. "I gave him that. Those are the keys to this office and his house and his car and his I-don't-know-what, his briefcase and his safe deposit box, and everything!"

"What does this mean to you?" the sheriff asked her.

"You mean the ornament? The fob? It's silver, a local artist. Okay, it's a marijuana leaf. So?"

"I know that," Blue said. "I mean how do you think it got on Pete's desk?"

"He left it there? When he left the office on Friday?"

"And left the office unlocked?"

She shook her head. "No way."

I said, "Looks to me like somebody took those keys from Pete after he was dead. Then came to the office and trashed it, probably the same night. Maybe that's why Pete was killed in the first place."

River was teetering on the edge of a breakdown. She tried to pull back from it, but it was too late, and she fell into a loud gasping, shuddering sob.

Blue put the keychain back on Pete's desk, pocketed his pen, and wrapped River in a comforting hug. He said to me, "Can you take care of her, Guy? Make sure she gets home safely?"

"Yup," I said. "I'm getting pretty good at that."

River and I said goodbye to Blue Heron and left the office of the *Nickel*, but we didn't get far. When we reached the mezzanine, she pointed at the restaurant and said, "I could use a cup of tea."

"Okay."

We went in and sat at the bar. I had a cup of coffee and she had chamomile tea.

"Listen," I said. "I don't know the first thing about publishing a newspaper. Maybe we'd better think this over."

"I know how it's done," she said.

"What do you know about selling ads?"

"We already have ad accounts."

"Are they paid up?"

"I don't know."

"What do you know about layout and design?"

"I thought you knew stuff like that."

"Just books," I said.

"Well, Pete had a template. He just wrote right into the design. No problem."

"Where's that template now?" I asked. "In Pete's computer, which is a tossed salad on his redwood desk?"

River laid her hand on mine on the bar. "He had back-up disks. We'll find them. Honestly, Guy, you have to trust that things are going to work."

I wasn't giving up. "What about circulation? Do you know where all the drop-off spots are?"

"Guy, please. If you don't want to write the paper, okay. I can't make you. I just hoped—"

"I'm just saying we're not ready. I want to do this, but I want to do it right."

"Okay," she said. "Okay, but what's right? I want my paper to tell the truth, that's what's right."

"And here's what I want," I said. "I want—"

"You don't want the paper to tell the truth?"

"Shut up and listen."

River swiveled her bar stool toward me and folded her hands in her lap. "What?"

Over the next hour, during which I drank two cups of coffee and she drank three cups of tea, River Webster and I came up with a business plan to bring the *Jefferson Nickel* back from the ashes.

She was the owner. That made her the publisher.

As for content, the paper had a few stringers—a movie reviewer, a restaurant reviewer, somebody who covered the city council and county board of supervisor meetings—and letters to the editor. I'd edit those. The local entertainment listings and a few syndicated columns would run as submitted.

As managing editor, I would write one big column a week. We argued about that. I said I stood for the truth, but I would not stand for controversy. I did not want to use the paper as a weapon, even a weapon for good. "And I'm not using the paper to solve any mysteries. I want to stay alive, thank you very much. No investigating, no politics."

She seemed reluctant to give up the banner of truth that Pete had waved, but she agreed to those terms.

"Okay," I said. "Now. Carol is the business manager. She's already agreed to that, and she's good."

"Good."

"And I think we ought to publish the paper out of the bookstore. We've got a lot of local history books there, and there's plenty of space. I think Carol and I can do it without a staff, although if you want to come in and work on things there would be room for you too."

"What's the matter with the Webster Building?"

"It's already been trashed once. No, really the thing is, Carol has to stay close to the bookstore. Besides."

"Besides what?"

"Three flights of stairs several times a day would be hard work for me."

"Bookstore it is, then. I'll quit paying rent to Seamus Connolly and pay it to you instead. Makes sense. Now we have to go get Pete's back-up disks."

"Do we really need them?"

"It took a long time for Pete and me to invent the wheel, Guy. What about the circulation routes, the ad accounts, the payroll, the I-don't-know-what, the business part of the business? Carol can't build that all from scratch. Then there's layout and design templates. You don't want to have to create them from scratch either."

"We may have to," I said. "If the back-up disks were in the office, they're probably destroyed by now, and even if they're not destroyed, they're off limits for who knows how long."

"Pete kept his back-ups in his home. No big deal. Let's go over there and get his Zip disks."

"Isn't his house locked up?"

River smiled. She opened her purse and pulled out a keychain. The fob was a silver marijuana leaf. "They were a pair. I still have his house key and his car key. We hadn't gotten to that stage of our breakup yet."

"But what if the police or the sheriff has sealed off his house too?"

"What if they haven't?" she answered. "We'd better hurry." She clinked my spoon against my coffee cup to get the bartender's attention and asked for the tab.

"Where does he live?" I asked, and then I felt like an insensitive idiot. My face went hot. "Did."

River put her hand on my cheek. "It's okay. Just three blocks. It's not raining. Let's walk."

I felt like a creep walking to the dead man's cottage, and I felt great relief when I saw that the premises had been wrapped up in yellow ribbon: CRIME SCENE DO NOT ENTER CRIME SCENE DO NOT ENTER CRIME SCENE DO NOT ENTER CRIME SCENE DO NOT ENTER CRIME SCENE DO NOT ENTER...

"Well," I said, "so much for that."

"Don't be silly," River responded. "We're going through."

"No we're not."

She gave me a challenging squint. "Okay then. I'm going through."

"No you're not," I hit back. "It's against the law."

She shook her head in disbelief. "I don't get you, Guy. We need Pete's Zip disks. It's not like we're going to rob the place. We need those Zips, and we're doing this for Pete."

"River, we are not crossing this line."

"Yes we are."

"No you're not." The voice from behind us made me jump as if I'd been caught doing something wrong. River and I turned around and faced a large woman in a beige bathrobe, a kerchief over her curlers. She held a mug of coffee in one hand, a spoon in the other. "I live next door. Help you with something?"

"What's going on here?" River asked. "This is my friend's house."

"Well, your friend was killed on Friday night. You heard about that?"

River and I nodded. "It was in the paper," I said.

"Well, his house was broke into, middle of the night last night. You didn't hear about that."

River and I shook our heads. River reached for my hand and squeezed.

"It's not in the paper yet," the neighbor continued. "I heard a big racket coming from the street, dogs barking, so I told my husband to check it out, and he said he saw a couple of men come out of Pete's house, get in a car, and peal out. I called the police. I mean I'm not a nosy neighbor, but like I says to my husband, this is a nice neighborhood and nice neighbors look out for each other." She dropped her spoon into the pocket of her bathrobe. "See, I got no problem calling the police, is what I'm saying. So I suggest you respect the signs and leave our neighborhood alone. You can read about this in tomorrow's *Republican.*" She turned and walked back to the house next door.

River and I walked back the way we had come, but when we were halfway down the next block she stopped and said, "Wait."

"What?"

She nodded at an old Volkswagen Bug that was parked across the street. Not one of those new yuppie Bugs that cost as much as a real car, but an old Bug from the sixties or seventies, once painted red and now colored rust and aluminum, a tail light held in place by duct tape. "Pete's car. Come on. I got an idea."

We crossed the street, and she pulled out the silver marijuana leaf and let herself into the passenger side. She pried open the glove compartment and pulled out three Zip disks. She smiled at them, then at me. She handed the disks to me and locked the car door. "Bingo," she said.

"Production—August," I read. "Good, that will probably have the layout template. Business. Good. Probably has all the circulation routes, the ad accounts, accounts payable and receivable, contract forms, everything we need. And this other one? Editorial—August."

"That's the one they were looking for, I figure," River said. "Somebody wanted that disk, and I want to know who that was."

"River, let it go."

"Let it go? Guy—"

"Okay. I admit I'm curious, but I still don't think—"

"At least we have it. We can decide later what to do with it. For now, you should take all these disks to the bookstore and keep them locked up. We're going to learn a lot from them, I bet. Like who killed Pete Thayer."

"We're not investigating a murder, River," I said.

She answered, "Who said we were?"

"You did."

She nodded. Shrugged. "Listen, I've got to get home. I need to take care of poor Freddy. He's taking this pretty hard."

When I got to the bookstore, Carol was sweeping the aisles. My job on Monday mornings. "Sorry," I said.

"No problem. I enjoy sweeping. How'd it go?"

So I told her about the staff walk-out at the *Jefferson Nickel* and the trashed office. I told her about Sheriff Heron's visit and my meeting with River and how we had decided to proceed. "She's going to give up the space in the Webster Building. I said we could publish the paper out of the store here.

Would that be okay with you? I was thinking we could clear some space on the second floor."

"Sure," she said. "Lot of unused space up there. We could each have a desk. Do we need more than that? There will just be the two of us, right?"

"River maybe, sometimes. Or she could mind the store while we're working. But mostly just the two of us. We'll need some office furniture."

"Hospice Thrift Shop."

"Computers?"

"Will our Macs be enough?"

I pulled the three Zip disks out of my jacket pocket. "Pete used an IBM clone, I think. Let's see if you can open these files."

We walked to Carol's desk behind the front counter. She shoved the Production disk into her Zip drive and clicked it open. The window displayed three documents, titled August 6, 1999; August 13, 1999; and August 20, 1999. "These are PageMaker documents. Probably the whole paper, for the fifth and the twelfth. If that's what they are, you'll be able to use one of them as a template. Just write the paper and pour the copy into the appropriate space."

"Too bad we don't have PageMaker," I said.

"We can buy it. You'll have to learn how to use it."

Then she tried the business disk and found spreadsheets in Excel, invoice forms and address lists in FileMaker, and business correspondence in Word Perfect. "Excel works. FileMaker works. We can't open Word Perfect documents. Probably not too important. I know how to write business letters."

"What about the other disk?" I asked.

She slid the Editorial disk into the Zip drive and double-clicked. A list appeared on the screen:." Looks like this week's paper in progress. Editorial, Lead, Feature. Letters. I hope you don't need this stuff."

"What's the problem?"

She double-clicked on "Editorial" and a dialogue box came on the screen. *This document cannot be opened. The application in which it was created cannot be found.*"

"Too bad. Well, we don't need it, but River's going to be upset."

"Maybe she has Word Perfect. If so, she could open the documents and save them in Word or Rich Text Format for us. Why don't you give her a call?"

"Sleeping dogs," I said. "Let 'em sleep."

"You're not curious?"

She had me there.

I spent the rest of the morning upstairs, taking books off the movable bookcases, then moving the modules closer together, clearing enough space to put three workspaces, one each for editorial, business, and production. I swept the floor of the space I had cleared. I wiped years of dust off the empty bookcases, then put the books back in place. The aisles were narrow, but not as narrow as the aisles downstairs. I made a list of furniture we needed. Desks or tables, chairs, lamps, phones. Filing cabinets we'd get later, once the police were done with their investigation of the old office.

At one o'clock Carol and I took her station wagon to the noodle shop for lunch and then to the Hospice Thrift, where we bought three used eight-foot sturdy work tables with folding metal legs. We got them into the back of the station wagon and drove back to the store, where we carried them up the winding staircase to the second floor, one at a time, and put them in place.

Something big was happening to me.

I had followed Carol north to Jefferson County three years before, for only one reason: to be with her for the rest of my life, wherever she wanted to live. And for the most part, I'd been happy, helping her with the house and the garden, helping her with the bookstore. But I had missed having a real job. I guess I'm nuts. All I know is, now, this morning, I was excited: I had a new career! Oh, and one more thing: I had a big itch to know what Pete Thayer had been writing at the time of his death.

Yes, definitely nuts. I should have known better.

I called River. When she answered, I asked, "Do you have Word Perfect on your computer?"

"Me? I don't have a computer. But Freddy does." I heard her call, *"Freddy, do you have Word Perfect?"* After a pause she told me, "Yes. Word Perfect."

I told her about the problem opening Pete's files and asked her if Freddy could save the files in Word or Rich Text Format.

"What does that mean?"

"Beats me."

"Just a second." I heard more yelling, and then she told me, "Sure, not a problem. Come on out. Better come now, because he has plans for later this afternoon."

Half an hour later I pulled off Bear Gulch Road onto her land and parked in front of the old Webster house. She held the door open for me and we walked up the stairs together to Freddy's room.

Freddy sat at his computer. When we came in he turned and nodded. "Sup."

I handed him the business and editorial disks and said, "I hear you can open these Word Perfect documents and save them in RTF?"

"No prob." He took the disks and shoved one into his Zip drive. River and I stood behind him and watched. He turned back to me and said, "This is going to take a little while. So, like, maybe you could, you know."

"I want to watch," River said.

"Mom, get out of here, okay? I'm not into people, like mothers and stuff, looking over my shoulder while I'm trying to do stuff, okay?"

"Freddy, for goodness sake."

I said, "River, will you make me a cup of coffee?"

"Thanks," Freddy said.

When we were seated at the kitchen table downstairs, River said, "Sorry about that. I guess I do hover a bit. But Freddy's got such privacy issues these days."

"How old is Freddy?"

"Fifteen."

"Privacy issues are normal."

"I guess. But I'm still worried. He's such a sensitive kid."

"At fifteen? Sensitive is normal."

"Were you that way at fifteen?"

"I still am," I said.

"Yeah, me too, I guess. Did you want some coffee?"

"Not really."

Ten minutes later, Freddy appeared in the kitchen door, holding the disks out to me. "Those business letters opened up just fine," he said. "But the files on the editorial disk are all totally bogus."

"Bogus?"

"Corrupted. Nothing but gobbledegook."

"Too bad," I said.

River said, "Damn."

Freddy shrugged. "Sorry. Not my fault, Mom."

"Nobody said it was your fault, Freddy. Guy, what do we do now?"

I stood up. "Let go of it," I said. "Nothing we can do. The hard drive was destroyed, the backup files are corrupt. It's like whatever it was was never written. I guess it doesn't matter. We were going to write new copy anyway."

River said, "Still. Let's see that gobbledegook, Freddy."

He took us back to his room and allowed us to look over his shoulder, where file after file was filled with stuff that looked like this:

bjbjÓFÓF

"0 å, å, © ˅ ˅˅ ˅˅ à h h h

ß ™ ≠ Ω √ Ó " Á ^ . T V $ O g l l Ñ

È'æ≠ü≠ç≠ç≠ü≠ü≠ü≠ü≠ü≠ü≠ ü ü ü ≠ ≠ ≠ ≠ ≠ç≠n≠ hāUk hG2– CJ OJ QJ
^J aJ hG2– CJ OJ QJ ^J aJ # hG2– hāUk 6 ÅCJ OJ QJ ^J aJ h; CJ OJ QJ
^J aJ hāUk hāUk CJ OJ QJ ^J aJ , h~#¸ hG2– 5 ÅB* CJ, OJ QJ ^J aJ, ph ˅
& hāUk 5 ÅB* CJ, OJ QJ ^J aJ, ph ˅ , h~#¸ hāUk 5 ÅB* CJ, OJ QJ ^J aJ,
ph ˅ + D E m n

Ó Ô   Ä Å " " ; < ¢ £ v w ö õ gdāUk © ¸ Ñ ß ´ À Ô

+ . e u ∫ ø Û ¯ ¸ J S ä í õ Ø ∫ æ - § ™ ∫ ª ∅ V W " ' ˜ - ' D E F } ~ â ® N j

∑ ‡ - É - Ñ - N

Ô·Ô·ÔœÔ·Ô·Ô·Ô·Ô·Ôæ∞æ·æ·æ·æÔ·Ô∞Ô·Ô¢·ëÔ·∞Ô·∞·Ô∞·Ôë·ÔœÔ
œÔë·Ô hāUk hG2– CJ OJ QJ ^J aJ hāUk CJ OJ QJ ^J aJ h; CJ OJ QJ ^J
aJ hG2– hāUk CJ OJ QJ ^J aJ # hG2– hāUk 6 ÅCJ OJ QJ ^J aJ hG2– CJ
OJ QJ ^J aJ hāUk hāUk CJ OJ QJ ^J aJ 9 - W X ' ' ó ò l } à â ß ® - - W- X-
g- u- É- ˙ ı ı ı gdG2– gdāUk É- Ñ- «- »- ® © ˙ ˙ gdāUk N- {- l- è- ß- ©- ™-
'- √- f- »- % & 2 j l m n ¶ ß ® © Ú‡ÚœÚ∑‡§‡Ûì‡ÚœÚ{‡§‡mœ hāUk
CJ OJ QJ ^J aJ / Å jÈ h´x

h; CJ OJ QJ U ^J aJ hāUk hāUk CJ OJ QJ ^J aJ $ h´x

h; 0J CJ OJ QJ ^J aJ / Å j h´x

h; CJ OJ QJ U ^J aJ hāUk h; CJ OJ QJ ^J aJ # j h; CJ OJ QJ U ^J aJ h; CJ
OJ QJ ^J aJ 1êh -∞-/ ∞‡=!∞ "∞ #ê† $ê† %∞

River said, "Damn" again. I thanked Freddy and said goodbye.

Carol said, "Don't give up."

"I'm letting it go," I said. I had told her about the gobbledegook. "It doesn't matter. The words have disappeared."

"We still have the files," she said. "I saved the documents to my hard drive. And then I made another backup Zip disk." She held a disk in her hand.

"But what good does that do if the documents are corrupt?"

"What if they're not?"

"But they are, Carol."

She tossed me the keys to her station wagon. "Go back to the thrift store and buy us three office chairs. Oh. Get us three desk lamps. And go to Ace Hardware and pick up a power strip with a fifteen-foot cord. I called the phone company, by the way. They'll be here Wednesday."

When I got back to the store with a carload of stuff for the new business,

Carol greeted me at the door with a kiss. "Congratulate me," she said.

"Congratulate you? I'm the one who found three desk lamps for under four dollars."

"And I'm the one who got the editorial files to open in Word, smarty."

This time I kissed her back. "How did you do that?"

"While you were gone I called up Mickey at Mac Mechanics. He came over with his laptop, opened the files in Word Perfect, saved them in Word, and we're in business."

"That's terrific!" I said. "I'm going to call River and let her know."

Carol dropped her smile. "I wouldn't do that. Not till after you've read what Pete wrote."

"Why's that?"

"I don't think she needs to know about this right now."

"But at least she'll be glad to know the files weren't totally lost," I said. "I mean that Freddy was mistaken about that."

"Was he?"

"Wasn't he?"

"Read the lead story," she said. "And the editorial."

The next day, Tuesday, I asked River to meet me in town for lunch at the community center cafeteria, next to the library. The afternoon was warm and the outside tables were full, so we carried our trays across the lawn. We straddled a low brick wall, facing each other, our trays on the wall between us. River lit a cigarette.

"How's Freddy?" I asked.

"He's getting better. It was a big shock, but he's a kid. He'll put this behind him. So will I, although it's going to take some time. And...what's the matter, Guy? So what's eating you, huh?"

"Me?" I picked up my sandwich, then put it down. Picked up my coffee cup.

"Your hand is shaking, and you haven't said hello to me yet. I drove all the way into town, and all you can say is 'How's Freddy?' You haven't looked me in the eye yet, either. Hello? Anybody home?"

I looked up into her face and tried to smile, but she blew smoke out of the side of her mouth, shook her head, and said, "Don't be phony with me, Guy Mallon. Something's eating you, and it has to do with me. You're not going to quit the paper, are you?" River's lips were twitching, just as I knew mine were.

I shook my head and put my coffee cup on the tray. "You haven't been straight with me, River."

Her face flushed in a whipstitch. "What are you talking about?"

"You know why Pete Thayer died, don't you."

She blinked. "Huh?"

"You know why Pete was killed."

"I what?"

"Are you hard of hearing, on top of everything else? Don't make me say it again, River. Just answer the question."

"It didn't sound like a question," she said. "It sounded like an accusation." She took a big drag on her cigarette and looked away from me, smoke seeping from her nostrils. She set the cigarette on the wall, took off her purple hat, and ran her fingers through her brown curls.

"Let's quit dancing around this," I said. "I read what Pete was writing at the time of his death. He knew all about what you were doing, and you knew he knew."

"I don't know what you're talking about."

"The fishing boats. You were talking about that the night he died, how Pete was doing an exposé of the fishing fleet."

"Well that's what he told me," she said. "He always had some dirt he needed to dig up. You know Pete. So?"

"And you know what he was writing about. Right? And knew about it last Friday night?"

"May I remind you Pete and I broke up three weeks ago. I have no idea what Pete was working on at the time of his death. And you don't either."

"I read the articles he was writing, River."

"You what?"

Jesus. "What, you want me to shout? I opened his documents, River. I read the lead story, which was unfinished but conclusive. You know what I'm talking about."

She dunked her cigarette in her coffee. "Oh shit."

"Right."

"I thought that document was corrupted. That's what Freddy told us."

"Clearly Freddy read the article and destroyed the document. Smart kid."

"Then how did you get it open?" she asked. "How could you read it?"

"Carol saved a copy on her computer, and she got it to open. She's a smart kid, too. What I want to know is: why did you want to save that disk, if you knew it was going to incriminate you?"

"I didn't."

"You did too. You found the disk, you gave it to me, you—"

"I mean I didn't know it would incriminate me," she said. "Freddy found out when he read the article, so he corrupted the document. For my sake. After you left the house he told me what the article said. I was glad he'd destroyed all that stuff. It would have made me look, I don't know—"

"Like you had a motive for murder."

She stared into my eyes, her face bright red and breakable. "I want you to get rid of that story, Guy. Please, I beg of you. Nobody needs to know about all that. You told me yourself you're not interested in controversial issues. You're not an investigative journalist, so please, please, Guy, just trash that stuff, okay?"

"I will if you'll tell me the rest of the story," I said.

"There's nothing more to tell," she muttered. She reached in her bag and brought out her smokes. She tried to light one, but her match hand was shaking too hard, and I didn't offer to help her.

"Okay," I told her. "I'll quit beating you up. But I can't help noticing how similar this is to the olden days, when the Websters first came to Jefferson Bay. In boats." I took a sip of my coffee. *"Plus ça change,"* I said.

"Plus c'est la même chose," she replied. "Yep. We still take our crop to market in boats. But that doesn't mean...you don't think I killed Pete Thayer, do you, Guy? I mean I loved that man!"

"No. Of course I don't think you killed Pete," I said.

"Thank God. I mean I couldn't stand it if you—"

"I think your friend Nails killed him."

CHAPTER FIVE

Wednesday morning Carol and I walked the six blocks to the store instead of taking our usual walk along the beach trail. I went right upstairs to finish setting up the newspaper office. I turned one of the work tables into a desk for myself and another into a desk for Carol. I carried both of our computers up the stairs and plugged them in. The third table I left clear, ready for production work, whatever that might entail.

The phone company arrived about ten and by eleven we were connected to the world by phone, through which we could access the Internet. In business. Publishers again.

My first phone calls were to Elizabeth Butler, Lydia Sweet, Jackie Haas, and Artie Miller, the former staff of the *Jefferson Nickel*. I got them all to agree to come to the store that afternoon for a meeting. They agreed to do this as a favor to Pete's memory, but they each made it clear they had no interest of staying on with the business. Fine, I said. We just need a few pointers. Right, they said, each in a different way. Like everything we learned over five years of full-time work, in one hour?

Please, I said.

They said okay. Four o'clock.

I went downstairs and said to Carol, "Why do you suppose the police haven't asked us anything about this murder case they're supposed to be on top of?"

"Maybe they don't need any help," she said. "Which is fine by us, right?"

"Don't you think they'd want to know what Pete was investigating at the time of his death?"

"Guy, keep your nose clean."

"Really. It's as if they don't really want to know—"

"Fine."

I took my fedora and my windbreaker off the coat rack.

"Where are you going?" Carol asked.

"I thought I'd go check out the harbor," I said.

"Why?"

"I don't know. Just curious, I guess."

"Guy, don't get in any trouble. Please."

"Me?"

"Yeah, you," she said. "And me. Don't get me in any trouble either."

It was a working harbor, full of fishing boats, not yachts. It smelled like fish and diesel oil, and the boards of the pier were scuffed and stained from heavy boots and fish guts. Gulls squabbled over the cement troughs on the north side of the pier, where fishermen could gut their catch, while otters and sea lions bobbed in the deep water underneath, waiting for whatever dropped. Fishing boats were berthed on the south side, tied to slips and bumping their rubber tires against the creaking wood.

Up on land was a parking lot for pickup trucks and boats on trailers. The parking ended up as a cement road down into the cove where boats were launched. On one side of the lot was the harbor master's shack; on the other side was Crabby's, the diner where fishermen ate burgers and fries. Both buildings could have used a coat of paint.

I walked out to the end of the pier, then turned around and walked back, turning out onto each slip and reading the names painted on the sterns of the boats. What did I expect to see, a boat named "Nails"? "Louie Luau"? I did see some good names: *Juana Dance, Les Dewitt, Little Mermaid, Piggy Sue*....

Back on solid land I walked into Crabby's and headed toward the counter in the back, but before I got there I saw Charles Connolly sitting in a booth talking to a large man with a gray crew cut, who was wearing a black leather jacket. I strolled over to the booth and smiled at the teenager. "Remember me?" I asked.

Charles looked up and said, "Hey. Yeah. The bookstore guy. Freddy tells me you're going into the newspaper business."

"No shit?" his big friend said. "Just like your old man, huh, Chunky?"

I took a look at the man who apparently didn't know we're not supposed to call Charles "Chunky" anymore. He was younger than I, maybe in his late forties, and at least a foot taller. That was just a guess, because he was sitting down, but I'm pretty good at guessing just how big men are. He was stirring his coffee with a massive hand.

"Sit down," he said. "Chunky, move over for your buddy." He gave me a poor parody of a friendly smile. "Want a cup of coffee?" He was chewing gum.

"No," I answered. "I already had some this morning. I just—"

"Then what are you doing in this dump? The food's not fit to eat."

I ignored that and turned to Charles. "You know a man named Nails?" I asked. "Fisherman?"

Charles glanced quickly at his friend then back to me. "Never heard of him."

"Hangs around with another fisherman, big guy named Louie Luau?"

Charles shrugged. He was no longer smiling, and he wasn't looking me in the eye, either.

The man across the booth said, "I believe you're talking about Mister Andersen. Nels Andersen?"

"That could be," I said. "I don't know him personally."

"Little guy?"

"That's a matter of perspective," I said.

He bobbed his head and grinned, his jaw still working his gum. "I guess it would be," he said. "I guess to you Mister Andersen's a pretty big fella."

Who was this asshole? "I don't believe I've met you either, come to think of it." I held my right hand out across the table. "I'm Guy Mallon."

The man stopped stirring his coffee and the spoon clattered against the side of the mug. He reached across the table too, but his right hand wasn't open like mine. It was a fist, with knuckles the size of marbles. Was this some kind of cool motorcycle-gang way of shaking hands? I closed my hand and bumped fists with him.

"What's that supposed to mean?" he whispered. "You don't really want to fight me, do you, Guy Mallon?"

"Absolutely not. What's your name?" I let my fist vanish and pulled my hand back across the table and down into my lap.

"Thomas." He began stirring his coffee again.

"Nice to meet you, Thomas. Now if you gentlemen will excuse me—"

"Thomas is my last name."

"Okay. And your first name?"

"Jefferson. You can call me Jeff. So you're a newspaperman?"

"It's just a hobby," I answered. "How about you? Fisherman?"

"Shit." Jeff Thomas grinned at me with an open mouth. One of his eye teeth was steel, and the other was missing. "I'm in business."

"What kind of business?"

"I'm in the business of minding my own business."

Sheesh. "Right. Got it. Well." I stood up. "Nice chatting with you Charles. Jeff. So long."

"Been good to know ya," Jeff said.

Charles Connolly snickered.

I walked out of Crabby's and into the fresh air of the harbor parking lot.

I got into my car and thought for a moment before starting the engine, trying to figure out why I had assumed "Andersen" was spelled with an E.

When the connection came to me, I took my key out of the ignition and got out of the car, locked it again, and strolled back to the pier.

The *Little Mermaid* was a small boat. Its deck was covered with machinery and heavy equipment that I knew nothing about. There was a cabin toward the bow and from the pier I could see that the cabin door was open. I hopped aboard.

Knocking on the open door of the cabin I shouted down the steps, "Anybody home?"

No answer, but I could tell from the rich smell of skunks that someone was down there, and I knew what he was smoking. This was clearly none of my business. I turned and prepared to jump back onto the pier.

I heard steps behind me. Heavy steps. Monster heavy steps.

I turned around and looked up into the placid face of Louie Luau. His eyelids were riding low, his eyebrows high. He reeked of weed. He advanced until I had to bend my neck back as far as it would go in order to see his face, which seemed to occupy most of the gray sky. He spoke, sort of. "Uhhh."

"I'd like to talk with Mister Andersen," I answered. "I need to tell him something."

Louie Luau moved even closer, breathing through his smelly teeth.

"We seem to have a communication problem," I said.

"Huh?"

"My name's Guy. Listen, if Nails isn't here, I'll just be on my way."

"Yah." Maybe an actual word, but maybe not.

"Okay, well—"

"YAH!" Louie Luau roared with a force that spun me around and flung me off the boat and onto the pier. I began walking toward land without looking back, picking up speed the farther I got from the boat, and the closer I got to the large man who was walking in my direction, the man in the black leather jacket. He seemed to be minding his own business at full throttle. I slowed back down and got my keys out of my pants pocket so I could make a fast getaway.

We met.

"Hello, big Guy," he said.

"Jeff."

"You in a hurry?"

"Yeah. I have to get back to the office." I jingled my keys

"Come here," he said. "I want to show you something." He put his arm around my shoulder and led me to the railing on the north side of the pier. We stood between two bloody, stinking troughs. He pointed down into the water below us, where seals poked their noses up through a web of kelp. "See that?"

"What am I supposed to be looking at?"

I heard him say, "You're supposed to be minding your own business." And I felt his huge claws grip the collar of my windbreaker and the seat of my pants and lift me until I was out over the railing, looking straight down into the curious gaze of a brown seal with black whiskers.

"God damn it! Let go of me, asshole! Put me down!"

"As you wish, little brother," he whispered.

My keys fell from my hand and hit the water before I did.

God damn, that water was cold!

I had to fight my way up to the surface through the tangle of kelp, then fight to breathe; the fall had knocked the wind from my lungs.

My clothes were heavy and my feet were held down by weeds, and I was scared that the seals would mistake me for fish guts, which I could hardly blame them for. I reached for a pier, and sliced the palms of both my hands on barnacles. I swallowed a mouthful of oily, fishy, ice-cold water, then forced myself to breast-stroke to shore. By the time I got there I was exhausted, shivering, barely able to hold myself erect. I stumbled across the narrow rocky beach and climbed the wooden stairs to the parking lot. My hands stung from salty wounds. My soggy clothes weighed a ton.

When I reached my car I remembered that it was locked. My keys were at the bottom of the harbor. Fuck.

I walked to the harbor master's hut and opened the door. A woman seated at a desk jumped up and said, "Ye gods! Did you fall in?"

I nodded, my teeth chattering. "Will you do me a favor?"

"Let me get you a towel."

She disappeared, then reappeared with a towel which she handed to me. I wiped my face, dried my head, and blotted my bloody palms.

"Do you have a change of clothes?" she asked.

"Yeah, but not here. Would you call the sheriff for me?"

"The sheriff?"

"Blue Heron," I said. "Tell him Guy Mallon's in trouble."

"Holy cow, Guy. All right, just what the hell happened?" Blue Heron opened the passenger-side door of his car. "Get in."

"I fell off the pier," I told him when I was strapped in. "Thanks for coming down."

"What were you doing here?" he asked me. He started the engine. "Jesus, we got to get you home. You need to get out of those wet clothes. So how did you happen to fall off the damn pier? Come on. What were you doing?"

"I thought I was minding my own business, but not everybody agreed with me."

"You were pushed?"

"Sort of."

"By?"

"A man who calls himself Jefferson Thomas. Heard of him?"

"Nope. What's he look like?"

"Large. Even if he were small he'd look large. Gray crew cut and a steel eyetooth. Sound familiar?"

Blue shook his head. "I don't think he's local. Well, enough for now. We have to get you home." He drove up out of the harbor and into the main part of town. "Where do you live?"

"My house is locked and I can't get in," I said. "You can drop me off at the bookstore, but I do want to ask you a question or two."

The sheriff said, "Tomorrow morning. Right now you need a hot bath and some dry clothes. Get Carol to take good care of you. And whatever you were doing?"

"Yes?"

"Quit," he said. "Okay, here's Scarecrow Books. Get out. See you tomorrow morning at my office. Okay?"

I thanked him again, got out of the car, and shivered my way into the bookstore.

Carol looked up from the counter. "Guy! What happened? Where's your hat?"

"Pacific Ocean," I said. "Can I borrow your keys?"

"What happened?"

"Carol, may I please borrow your keys?"

She shut her mouth and frowned. She reached into her purse and pulled out her keys, which she tossed across the counter to me. I missed, and they clattered on the wooden floor.

"You have to tell me what happened," she said.

"I will. I promise. But right now I'm going home to get warm. I'll be back by four o'clock."

"Four o'clock?"

"We have a meeting, remember?"

"Are you okay?"

"I'll be back by four."

Which I was, in warm dry clothes and with bandages on my hands. Lydia and Jackie were already at the store when I got there, so I didn't have a chance to tell Carol about my adventure until after the meeting.

The meeting went well. Jackie Haas gave Carol a list of her responsibilities as business manager, and Carol looked it over and said it all made sense to her. After all, Carol had run a publishing company for years. Lydia Sweet gave us a list of all the drop-off spots where the *Jefferson Nickel* needed to be delivered each week. Elizabeth Butler brought a list of ad accounts, with the names and phone numbers of the contacts. She gave me a brief lecture on how to sell ads. "Make it clear you're overjoyed to be doing them a favor."

That left design, layout, and production. Artie Miller said, "What do you got, Quark or PageMaker?"

"Neither one," I said. "Just word processing, spreadsheets, a mail-merge program, that's pretty much it."

"You're going to have to get PageMaker or Quark. Also Illustrator, Photo-Shop, you need a good scanner, and…what's the matter? I thought you guys were publishers."

Carol and I exchanged a look of dismay. "We don't know how to do all those things, Artie," Carol said. "We had our books designed and typeset by a free-lance book designer in Santa Barbara. Do you think there's anybody in Jefferson City who could manage our layout and design on a free-lance basis?"

Artie grinned and said, "Aw shit. Thought you'd never ask."

"You'll do it?" I asked.

"I got to make a living. Why not? But I get to work at home. I don't want to be in the building when the paper gets bombed."

"I just want to know one thing, Guy," Carol said when I handed her her martini that evening. I had chicken on the barbecue and rice and artichokes on the stove. We had half an hour to relax before dinner would be ready to dish up. I had a lot to tell her, and telling her was not going to be relaxing. I wondered, in that moment, when I'd ever get to relax again.

"What's that?" I asked.

"Are you out of your fucking mind? What in the world were you thinking of? Don't you know that man is dangerous? Those men, I mean? Didn't you hear me ask you not to get us in trouble? Guy?"

I held my bourbon up to the sunlight, which had finally arrived late in the afternoon, as usual. The ice cubes sparkled and the liquor gave off a warm luster. I caressed the glass between my hands, letting the cold soothe my wounds.

"I'm waiting."

I set my drink down on the coffee table and crossed my legs. "It seemed like a good precaution to take," I said. "I thought that if I approached Nails first—"

"That's crazy! The man's a killer."

"We don't know that. He might be, or he might not. But either way—"

"Either way you were putting us both in danger."

I took a sip. "If you'll let me finish a sentence or two, maybe I can explain why I went to see Nails, and what I wanted to say to him. You may still think I was nuts, but at least you'll know I had a reason. Maybe I made a mistake, but you can't ask me 'just one thing,' as you put it, and then swat down everything I try to say."

Carol blushed. She has a great Irish blush that starts at the base of her throat and spreads up across her cheeks and almost closes her eyes. "Sorry," she said. "Go ahead. Please."

One more sip, and then I put the glass down. "If Nails or Louie Luau or both of them murdered Pete Thayer, it was because Pete knew too much about the way marijuana is shipped out of Jefferson Bay. Not just that Pete knew too much, but that he was going to say too much in his newspaper. Right?"

Carol didn't answer. I expect she would not be able to confine her answer to a simple yes or no, so she nodded for me to go on.

"It's no secret that you and I are taking over the *Jefferson Nickel*. Officially River will be the publisher, and you'll be taking care of business matters, but I'll be the editor and I will be the one to decide what goes in the paper. I think we agree on that, and we've already put the word out. The whole plan will be published in the *Jefferson Republican* tomorrow morning. Nails may already know I'll be the new editor, but in any case I wanted to tell him myself before he read it in the paper, if he reads the paper. And the main thing I wanted to tell him was that I have no interest in whatever story Pete was writing for the issue of the *Nickel* that never came out. I am dropping the story, willing to forget it entirely. I have no interest in how Nails makes a living. I want him to know we are not a threat to him. It's a small town and we drink in the same bar. I don't want him to fear me, and sure as hell don't want to fear him. You are now welcome to tell me how big a mistake I made."

I took another gulp of bourbon, which tasted like just the right medicine to take at the end of a day when I'd been yelled at by a giant, tossed like fish guts into the harbor by a black-jacket thug, and bawled out by the love of my life.

She smiled at me. "I guess you did the right thing," she said. "Or at least you tried to. Now promise me one thing. Promise me you'll stay away from the harbor from now on."

"I can't."

"Guy—"

"I have to go get our car tomorrow morning. It's parked at the harbor."

"I'll get the damn car," she told me.

CHAPTER SIX

"Well, supposedly it doesn't concern me," Blue Heron said the following morning. "I am, as of yesterday afternoon, officially off this investigation. That's why I'm talking to you. If I were the investigating officer, I wouldn't be allowed to speculate with you. But since I've been told I'm just a private citizen as far as this case is concerned, I'm free to gossip all I want."

"Who told you to stay out of it?"

"Chief Marvin of the Jefferson City Police Department. It's a city matter. Which is funny, because usually they want me to do their dirty work. All those dickheads usually want to do is bust the homeless and interrupt loud parties. Good thing we never have any serious crime in this town."

"Unless you count murder," I added.

"But Marvin takes orders from Connolly. That piece in Sunday's *Republican*? About Connolly pledging his support to the police? Right. I'm not saying Seamus knows who did this crime, but he doesn't want anybody to go any further with it."

The sheriff got up from his desk, walked over to the hotplate on top of his filing cabinet, and poured himself another cup of coffee. "You sure you don't want some more?"

"I had two cups before I got here," I said. "And you've already given me two more. I didn't sleep much last night, and now I'm wired as an all-talk radio station."

"Bad dreams?"

"Jesus. In one of them I was wandering around a parking lot looking for books, and there was this old pickup truck with a Rottweiler in the back. I saw some books there, so I climbed up into the back of the truck, and the Rottweiler tried to chew my undershirt off."

I stretched back in my metal folding chair and looked around the sheriff's office. Every horizontal surface was piled with paperwork, and the piles appeared to be built by amateurs. The desk itself looked like a game of 52 Pickup. This office drove me nuts, and it wasn't even my office. I believe in tidy right angles. The sheriff's office was in a concrete block building on the east side of town. The county jail was in the back, and up front was a reception area and Blue's office, a twelve-by-twelve Mixmaster of work in progress. There were certificates and award plaques on the wall behind his desk. On one corner of the desk was small plate that still had crumbs from a Danish out of the past.

Blue sat back down. "Well, I went down to the harbor again," he said, "after I dropped you off. I asked Eloise in the harbor master's office, and I asked Bob at Crabby's, and neither of them ever heard of anyone named Jefferson Thomas, and they didn't remember anyone who matched the description you gave me, either."

"He was there," I said. "I assure you. Him and Charles Connolly both."

"Chunky? You didn't tell me that yesterday."

"My teeth were chattering too hard. I was cold."

"You were scared, Guy. I don't blame you. So what were you doing down at the harbor anyhow? Bob makes the worst hamburgers in town."

"I wanted to talk to a fisherman," I said. "That guy Nails."

Blue scratched his cheek. "What the hell did you want with him?"

"I wanted to tell him something. But I never got a chance. His first mate yelled me off his boat."

"You were on his boat? Who invited you onto his boat?"

"I just walked on. I—"

"Guy, you don't do that. It's considered rude."

"Well, I didn't mean any harm by it. I was just—"

"You know how a Rottweiler feels about his master's pickup truck?"

"Ah."

"So what did you want to tell our good friend Nails?"

I took my time deciding, and then said, "I think he had a reason to kill Pete Thayer, and I wanted him to know he had no reason to kill me."

"Nails? Why would Nails want to kill Pete Thayer?"

"They were both out there, behind the Redwood Door, when—"

"Opportunity, maybe. But what was the motive?"

That took another decision, but I was already in with both feet anyway. "I think I ought to tell you about what Pete Thayer was writing at the time of his death," I said. "What would have appeared in the *Jefferson Nickel* today, if he had lived."

"You mean the marijuana traffic through Jefferson Harbor?"

"You know about that?"

"I know about the traffic. Go on."

"Well, I read the story. It's pretty damaging."

"Name any names?" Blue asked.

"No. But he does say it's big business. Thousands, maybe millions of dollars, street value, leave here, bound for southern California, Oregon, Washington."

"I hate to break it to you, Guy, but that's not news. How long have you lived in this county?"

"Three years."

"And you never heard about our primary cash crop?"

"Well sure, but there's more. According to Pete's story, the medical growers are getting into the act."

"So?"

"Well, that's what Pete's story was really about. Not the shipping industry, but the people taking advantage of their permits to grow more than they're entitled to grow, shipping the surplus out illegally."

Blue Heron shrugged. "No big deal. And I knew all about this story, by the way."

"How did you know about it?"

Blue chuckled. "Nails told me. And by the way, he's not transporting pot to the streets of Oakland. That stupid boat of his wouldn't get past Port Silva. And if you think he or Louie Luau was responsible for Pete's death, you're wrong. They were out in the town square, smoking dope at the time. I was there with them, giving them the usual warning, at least fifteen minutes before Gloria called the switchboard."

"Couldn't they have killed him as soon as they went outside with him, then gone to the square, leaving him to be discovered, which River did, maybe twenty minutes later?"

"Possible. But the wound looked fresh to me, no more than five or ten minutes old. I'm no expert, I admit. But I am an expert on how people act under stress, and the guys I was talking with out there on the square were not one bit nervous. As a matter of fact, Nails and Louie were laughing about Pete's supposed exposé when my cell rang, telling me there'd been a murder."

"How did Nails know so much about the story Pete was writing?"

"Nails was doing some investigating for the paper. He was what they call an unidentified source. Now he's pissed off because he won't get paid."

"Oh."

"Don't feel bad, Guy. Even real detectives go down blind alleys."

"So you don't think what Pete was writing had anything to do with his death?"

"Nope. Nobody cares, Guy. Everybody knows."

"Well, I'm still not going to get mixed up in it. I'm going to stick to non-controversial subjects."

"Like that local history thing?" Blue asked. He pulled a copy of that morning's *Jefferson Republican* out of a pile of papers on the floor beside his desk. "Your piece in this morning's paper? The one where you declare the new mission of the *Jefferson Nickel?* The so-called local history project?"

"What about it?"

"Hot issue, dude. It's a closet full of spiders. That's what killed Pete Thayer, is my guess. He kept quiet about it, but he was carrying a rocket in his pocket when he died."

"What are you talking about?"

Blue Heron got up from his desk. "Let's go for a drive. I want to give you a history lesson."

I looked at my watch. "I'm already late. Carol's waiting for me so we can have lunch together."

"You can call her from my car," Blue said. "We'll take her to the casino for lunch. That's the place to tell this story."

Blue Heron cut an impressive figure as he led Carol and me through the noisy front room of the Steelhead Casino to the coffee shop in the back. A tall man with inky black hair and a substantial gut, he wore his starched tan uniform well. We sat in a booth by the window, overlooking the Steelhead River. Casinos are usually noisy, nervous places, but this coffee shop was a serene oasis compared to the food court in the Steelhead Mall just a hundred yards upriver.

A waitress wearing a tag that said "Nancy" patted Blue's cheek and gave each of us a menu and a smile.

"What'll you have?" the sheriff asked. "Want some coffee?"

I laughed at him. "How many cups a day do you drink?"

He raised his eyebrows. "When are you going to learn not to ask personal questions?"

"Sorry."

He shook his head and brushed the question away from his face. "Just yanking your chain. I drink my fair share. Carol, what looks good?"

"How's the clam chowder?" she asked. "Nice view, by the way."

Blue waited until Nancy was done pouring his coffee before he answered. "Chowder's excellent. And yes, nice view," he agreed. "I was born right over there, on the other side of the river. House is gone now. Now it's a county park. How much do you know about this place, the Steelhead Rancheria?"

"I assume it's an Indian reservation?"

"Was. What else have you heard?"

"I know there was some trouble back in 1986 when Seamus Connolly decided to develop the mall."

"There's a lot more history than that."

"I expect there is."

Carol and I each had a cup of clam chowder, and we split a club sandwich. Blue had a heaping plateful of scampi on pasta, with a side order of Cobb salad, followed by huckleberry pie à la mode, which he washed down with coffee.

"Here's the deal," he said when the dishes were cleared away and he was sipping his second cup. "And I think I should be talking to both of you, right?"

"Saves time," Carol said. "We tell each other everything anyway."

"Figured. The thing is, Pete Thayer wasn't killed for what he knew about pot going out on the fishing boats. I think someone was afraid he was going to take the wrong side in a family feud that's older and thornier than anyone alive. And now, according to this morning's *Republican,* you two want to get into history business too. Can of worms, friends. Can of worms. I can't tell you everything I know, because some of it I don't know for sure, but let me tell you this: you're better off not publishing any stories that deal with family secrets. The history of the Steelhead Rancheria is public knowledge, but there's other stuff I won't even bring up because it would be dangerous for you to know. Grudges kill people. Is that warning enough?"

I took the hint but I could still say, "So you think Seamus killed Pete? That was his BMW behind the bar."

"No, as a matter of fact, it wasn't Seamus who killed him. Seamus was with his girlfriend in Redding, on the other side of the Alps. They were at the country club there all afternoon and all evening. He didn't come home till the following day."

"But his car."

"Well, whoever drove that car there wiped off all the fingerprints on the steering wheel. There were no prints on the wheel or on any of the manual controls or on the door. Kinda weird, huh."

"The Connolly boy?" Carol suggested. "Charles?"

"I wish," Blue said. "But at the time of the crime, Chunky was in the security office out at the mall. He was caught trying to shoplift a portable CD player from Radio Shack."

"How do you know?" I asked.

"They fax me reports. The mall's County, not City."

"Do you press charges?"

Blue smiled. "Not when it's Seamus Connolly's kid. He gets a talking to, for all the good that does."

"I saw him Saturday morning," I said. "He and Freddy seemed to be friends, which struck me as odd."

"I'll say this much," Blue said. "If Freddy and Chunky are friends now, it's not because Chunky's gotten any mellower. Freddy must be moving over to the wild side, which is a shame, if you ask me. Of course nobody asks me. But Chunky's no murderer. He's an asshole, but he's just a kid. However, if he didn't have an alibi, I'd be pretty suspicious. Presumably he'd have access to the BMW car keys. And somebody drove that car to the parking lot and made sure it stayed there. Somebody without fingerprints."

"Who else didn't do it?" Carol asked. "River was out back in the lot. So was Guy."

Blue Heron rubbed his fingers over his brow, his eyes, his nose, his upper lip. Nodded and said, "Here's what I do know for sure. That knife did not come from the kitchen of the Redwood Door. And I have a feeling the murderer was a man, not a woman. Why? Because the men's room window was wide open and it looked as if somebody with muddy boots had crawled up on the back of the toilet to get out of the building, maybe came in to wash the blood off his hands and then heard the commotion. Of course maybe somebody was just trying to get out of paying his bar tab.

"I also know it wasn't Guy. Why? Because he told me so. And I know it wasn't River. Why? Because that's not something River would do. Believe me. She might have been pissed off, but she is completely nonviolent. She wouldn't even let me shoot a rabid bear one time on her property. Any other questions?"

"Seems to me you've ruled out every possible suspect," I said. "So where do you go from here?"

"I don't know. Like I said, it's not my case."

"But you must be curious."

"Damn right I'm curious, but my hands are tied," Blue said. "Yours aren't. If you're as curious as I am, you'll give the matter some more thought, and I hope you'll let me know what you come up with. But don't be obvious about it, okay? Don't be dumb. Don't ask a bunch of nosy questions, and don't publish a bunch of dirty laundry in that newspaper of yours. I don't want to lose any more friends."

"So tell us about this Steelhead Rancheria business," Carol said. "You said there was more to the story."

The sheriff sipped his coffee. He put down his cup, wiped his upper lip, and folded the paper napkin with careful creases.

INTERLUDE
The Steelhead Rancheria

I

Dorothy Webster was only five years old the evening she became an orphan, the first Tuesday of November, 1960. Her parents, Joseph and Holly, were killed in an automobile crash on Connolly Avenue, coming home from the Redwood Door, where they had raised their glasses once too often in celebration of John Kennedy's election. Whoever rammed their car never reported the accident, but it happened outside the Connolly family home, after what was to have been a victory celebration for President-elect Nixon, but turned into a brawl between the Connollys who were proud Republicans and the Connollys who remembered they were Irish. Little Dorothy was spending the night with her grandparents, Henry and Amanda, out on Bear Gulch Road.

And there she lived for the rest of her childhood.

She wept for her parents, but she already adored her grandparents, who taught her to be proud of the Steelhead blood in her veins. She grew up a country girl, but her grandpa drove her into town each day to attend the grammar school, then the junior high, then Jefferson High School. She was tall and athletic and as good as a high school girl could be expected to be in the late-nineteen sixties, and if she lost her virginity in her sophomore year because a stunning, handsome boy five years older than she took her to a hunting lodge in the Jefferson Alps on the night of the hunter's moon, it was nobody's business but her own. It didn't stop her from graduating at the top of her class from Jefferson High, then going on to Stanford, like her father and grandfather before her.

Unlike her father and her grandfather, Dorothy did not last at Stanford. She moved to the Santa Cruz mountains after her sophomore year, and there she joined a women's commune, learned the art of shiatsu massage, played a hammer dulcimer, gardened, knotted macramé, and fended off long-haired, patchouli-oil-scented suitors, remembering that lover she had left in Jefferson County, the young man to whom she had given her maidenhead. The one who had explained that he could not be tied to one pussy, and the only man she would ever love, she just knew it. As Cathy loved Heathcliff, but his name wasn't Heathcliff. It was Connolly. Billy Connolly.

It was because of Billy Connolly that Dorothy stayed away from home. She dearly loved her grandparents, and saw them whenever they came as far south as the Benbow Inn in southern Humboldt County, but she never went north with them, back into Jefferson County, where her broken heart and her broken hymen still tainted the land.

Instead, she moved from commune to commune, remaining almost a virgin. She was a cook-gardener-massage therapist at Karma Hot Springs on Mount Shasta when she received word, in April 1978, that her grandfather and grandmother had both died, one day apart. And, incidentally, that she had inherited what was left of the Webster fortune, not that she cared about fortune. She was now the only Webster left in Jefferson County, although she was not in Jefferson County at the time, and for some reason that mattered to her. She knew it was time to move home. Besides which, the reason she was not in Jefferson County at the time was the reason she wanted to return.

The day after the double funeral, Dorothy met with Bradford Parker, the executor of the Webster estate. His office was on the top floor of the Webster Building, which the Webster family trust still rented from the Jefferson Lumber Company.

Bradford was a tired, kindly man in his middle years, balding, boring, and bulging at the waist. He looked over the top of his wire-rimmed glasses, across the desk that had been in the Webster family since San Francisco, and said, "Dorothy, sweetheart, there's not much left."

"What does that mean?" asked the twenty-three-year-old heiress. "How much is not much?"

"Ezekiel Webster was one of the richest men in California in the nineteenth century," Bradford explained. "Since then, not one Webster in four generations has earned a thin dime. Well, your great-great-grandfather Jonathan tried to make a go of it in the ice business, but that was a disaster. Your great-grandfather, your grandfather, and father spent what was left on harmless hobbies. What you have, what is left, is worth about thirty thousand dollars in various pieces of paper, as well as three pieces of real estate. You have the house in which you were born, at the corner of Connolly Boulevard and Webster Avenue. You have your grandparents' place out on Bear Gulch Road, a hundred acres of forest and farm, where you were raised. And you have that ranch, the Webster Ranch out by the river. That's the one you need to sell."

"Sell?"

"You have a buyer. Seamus Connolly wants that land, and he's willing to pay a fair price. Then we'll be able to restructure your assets, so you'll receive an annuity that will keep you going indefinitely. So there's really nothing to be worried about."

Dorothy said, "But don't people live on the Webster Ranch?"

Bradford Parker shrugged. "Indians," he said. "Squatters, really. Your family has been good enough to let them live out there rent-free for generations, but we have to keep up with the times. I mean the Indians are nice people, most of them, but—"

"Give it to them," Dorothy said.

Bradford took off his wire-rim glasses and folded them in one hand. "I beg your pardon?"

"You heard me." Dorothy was remembering Blue Heron, a sweet boy in her high school, her best friend, really, a shy doofus who had grown up on that ranch. She was not about to make her friend Blue the tenant of any Connolly. Especially Seamus Connolly, that horse's ass. "I want to give the Webster Ranch to the Steelhead Tribe. Sell Seamus the house in town, if he wants it. I'll live out on Bear Gulch Road."

"That doesn't make sense," Bradford Parker said. "Dorothy, let's act like grown-ups. The house in town will bring maybe forty thousand dollars. The ranch could be worth a hundred. Or more. Unless you have some way of making a living—"

"He will provide," Dorothy said.

"He?"

Dorothy smiled. "Tchlkmsh," she said.

"Oh for God's sake."

Dorothy fumbled with the handles of her straw bag. "Seamus Connolly? Is his brother still around?"

II

The old farts came all the way up from Willits, two counties to the south, to attend the sunrise ceremony and celebration on the twenty-first of June, 1978. None of the elders, in fact no Indians over forty years old, still lived on the Webster Ranch, even though they could live there rent-free. The old folks preferred to hang out on the Mendo Intertribal Rancheria in Willits, where they could watch television, play bingo, and receive BIA benefits. It was called Intertribal because the BIA said Indians of any tribe could use it, but the only Indians there were Steelheads, formerly of Jefferson County. They were the elders, the ones who made the official decisions, but they left the decisions of daily life to the young people they'd left behind.

The Indians still on the ranch were hard-working and proud. There were about thirty-five of them, a dozen men, eight wives, three unmarried women, and a bunch of kids running around. The kids were bussed to school in town. Some of the men worked in construction or for Jefferson Lumber; the other men fished and hunted, cured meat, tanned hides, and smoked salmon. The women farmed the land, sold their produce on the Jefferson City town square on Saturday mornings, and canned whatever they didn't sell. The ranch had no electricity or gas, no alcohol, and no religion other than the old ways, which few of them knew much about. The community lived in cabins they had built themselves, and they ate, danced, and played Ping-Pong in a common rec hall, where there were toilets, showers, wood-burning stoves, kerosene lamps, and a giant communal kitchen with ten propane refrigerators and three twelve-burner propane stoves. There they held their weekly meetings, presided over by the biggest, friendliest, and smartest Steelhead Indian, a young man named Blue Heron.

Blue Heron stood on the porch of the rec hall and looked out over the assembled group. Before him stood the entire Steelhead Tribe or what was left of it, including the old folks from Willits, as well as a few white people: the mayor of Jefferson City and his wife, the chief of police, three members of the Jefferson County Board of Supervisors, a reporter and a photographer from the *Jefferson Republican*, and the Woman of the Day, the tall, strong star of Blue's heart. Wearing a straw hat with flowers around the rim and a calico granny gown, smiling like the summer dawn. He'd been in love with her since ninth grade.

He smiled into her smile, then addressed the gathering. "You know I don't use up a lot of my brain talking. But I do try and say what's important, and this Solstice morning an important thing is happening to us all. Right down there in front of me stands the most generous person I know. Her family for generations has allowed our people to live on this land, and now, as the sole surviving member of that generous family, Dorothy Webster is giving to the Steelhead People, tax-free, possession of our home, a home we have loved since the old days!" He held out his hand, and Dorothy trotted up the steps to join him on the porch. She threw her arms around the big Indian, squeezed him and kissed his cheek.

Victor Two Elks, the ancient Chief Elder of the Steelhead Tribe, limped up the stairs and stood on Blue's other side. He shuffled, dusted off his denim jacket, and slapped his cowboy hat against his jeans. Blue backed away and let the old man and the young woman exchange bows, a handshake, and a hug.

Dorothy said, loud enough for the hushed gathering to hear, "It was always your land. You know that. I know it too. I am pleased to announce that this land is now yours legally, and we are filing papers to have this land recognized by the federal government as an official Native American rancheria. You will have sovereignty!" She handed a manila envelope to the Chief Elder.

Old Victor Two Elks took the envelope with a trembling hand. He drew a deep breath, frowned, then chanted the speech he must have labored to remember: "Thank you, Miss Webster, on behalf of the Steelhead People."

"There is no need to thank me." Dorothy replied. "I wish I could do more."

You can, Blue Heron thought. *But I'll never ask.*

He escorted Dorothy Webster and Victor Two Elks down the stairs. The women had tables set up in the meadow, where they served coffee and cakes to the entire group. Dorothy and Blue Heron answered questions for the reporter, posed for the photographer, and shook hands with the politicians.

When all the white people except Dorothy were gone, she and the Indians made a large hand-holding circle in the meadow. The sun was high in the east now, warming the meadow and lighting up the silver surface of the Steelhead River.

When the people, even the children, quieted down, Blue spoke. "Dorothy, you are related to every one of us. Your great-grandmother, Little Shell, was a Steelhead Indian, and so are you. You are always welcome on our Steelhead

Rancheria, and me and my boys are going to build you a house to stay in whenever you come to spend time with us. Or..." the big man trembled "...or to live in if you want."

Dorothy grinned. "You're too generous, Blue. You want me to live here on the Rancheria?"

"You're one of us." Blue looked around and saw all his cousins smiling their approval. He looked into her face and saw the blush on her cheeks, eyes like the sky, teeth like white agates, hair a forest of curls with flowers woven in, her breasts swelling against the calico. "Aw jeez," he cried. "I want to change your name!"

"Be my guest," she murmured. "What will you call me?"

Blue shut his eyes and listened. The breeze in the far-off forest. The crying of a hawk, the squawk of a raven, the rush of the river where the steelhead swam.

"River," he said.

"River," the tribe repeated.

River wept and murmured, "Thank you."

The gentle sounds of the morning were bothered by a buzz that grew into a roar as a Harley Davidson tore through the gates of the Rancheria, rattled and blasted down the dirt driveway, then screeched to a stop in a spray of gravel. A long, brawny man in a leather jacket with steel studs and wrap-around mirror glasses, an ape with a thundercloud of curly blond hair and a beard like a briar patch, climbed off the chopper, stretched, and stomped into the circle.

Grinned. Grinned his shiny big teeth right at the tall young woman and chuckled. "Hey, Dodo. What's shakin'?"

"Sweetie-pie!" River cried. She let go of Blue's hand and rushed into the arms of the biker. She planted a long, involved kiss on his mouth and announced, "Guess what! I have a new name!"

The man took off the shades and cocked an eyebrow. "Yeah?"

She nodded, turned and smiled at Blue Heron. "Tell him, Blue. Tell him my new name."

Blue took his time, then said, "We call this woman River."

The biker laughed. "That's classic! Terrific! Hey, man, I want you to give me a new name too. Come on, Blue. What's my Indian name? Huh?"

Blue Heron shut his eyes. Squeezed them tight. Tried to listen, but all he could hear was the anger in his ears. He thought of the worst name he knew, then opened his eyes.

"Connolly," he said. "Your name is Billy Connolly."

Shit.

It was a mistake, Blue knew it almost from the beginning. Yes, it felt good to have the land belong to the Steelhead People, to be sovereign, whatever that meant, but how was it going to change their lives for the better?

Yes, it was a joyful day when River arrived with a moving van and settled in the house that Blue and his cousins had built for her over the summer. But her boyfriend helped her move in and then began visiting, then staying overnight, then moving in his clothes, his motorcycle, his bottomless supply of weed, and his boom box running on car batteries. By wintertime Billy Connolly had become a full-time resident of the Rancheria, and there was nothing Blue could do about it, because River seemed to want it that way.

She was wrapped up and sold to this man five years older than her, handsome as a wolf and mean as a skunk in a trap.

Another reason Blue couldn't do anything about it? Because the other Indian guys actually liked Billy. Or liked his dope. Took turns riding on his chopper. Went drinking with him at the Redwood Door, on the town square, on Friday nights. And the Indian girls? The unmarried ones? They followed him around, laughed at his smutty jokes, gave him little presents—feathers, flowers, buttons made of oyster shells, bay leaf wreaths for his bushy blond head. As if he deserved to be so damned handsome. The kids liked him too, played soccer and Ping-Pong with him. He gave them Coca-Cola and cigarettes. He was such an asshole.

Worst, River loved him. Even when he slept with one of the Indian women, that time. Even when he stayed in town and slept with God knows who. Even if he used her and cursed her and made fun of her in front of her friends. He never stopped calling her Dodo.

And there was nothing Blue could do about it, because that's the way she wanted it. River Webster, the sweetest, most beautiful woman in the world, but, Blue had to face it, a complete fool when it came to men.

Billy stood before the tribe at the community meeting on the evening of the first Sunday after the Spring Equinox, 1979. He wore beads and the fisherman's sweater River had knitted for him all through the winter. His smile shone and his halo of hair was orange in the kerosene glow.

"Listen up, braves and maidens," he said. "Gather 'round, chillun, and listen to what's goin' down. Big changes, we're talking serious shit, so sit tight and listen.

"Number one. Dorothy is starting a massage school. Right, babe?"

River nodded and added, "Call me River."

"Right," Billy said. "We're bringing five couples over from Karma Springs to set up a massage business. They're bringing their own tepees. Guys, you wouldn't believe these chicks, and they're going to give us free massages. And their old men can help us with the other business at hand. You probably want to know what that other business is, and here it is, ladies and gentlemen. A cash crop. Some real money, for a change. We're going to get this enterprise smokin'!"

Blue Heron stood up at the back of the hall. "What the hell are you talking about, Billy?"

Billy threw his mouth open in a silent laugh. "You're a stitch, Blue," he said. "Every man in this room knows what I'm talking about. Am I right? Huh?" He swept the room with his grin, and most of the men shrugged and grinned back. "Blue, baby, grow up. We're going to grow the finest crop of herb in Jefferson County. This valley is *perfect*. Forget zucchini, forget melons, forget fuckin artichokes. Man, we're going to be solvent for a change. I have distribution all worked out, and I've got the seeds. Five gallons of seeds. Tomorrow we plant. In six months, we'll be rich. Next year, who knows? Maybe a swimming pool? Coupla hot tubs? A new truck? Electricity! Think about it, people. Television?"

"Illegal," Blue Heron said.

"Fuck that," Billy said. "This is a sovereign nation, remember. Besides."

"Besides what?"

Billy smirked. "Let's put it to a vote."

Blue shook his head. "That's not how we decide things."

"What? You want to duke it out, take it outside? Pistols at dawn? C'mon, man, get real."

Blue could feel the anger growing in his belly, glowing on his face. "Our people decide by consensus, that's how."

"Ah." Billy held his arms out like Elmer Gantry. "Consensus. I get it. Fine and dandy." He bowed to Blue, then addressed the room. "So how many of you want one of those new satellite dish TVs for the rec room. Huh?"

III

The Steelhead Rancheria changed more in its first year than the Webster Ranch had changed during its ninety-four years, and far more than the same land had changed for hundreds of years before that, before the arrival of the Connollys. By summer 1980, what had been a simple farming commune was dotted with two dozen tepees inhabited by white young men and women who pretended to be Indians, which they believed included banging on drums late into the night, swapping sexual partners, staying stoned, and walking about the compound naked whenever the weather permitted. The weather was not always warm enough for that last one, but whenever the sun shone the population swelled with visitors and onlookers from town. Free looks, as long as they weeded in the garden, cleaned the toilets in the rec hall, helped repair buildings, cleared brush, or whatever else Blue Heron told them to do.

The garden prospered. Under Blue Heron's direction, it continued to yield fruits and vegetables, which the Indian women continued to take to market in town on Saturdays; but under Billy Connolly's direction it also yielded a bumper crop whose legal status was questionable, depending on how one interpreted the word "sovereign." Billy's business associates, a couple of scuzzy commercial fishermen from the harbor in Jefferson Bay, had arrived at the end of the first summer and had bought over a hundred paper sacks full of marijuana buds. Billy kept his share of the money (the Indians never knew how much) and gave the rest to the Rancheria, advising them how to spend it. The Indians took his advice (ignoring Blue's advice to give the money back and get out of the marijuana business), and within a month of the harvest the Rancheria had a generator, which furnished electricity, which in turn fueled two hot tubs and powered a satellite-dish television that was kept on all day.

River ran her massage school, which certified a few students and also earned money by laying hands on horny men from Jefferson City. No hanky-panky, River insisted, but nobody told what really went on inside some of those tepees in the meadow, or how much money exchanged hands. Or how that infestation of crabs sneaked into the commune. The Indians blamed the white visitors. The ashram transplants didn't believe in blaming people.

Each year's marijuana harvest was bigger than the one before, and the community continued to thrive. Under Blue's direction, and with the help of gawking day laborers, more plumbing was laid and more toilets were built, as well as a laundry facility, a workshop, and a barn, which was used once a year for drying and curing the crop. After the harvest of 1981, Billy bought the community a pool table for the rec hall; in 1982 it was a tinny upright piano so Indian kids could play "Heart and Soul" ad nauseam. White women helped the Indian women in the kitchen, and the community ate well, a cuisine of blended cultures: smoked fish, venison, brown rice, tofu, and ice cream, for starters. Still no alcohol, still no religion. Unless you count those damned drums, which kept everyone awake far later than the Indian farmers wanted to stay up.

Billy Connolly and Blue Heron divided the authority. Blue was in charge of maintenance, the buildings, and the garden, and remained the leader ("chief," as Billy called him) of the Indian residents. Billy bossed the white people around and was in charge of the cash crop. The two leaders stayed out of each other's long hair. Blue often felt like murdering Billy, but no Steelhead Indian had ever—ever—killed a human being intentionally. He suspected Billy hated him just as much, and perhaps Billy would try to murder him one night, in which case Blue would welcome the chance to strike back.

In April 1982, Billy's brother, Seamus Connolly, married a girl from Yuba City. For no logical reason, Billy was the best man—Billy, whom Seamus despised and who was "best" only when it came to being the worst. The festivities took Billy off the Rancheria and out of the commune for two weeks. When he returned to the Rancheria, he brought with him one of the bridesmaids, a short, buxom junior college dropout named Mindy, who chewed gum with her smile wide open and who snorted when she laughed, which was all the time. Billy introduced Mindy to the members of the community as they gathered for supper. Including River, whose frosty smile was barely gracious.

The following morning, Blue walked down to the river's edge to meditate to the sound of flowing water. When he reached his place, he found River there, sitting on the bank, tossing pebbles into the Steelhead, tears flowing down her cheeks.

He sat beside her and she grasped his hand without looking at him. "Hi, Blue," she snuffled. "Sorry."

"Sorry?"

"I'm such a wimp." She let go of his hand and wiped the tears from her face.

Blue put his arm around her shoulder. "Tell me."

She took in a deep breath and let it out in a jagged sigh. "He wants a ménage-à-trois," she said. "So does she, that Mindy person. They did it with two of the other bridesmaids, three nights in a row, she tells me. Mindy tells me there's enough of Billy to go around. To satisfy all the women in the world! Don't I already know that, Blue? Don't I know what a fucking sex-freak that man is? Don't I?" Her voice grew to a wail and she sobbed into her hands.

"River."

She shook her head.

"River, that man is an asshole."

"Of *course* he's an asshole," River whimpered. "Don't you think I know that? Doesn't everyone know that? That's not the problem. The problem is, I wish he were *my* asshole. *That's* the problem."

Blue held her shoulders tightly with his arm and his large, leathery hand. She dropped her head against his body and they rocked side to side, slowly in time with her ragged sobs.

"Hey hey *hey!* What's going on? Looks like I got to get up early in the morning to keep you two in line, huh? So, is this what you two been doing while I've been gone? Huh?"

Blue and River parted their bodies and slowly rose to their feet. Blue faced Billy and found him grinning fiercely. "Huh?" Billy said again.

River spoke softly. "Are you finished fucking Mindy?" she asked Billy.

"For now." Billy winked at Blue.

Blue said, "I want that woman off the property by noon."

Billy's jaw dropped slowly, wiping out the grin. "Dream on," he said.

Blue took a deep breath, put his hands on his hips, and said, "This here's an Indian rancheria. That means reservation. That means it's reserved for Indians. So far we've allowed you to live here, and your friends from that abbey. That's temporary. You've never been formally invited to live here, and you may be formally asked, *told* I mean, to leave. For now, I want that woman, Mindy whatever her name is, off the premises."

"Dude, it's none of your fucking business. Get real."

"And at the community meeting on Sunday, we'll decide whether or not you white people are welcome to stay. This shit is getting old."

Billy took his time. His shoulders jerked and his knuckles turned into gravel on his clenched fists. "Seems to me," he said at last, softly and clearly, "Dorothy

Webster should decide who's welcome to stay on this land and who should get the fuck out." He turned to River and said, "So, Dodo, what's it going to be? You want to kick us white folks off the old plantation? It's the Webster Ranch, you decide."

She looked first at Blue, then at Billy. "It's not the Webster Ranch anymore, Billy. This is the Steelhead Rancheria. It's not for me to decide."

"I'm telling you, Dorothy—"

"River, I'll go along with whatever you want," Blue said.

"Oh, yeah," Billy said. His lip curled, his eyebrow twitched. "You're so sweet on my woman. Okay, Dodo. What? What is it you want?"

River continued to look back and forth between the two massive men. Quietly, she said, "I want you to get rid of Mindy. I don't want you bringing any more girlfriends to my home. Otherwise, I don't care."

Billy smiled and put a hand on his woman's cheek. "Okay, baby. You don't know what you're missing, but okay. If you'll stay away from Straight Arrow here. Is it a deal?"

Before River could answer that one, Blue said, "Another thing. Okay, you can stay on the Rancheria for now, but the marijuana farming has to stop. Do you hear me? No crop this year."

"You're out of your fucking tree, Chief."

"I'm serious. We had helicopters buzzing us last summer. I don't want trouble, and marijuana is trouble."

Billy shook his head and treated Blue to a belittling smile. "Blue, bro, you gotta relax about that. Nobody's going to bust us. My brother runs this whole county, and he's not going to hassle me. Believe me."

"Why should I believe that?" Blue Heron asked.

"Because," Billy Connolly answered. "Because Seamus knows that if he hassles me, I'll beat the living crap out of him. I don't tell him what to do, and he doesn't tell me what to do. But he knows what I'll do if he gives me any shit." He raised his right fist and turned it around like a gem on display.

"You're both cretins," Blue concluded.

"And the same goes for you, my friend," Billy added. He touched Blue Heron softly on the chest with his knuckles. "Nobody gives me shit. So, best if you stay away from my woman." He put his arm around River's waist and said, "Right, Dorothy? Huh?"

Later that year—six months later—Seamus's wife gave birth to a son, whom Seamus named Charles. The newlyweds called the baby "Choo-Choo," but by the time he could pull himself up, bellow, and push things over, he had

earned the name "Chunky." Little Chunky had a remarkable effect on the
Connolly family: he brought the snarling brothers together at last. During that
first year of the baby's life, his Uncle Billy spent more and more time in town,
often staying overnight in the house on the corner of Connolly Boulevard and
Webster Avenue, which Seamus had bought from the Webster estate. Billy was
becoming a family man.

Or so he told River. She never accompanied him into town. She knew what
her friends thought of him, and she knew what she thought of Billy's brother,
Seamus. What she did know about Billy's town trips, what everybody including
Blue Heron could see, was that he always returned to the Rancheria charged
with energy. "My God, that man's amazing," she told Blue one morning by the
river. "It's almost worth having him away for a few days to have him come
back so happy." And she was smiling while she said that.

"River—"

"I know, I know. I'm crazy, and you wish I weren't so crazy. But it's just how
I am. You're my best friend, Blue, and I have to talk about it with someone!"

Then late in the fall of 1983, Seamus's wife left town. She abandoned her
husband and her son and disappeared forever. That was the official story. After
that, Billy stopped spending time in town with his brother and his nephew.
Because by that time, Billy Connolly, the family man, was making a family of
his own, proudly rubbing his huge hand over River's huge belly, feeling his
son's first kicks.

Little Freedom Webster was born in February 1984, a blessing to his mother,
who worshipped everything about him. A source of pride to his strutting father.
A healthy baby who turned into a charming, mellow little boy, the darling of
the community, Indians and whites alike. He saved the Steelhead Rancheria
from discord and decay. The child restored harmony to the commune with
his laugh, his shrieks of glee in the tire swing, his hugs for anyone who'd take
them, any time of day, his dreamy wandering through the crops in summer, his
merry dance in the center of the drummers' circle.

He was a miracle: born an angel, and a saint by the age of two and a half in
August, 1986, when the shitstorm hit the fan.

IV

Blue Heron was the first to hear what Billy's brother Seamus was up to.
Earlier that year, in April of 1986, Seamus had sold his Jefferson Lumber Company to a wildcat Texas marauder who had come to the North Coast with a team of bean-counters, head-hunters, management consultants, and mavens of mergers and acquisitions. They made a hasty deal. Seamus, now several million dollars wealthier, was happy to be out of the lumber business, and a lot of JLC employees, including a lot of Indians, were distressed to be out of a job. The marauder and his gang, the Dallas Cowboys as they were called in the bars on the town square, had no interest in the local community or even the local forests except for what they could clear-cut in a hurry for a fast profit.

Many of the out-of-work loggers were from the Steelhead Rancheria community. Unskilled and unschooled, they could find no other employment in Jefferson County; and over the summer one by one they took their wives and children down to Willits to live on the Mendo Intertribal Rancheria. They were assured they could help out with the expanding bingo parlor and work in the fields during the harvest. By August, the Indian population of the Steelhead Rancheria had dwindled to twenty people, of whom five were children. The garden was suffering from neglect—except for that part of the garden that had already gone to pot; Billy and the white boys looked after the marijuana crop for all it was worth.

Blue got up early on the first Sunday morning in August, ate a bowl of granola and yogurt in the rec hall, then climbed into the Rancheria pickup truck. He had a second breakfast in town, in the Steelhead River Café on the square, before hitting the road south. Four hours later, he reached Willits and turned west on Highway 20 until he came to Lantern Valley, where he drove through the gate of the Mendo Intertribal Rancheria.

The Mendo Rancheria still had the original fake log cabin buildings from when it had been a tourist camp back in the 1950s, as well as a trailer park, a convenience store, and large dining hall where the tribe hosted a bingo game every Thursday night. Blue parked the truck in front of the old office cabin, which now served as the rancheria headquarters. He climbed down from the cab and walked up the steps to the front door.

Victor Two Elks looked up from his desk and grinned. "Blue Heron!" he said. "You're my sister's boy. She's not here, you know."

Blue smiled back at the old man. "Greetings, Uncle. Yes, I know. Mother died five years ago. How are you doing? Don't get up."

Victor Two Elks struggled to his feet, as if to prove he could do it. "Me, I'm doing good. You come to talk about us getting rich?"

"We do need to talk," Blue Heron said.

The chief elder nodded and scratched his chin. "Then we better go to the lodge and have a smoke first."

They left the office and walked slowly across the court and down the gravel driveway to the dining hall. They sat down in Adirondack chairs on the porch, and Victor Two Elks said, "Smoke, nephew?"

"Okay."

The old man reached into the breast pocket of his plaid shirt and pulled out a box of Marlboros. He offered the box to Blue, who took a cigarette and handed the box back. "Cowboy cigarettes," Blue remarked.

Victor Two Elks grinned and shrugged. "Those Indian cigarettes are too damn expensive." He fired up his Bic and they both lit their smokes.

They sat together, side by side, the young leader of the Steelhead Rancheria and the old leader of the whole tribe. They smoked and fanned flies away from their faces. When they had finished their cigarettes, Victor Two Elks asked, "So how's things up there on the river? That girlfriend of yours being good to you?"

"She's not my girlfriend."

"Crops okay?"

"Things aren't so good up there right now, Uncle," Blue said. "Lot of our people been coming down here."

"Glad to have them," Victor Two Elks said. "They're going to get rich. You too."

"What is all this about getting rich? We have our land, but we can't make that work if you keep luring our boys down here to play bingo. Can't get rich playing bingo, Uncle."

Victor Two Elks chuckled. "You don't get it, because you don't know. Nobody knows, but we're in for good times, boy. Pretty soon you'll all be down here, the Indians anyway. Not those white people. And we're going to build this place up. Pave the roads. Put in town houses. Safeway store. Swimming pool for the kids. Turn this lodge into a bingo palace, make some real money for a change. Put this place on the map. I'm going to get me one of them BMWs. I've had a vision."

It's official, Blue Heron thought. My uncle's lost it. He's howling at the moon. "Good luck," he said. Whatever that meant.

"It ain't luck, boy. It's brains. And you'll be living down here too pretty soon. Better be a part of it, because good times ahead. Be part of the vision."

"I'm happy where I am, thanks. And I want to take some of my cousins back home with me." All he had to do was talk to them and let them know. They were needed on the Steelhead River. They'd get rid of Billy and the hippies. They'd have the old ways back. They wouldn't be stuck down here with a bunch of old farts, playing bingo, for God's sake.

"Ain't going to be no home up there pretty soon," Victor Two Elks said. "Blue Heron, you better be moving down here where you belong, you and your people. We have a future down here in Mendo. All's you got up there in Jefferson County's a damn past. Shit."

Damned fool. "We have our home. Our rancheria. Where we've lived for—"

"Not anymore. You'll be off that land within the next six months."

"Bullshit."

"I shit you not, nephew, so get used to it. That old Webster Ranch is going to be a shopping mall."

"Says who?"

"Says the Council of Elders of the Steelhead Tribe is who says. This deal's been in the works since April. We're leasing the Steelhead land to a commercial concern. For a shitload of money, boy. How do you think we're going to be able to afford all the improvements around here?"

"You can't do that!"

Victor Two Elks smiled, but Blue couldn't figure out whether it was a happy or a sad smile. The old man said, "Can do it. It's our land, thanks to your girlfriend. Did do it. We signed the papers last week. I'm not supposed to tell anybody about this yet, but I figure you young people better get ready for changes."

Blue Heron was on his feet, glaring down at his smug, ancient, crafty, senile son of a bitch of an uncle. "Signed the papers with who?"

"That Connolly kid," the old man said. "Seamus Connolly. He drove all the way down here with his lawyer in his new BMW. I'm going to get me one of those."

That evening Blue heard the news from River that four young Indian men, former loggers for Jefferson Lumber, had taken jobs with the Connolly Construction Company. "There's a big project happening, I guess," she said. "I don't know what it is."

Blue knew, but he couldn't tell her. Couldn't bear to tell her that his people had sold her out, traded her generous gift in on a damn bingo palace. He'd have to tell her sometime soon, but...

Turns out he didn't have to tell her. The deal was announced the next morning in the *Jefferson Republican*.

PLANS FINALIZED FOR MALL CONSTRUCTION

Final agreement has been reached in negotiations between the Steelhead Native American Tribe and the Connolly Commercial Development Company, allowing a long-awaited dream to come true. Thanks to a fifty-year lease generously granted by the area's original inhabitants, a shopping mall in the scenic Steelhead River Valley will bring Jefferson City and County "into the twentieth century—and just in time, too!" according to Planning Commissioner Leon Conrad.

The mall will be located in what was formerly called the Webster Ranch until it was acquired by the Steelhead Tribe in 1978. The tribe's Council of Elders, currently residing in the Mendo Intertribal Rancheria in Willits, granted the lease to Connolly Commercial Development under the condition that the land be developed to serve the best interests of the people of Jefferson. "We figure it's time to give something back to our neighbors," said Victor T. Elks, the tribe's Chief Elder, "after all the people of Jefferson County have done for us."

The Steelhead Mall, as the commercial property will be called, will feature a supermarket, two department stores, retail shops, a food court, a children's play area, and a six-screen movie theater. The Connolly Commercial Development Company has begun the search for suitable commercial tenants. Supervisor Conrad, also vice president and chief marketing officer of Connolly Development, expects all available space in the Steelhead Mall to be rented by Spring 1987, the time scheduled for groundbreaking and construction to begin.

Official visitors began appearing at the Rancheria the following day.

A surveying team showed up in a yellow truck and crawled out with transits, tripods, levels, compasses, measuring string, lunchboxes, calculators, and notebooks. "Aren't you guys jumping the gun a bit?" Blue Heron asked them. "Ground won't be broken till next spring."

The leader of the crew consulted his datebook and his clipboard. "Order's right here. My report's due this week. Step aside, please."

"This is our *home,*" River complained.

"Not for long, ma'am, is what I heard."

The building inspector Wednesday afternoon. "Not that it matters much at this point, because these buildings are going to come down in a few weeks, but I'm required to file a report showing you're not up to code with the electrical wiring, your plumbing is substandard, and those tents are not legal dwellings."

"What do you mean the buildings are going to come down in a few weeks?" Blue Heron wanted to know.

"Oh, and I'll have to report that kitchen to the County Health Inspector. Community kitchens are required to have chrome sinks, not porcelain. And he'll want to look at that hot tub. Frankly, it smells pretty bad."

Thursday it was County Sheriff Wayne Marvin. Blue never could stand that guy. A tall, skinny man, still in his thirties but already balding, he looked more like an undertaker than a law enforcement officer, and he acted more like a horse's ass.

Blue Heron and Billy Connolly, in a rare display of unity, met him as he crawled out of his blue-and-white sheriff's department car.

Blue said, "What?"

Billy said, "What do you want?"

"Gentlemen," Wayne Marvin said, "I understand there are illegal activities occurring on these premises."

"By whose laws?" Billy demanded. "Huh? This here's Indian land, sovereign territory of the Steelhead Sovereign Nation, and we don't recognize the laws of Jefferson City, Jefferson County, the State of California, or the United States of America. We suggest you get your skinny butt off of this sovereign nation, where you're not welcome."

The sheriff smirked. "Who's we?" he inquired. "You don't look like a Steelhead Indian, Billy."

Blue Heron set his jaw, squinted his eyes, and looked as much like an Indian as he could. "I'm we," he said.

Wayne Marvin nodded and said, "Okay. Mind if I take a look around?"

"Nothing to see here," Billy answered.

But that wasn't true. Just at that moment a woman named Morningstar walked out of the garden, her skin dripping with sweat, a red smile as big as Texas on her face. She wore thongs on her feet, beads around her neck, and nothing else. Rippling belly, ripe breasts, a halo of blond curls emanating from her head, she moseyed over to the three men and reached up to lay a finger on Wayne Marvin's lower lip. "Nice to see you again, Sheriff," Morningstar murmured. "You want another massage? Decided to come out here this time?"

The sheriff shook his head at Morningstar, frowned at Blue Heron, scowled at Billy Connolly, crawled back into his vehicle, and sped back to the highway.

"What was that all about?" Blue asked her.

"He picked me up on the town square last month, accused me of soliciting. I said, 'Prove it.' We worked something out."

Friday afternoon River and Blue sat on the front porch of the rec hall, drinking lemonade and telling little Freedom a long story about Coyote and Raven. Freedom probably didn't understand much of the story—or maybe he did—but he bubbled with laughter every time Blue howled or River squawked. The child toddled between the two of them, turning back and forth, dancing to the rhythm of their tale, giggling and shaking his long blond curls.

The story wound to a close when a midnight blue BMW pulled in and parked in front of the rec hall. The driver got out and walked up the steps, taking off his wrap-around mirror glasses. Blue and River stood up.

"Just the two people I was hoping to talk to," the man said. He wore a green golf shirt, pressed jeans, and a Jefferson High School baseball cap. He held an envelope in one hand.

"Hello, Seamus," River said.

"Dorothy."

"You know Blue Heron?"

"Of course," Seamus said. He and the Indian shook hands. Seamus smiled. Blue did not.

"So what brings you out here?" River asked. "Did you want to say hello to your nephew?"

Seamus grinned at Freedom, who grinned back and slapped his hands together. "Cute kid," Seamus said. "So's my Chunky, but Chunky's a little older and a lot bigger."

"So, Seamus," Blue Heron said. "Victor Two Elks told me about your deal. You paid the tribe one million dollars for a fifty-year lease on the land? With an option to renew? Sounds like a pretty sweet deal for you."

Seamus smiled. "Win-win," he said.

"Right. My people win a million dollars to blow on improvements to a fucking bingo palace, and you win a life-long money-maker."

"Give your uncle some credit," Seamus scolded. "He drives a hard bargain. The Steelhead Indians will get ten percent of the property's profits, forever.

That annuity alone will double the standard of living for the whole tribe, yourself included."

Blue glanced at River, who was weeping silently. He reached out and put a hand on her shoulder. "I'm sorry," he whispered.

She shook her head. "Don't be. Not your fault."

Seamus said, "Look, I know it's hard to have to move. To have to leave a place you call home. But come on. It's just business. No hard feelings, I hope?"

River filled her lungs with air and breathed out in a rush. "I fight against hard feelings, Seamus," she said. "But sometimes the fight's harder than the hard feelings. I'm not making sense, am I? You shouldn't have anything to do with the Steelhead Valley, Seamus. You had no right. The ranch was given by your ancestors to my ancestors, and I gave it back to the Steelhead people, whose land it should have been all along, and I want to know how in the world you can justify—"

"I'm just a businessman, Dorothy, and I'm doing it for all of us."

She pressed her fingers to her lip and turned away.

"Anyway, I came out here today to let you know we're going to have earth-movers in here the last week of August." He handed Blue Heron the envelope. "I've given you written warning, and that's all I'm required to do. It would be wise of you all to be gone—"

"This is our home!" River exclaimed. "You won't be needing the land till next spring, and—"

"The lease is already effective," Seamus said. "I want to do some landscaping before the end of summer, while it's dry. I've hired my crew. We'll be here Monday, August twenty-fifth. That gives you a little over two weeks to relocate. Victor tells me all of the Steelhead people are welcome to move in down there at Mendo. Dorothy, you and your little boy have a home out on Bear Gulch Road. As for your hippie friends, well, that's not my responsibility, and it shouldn't be yours, either."

The screen door whammed open, and out onto the porch stomped the heavy, angry boots of Seamus's younger bother. The expression on Billy's face was somewhere between a sneer and a snarl. "Fuck you doing here, dipwad?"

"Billy."

"I said, fuck you doing here, dipshit?"

"Don't call me dipshit, dipwad."

Freedom looked up at these giants. His lower lip quivered and his eyes filled with tears.

"This is my home," Billy said. "I live here. Get out of here. Nobody invited you. And stay away from my land and my woman and my son. You got that,

Shame? You got that, dipshit?" Billy picked the little boy up.

"Billy, you're advised to get off this property within two weeks. Oh, and by the way, I'm taking out that illegal garden. You have two weeks to move."

"You touch my plants and I'll blow your head off, Shame."

"I'll be back on Monday, August twenty-fifth."

"I'll be waiting."

Freedom struggled in his father's arms and held his hands out for his mother. But River couldn't take him from Billy because her face was pressed against Blue Heron's chest, soaking his denim shirt with tears.

Seamus trotted down the porch steps and got into his car. Started the engine and roared away.

Billy turned to Blue and said, "Get your hands off of her, you asshole."

Freedom screamed.

V

B y the time the last Monday of the month arrived, only five Indians remained on the Steelhead Rancheria. All of the women and children had gone south to Willits, a couple of the young men had disappeared into the forest of the Jefferson Alps, and three others had moved down to Eureka to try their luck on the streets.

The scheduled confrontation was not exactly announced to the people of Jefferson City, but the *Jefferson Republican* made it clear something was coming. Every day some news story, some editorial, some letter to the editor appeared in the paper: stories about the hiring surge at Connolly Construction, editorials boosting the need for a shopping mall, letters complaining about the shameful behavior—dope, nudity, fornication, just plain lazy, unsanitary hippies, is what they were, let's face it—out on that so-called Indian reservation.

All this ink in the *Republican* caught the attention of Pete Thayer, a freelance journalist in Berkeley, who worked mainly as a West Coast stringer for *In These Times*, a left-wing monthly out of Chicago. If a small-town newspaper had that many bad things to say about a nearby commune, one with Indians, marijuana, and sexual freedom, there must be something good about the place, and certainly there must be a story.

Pete Thayer was a Berkeley man in his mid-forties, fully equipped with gray beard and Birkenstocks. He was painfully between relationships, he hadn't had an adventure in months, and he longed for a steaming pile of political dirt to dig in.

So Pete chugged north in his VW Bug. He left Berkeley at six in the morning, Sunday, August 24, and pulled into the Steelhead Rancheria at four that afternoon, just in time for a soak in a hot tub and a massage in a candle-lit, oil-scented tepee. River Webster, the woman who did his massage, invited him to stay for supper, and when he told her he was a journalist, she told him he might be interested in the community meeting after supper. And did he have a place to stay? There were some vacant cabins, she said. Pete Thayer decided right then, still naked, prone, and buzzing from his massage, that the Steelhead Rancheria had a lot to offer. And so did River Webster.

Dinner was served at six for what was left of the community: five Indians, including Blue Heron, and twelve whites, including Billy Connolly and River Webster. The visiting reporter made eighteen. Pete enjoyed the feast of brown rice, tofu, beans, and squash from the garden, served with kitchen-baked bread and iced mint tea. Zucchini cake and watermelon slices for dessert.

He sat with Blue Heron, the leader of the Indians, who told him the history of the Steelhead Rancheria, right up to the present worrisome day.

"Tomorrow?" Pete said. "You're expecting this invasion tomorrow?"

"Why are you smiling?"

"Sorry." Pete took the grin off his face. "It's just that this is going to be a hell of story. Big-time. Important. I'm going to get your struggle known nation-wide."

Blue Heron shook his head. "No way," he said. "We don't need that kind of publicity. I want you off the land first thing in the morning."

Pete smiled and said, "Think about it, Blue. How's this Connolly guy going to go forward with a mall for white people when the nation's press is exposing him as an exploiter, a racist robber baron? Somebody's got to get the word out, tell the world what's going on here."

"I want you to leave first thing in the morning," Blue said. "I mean it."

Across the table a plump-faced young blonde smiled at Pete and said, "You're going to spend the night?"

Pete smiled back and nodded. "In one of your spare cabins."

The woman paused a beat, then stretched her hand across the table. "Awesome. My name's Morningstar."

"Settle down, people. We got a lot to cover here." Blue Heron stood in the center of the rec hall while what was left of the community set up the circle of chairs. River laid her sleeping child on a sofa at the side of the hall. When folks were seated and quiet, Blue took the one remaining chair and said, "Okay. Shall we do our ten minutes?"

"Let's skip the meditation tonight," said the large man sitting across the circle on River's right.

"Billy!" River protested. "We always—"

"Yeah, yeah, yeah. Baby, we don't have time for the lovey-dovey shit tonight. Know what I'm saying? We're going into battle tomorrow, and—"

"All the more reason to get centered," one of the young men said.

Billy muttered, "Sweet Jesus," laid one massive hand in the lap of each of his neighbors and slammed his eyes shut. "Awright, let's get it on."

Pete Thayer held hands with Morningstar on his right and Blue Heron on his left. After a silence that seemed to last an hour, he felt the squeeze and opened his eyes. The room was full of serene smiles, and the lanterns glowed brighter in the darkening evening.

Billy said, "Okay, listen up. I want—"

"Wait your turn, Billy," Blue snapped. "I want our guest to introduce himself. Pete?"

Pete cleared his throat and said his name, where he was from, and what he did for a living. "I champion the working man and woman, and I stand up to bosses, tyrants, and exploiters. I am for human rights and I abhor racism. I am also for the freedom and the power of the press. I only just learned that tomorrow this land of yours will be the arena of a struggle between people who would live a peaceful, productive life and those who would take their home away from them. I will be here, and I will tell the world what happens tomorrow."

River said, "Welcome, Pete. You should know that we here at the Steelhead Rancheria are nonviolent people, and what you observe tomorrow, the struggle as you call it, will demonstrate the power of peaceful protest."

Billy stood up and said, "Awright, listen. Peaceful protest, fine as long as it works. But we're not leaving this land. Period."

"Of course, Billy, but—"

"Shut up, Dodo. I said okay, peaceful protest, sit-down type-thing, but I want everybody in this room to know about Plan B, 'case push comes to fuckin shove."

The room was quiet, except for the squirm of butts on metal folding chairs and the sputtering of a kerosene lamp.

"Okay," Billy said. He sat back down and leaned forward into the circle, his elbow on his knees. "I drove up to my lodge today. I loaded the gun rack in the back of my pickup. Two rifles, two shotguns. Plus a couple more shotguns in the pickup bed. So we're armed if we need to be. I don't want it to come to that, but we've got to be ready. So what I want to know is, how many of you guys have any experience with firearms?"

The room sat in shocked silence.

River said, her voice soft and trembling, "This protest will be peaceful. Nonviolent."

"Yeah, right," Billy countered. "These guys are going to come onto our land unarmed? Dorothy, get real." He stood up. "Guys, listen. You Indians know what I'm talking about, right?"

A chant began as a whisper across the room and grew to a one-note song: "Peace, Peace, Peace, Peace…"

Billy shook his head. His face glowed scarlet with fury, and his thicket of blond curls turned to flame in the lamplight. "Okay, pussies. Have it your way. But nobody touches me, my woman, my son, or my plants. That's final."

The next morning the Steelhead River Valley was a pillow of fog. Pete stood on the front porch of the cabin, buttoning his jeans and scratching the sleep out of his beard, and looked across the meadow at the marijuana garden beyond the tepees, its tall, bushy stalks gray and still. Even the dawn songs of birds were muffled by the morning mist. He walked back into the one-room cabin and picked up a sizable roach from the ashtray on the bedside table. He fished a book of matches out of the pocket of his jeans, set fire to one end of the roach, and sucked a gummy lungful of pungent smoke through the other. Held it in till the room got as soft as the meadow outside, then laid what was left of the roach back in the ashtray, sat on the edge of the bed, and stretched out next to the lump of woman he barely knew and hardly remembered. She stirred, smiled, threw back the sheet, scratched her fragrant pubis, then reached her fingers into his beard and said, "Hi, handsome."

He didn't remember her name, only that her name wasn't River.

He kissed her nose. "What time does the show begin today?" he asked.

"Right now?" Her fingers drifted down across his chest and belly to the button of his jeans.

"No, I meant the protest."

The woman's eyes flew open. "Oh Jesus, that's right!" she whispered. "God, I have to clean up. I have to get dressed. Man, I have to *pee,* is what I really have to do! Are you really going to stick around for this?" She got out of the bed and stretched her hands high above her head, giving Pete one more eyeful of all her glory.

Morningstar, that was her name.

Morningstar pulled on her T-shirt, underpants, and jeans and said, "Come on, let's get some coffee. That was great by the way. That was awesome." She kissed him. "Come on, get a shirt on."

Granola, yogurt, fruit, and coffee.

Pete followed Morningstar down to the center of the meadow, between the tepee village and the vegetable garden, where the other white community members were twisting their bodies in a slow-motion ballet. River, tall and graceful, did her moves out front, as leader of the dance. She threw Pete a serene smile without moving her head.

"Tai chi," Morningstar said. "Do you do it?"

"I'll watch."

"It's martial arts," Morningstar explained. "To get us ready." She kissed a finger and placed the finger on his forehead, then slipped into the ranks and joined the flow.

Pete ambled back to his cabin, feeling the sun burn through the morning mist to warm his back. He pulled equipment out of his duffel bag: steno pad, pens, hand-held tape recorder. He went back out onto his porch and sat where he could view whatever might happen that day.

Nothing much happened during the morning. The tai chi ended, the sun grew warmer, men and women gardened in the vegetable patch and the bigger, lusher, patch behind it. Pete sat on his porch smoking Camels and writing the background story, the history of the Steelhead Rancheria as he had heard it from River and Blue, and the proceedings of the community meeting where it had been resolved that today's resistance should be nonviolent.

Late in the morning, Blue Heron walked across the meadow and up the steps to Pete's porch. "Howdy," he said. "You're still here."

Pete offered Blue a cigarette and the two of them sat in the shade, smoking silently until Pete said, "That woman, River. She really is partnered with that cretin? That Billy?"

"She's an idiot," Blue explained.

"But she's such a beautiful soul."

"Tell me about it. She's still an idiot."

"You're sweet on that woman, aren't you, Blue?" Pete said.

"You don't know jack shit," Blue Heron said.

"Unfortunately, I do."

"What's that supposed to mean?"

Pete sighed. "I guess I'm sweet on her too. Known her less than a day, and I've spent the night with another woman in between, but I can't wait to see River again, just to spend a minute in her company. But between you and that cretin—"

"I think it's time for you to leave," Blue Heron said. "Pack up your things and go."

"Wait a minute. All I meant was—"

"Things are complicated enough around here as it is."

Pete knew Blue wasn't talking about the protest anymore. Damn it. He was right, Pete knew it. The last thing River needed was another panting puppy dog. "Okay," he said. "I'll go stay in town for a couple of days. But I need a story. What happens when the pigs come in here with armed force? Are your boys going to go to Plan B? Billy's guns?"

Blue stubbed out his cigarette and narrowed his eyes. He opened his mouth to answer Pete's questions, but suddenly it was too late. They both heard the loud, lumbering approach of big machinery. No more time for what-ifs. Blue ran down the steps and out across the meadow toward the rec hall.

Pete focused his binoculars.

It was a small army that invaded the Steelhead Rancheria at 11:56 a.m. Six officers and two German shepherds from the Jefferson City Police Department; the Jefferson County Sheriff and three of his deputies; and two federal drug agents operating big yellow monsters borrowed from Caltrans, the state department in charge of tearing up the earth. And—representing the private sector, the Chamber of Commerce, and the Fourth Estate—Mr. Seamus Connolly drove at the head of the parade.

Seamus parked his BMW in front of the rec hall just as Blue Heron was ringing the triangle, calling his community to action.

People emerged from tepees, cabins, and both gardens and trotted to where the community had done tai chi earlier that morning. They spread out, forming a human chain to protect the vegetables. Chanting *"Peace, peace, peace, peace..."*

Billy Connolly stormed out through the rec hall door and confronted his brother on the porch. From where he was walking, Pete could not hear what they were shouting, but he heard all three voices, Billy's, Seamus's, and Blue's.

And under all the voices, the constant, growing drone of engines, as the law marched in like Hannibal on elephants, over the Alps and through the gates of Rome.

The little curly-haired child screamed in the meadow, and his mother left the peace circle, rushed to pick him up, cover his ears, and run off to their cabin.

Approaching the rec hall, Pete saw one Connolly brother hit the other Connolly brother in the face, and Blue Heron step between and push the two of them apart. By the time he reached the rec hall steps, he had heard these brothers call each other asshole, dipshit, motherfucker, pissant, and peckerbreath. Blue called them worse than that: he called them Connollys.

Still they came, onward, onward, those twin giant crawler 'dozers, until they reached the end of the road and the beginning of the meadow. There they divided, one monster headed slowly toward the garden and the chanting circle of squatters. The other 'dozer picked up a bit of speed and charged into the meadow and the village of tepees. It crunched into a tepee and brought it to the ground, then flattened it and moved on. A second tepee. A third. Each dwelling took less than five minutes to ruin.

The white people had broken their peace circle and were screaming and scurrying about, ducking into their shelters and grabbing whatever they could before they lost everything they had in the world. Their screams were barely audible over the roar of the 'dozer.

And the other 'dozer? Straight into the vegetable garden. Slowly, like a methodical plague of locusts, it took down and gobbled every plant, every stake, every irrigation furrow in its march through Eden. Leaving torn earth in its path, torn earth to be paved over.

Billy took off running. He reached the Rancheria parking lot, jumped into his pickup, and started the engine. Sped down across the meadow, past the 'dozer in the vegetable garden, parked next to his plantation. Slammed out of the cab, scrambled up into the bed of the truck, and pulled a shotgun from the gun rack.

The whole drama took only a few minutes. Pete saw most of it through his binoculars, and the rest of it he pieced together from the shouting voices that replayed the scene for an hour thereafter.

Billy pulled the trigger just as the crawler 'dozer crunched into the marijuana plantation. "That was a warning shot!" he screamed, but the damage was done, and he'd never get that moment back. The federal agent fell out of the cab of the moving machine, onto the track roller. His left trouser leg was caught between the steel plates of the roller, and he was pulled forward to the earth, where his left leg was squashed like a penny on a railroad track.

Within two minutes, the pickup truck was surrounded by firepower. Billy Connolly stood on the bed of the truck, glaring down at three sheriff's deputies, six police officers, a federal agent, and his brother. Every one of them, including his brother, had a pistol pointed at Billy's heart.

VI

T urned out the federal agent didn't die in that accident. That was fortunate for him, if you count living blind with only one leg fortunate. It was fortunate for Billy, because they couldn't get him for murder or manslaughter. However, he was charged with resisting arrest, attempted murder, assault with a deadly weapon, and marijuana cultivation. Seamus also tried to have him charged with trespassing, because he, Seamus, had delivered that eviction notice, but the judge threw that one out. Didn't matter. Billy was convicted of all the other charges, wrapped up in chains, and sent to the men's prison in San Luis Obispo for the next twenty years. Blue Heron never stopped hating his guts.

The hippies scattered. Some went back to Mount Shasta, some on to Harbin Hot Springs, others to Oregon, or Canada, or the moon.

Pete Thayer never did file the story of how the Steelhead Rancheria was stolen. Instead, he remained in Jefferson County, teamed up with River Webster, and started a newspaper, the *Jefferson Nickel,* which operated out of the Webster office on the top floor of the Webster Building. Pete made it the paper's business to needle Seamus Connolly every week. He joined Rotary for the gossip. He became River's lover, giving Blue Heron another pain in his aching heart.

Seamus Connolly did well with his million-dollar lease of the Steelhead Rancheria property in the Steelhead River Valley. The Connolly Construction Company broke ground in the spring of 1988, and within a year the mall was finished and filled with shops, restaurants, services, a theater, a vast parking lot, shiny, clean restrooms, and customers. Four years later came the Steelhead Casino, entirely owned by the tribe, of course, but built by the Connolly Construction Company and managed by a subsidiary of Connolly Enterprises. The Steelhead Tribe got a fraction of what Connolly Enterprises got out of the arrangement. Another reason for Blue Heron to wish Seamus Connolly would go die somewhere.

Blue Heron joined the Jefferson County Sheriff's Department after he lost his home on the Rancheria. He trained, did well, and became a deputy. In the early 1990s, he ran for sheriff and won easily. The defeated incumbent, Wayne

Marvin, was promptly installed as chief of police, thanks to the patronage of his friend and classmate, Seamus Connolly.

River and little Freedom moved out to the Webster place on Bear Gulch Road, where River had grown up. Freedom became Freddy when he started in public school. He grew up a slightly odd, strangely happy child who found his niche as soon as he first laid his fingers on the keyboard of a computer.

As for River Webster, she was almost out of money, but she got by with a bit of income from the newspaper, and in 1996 when the state allowed the cultivation of medical marijuana she was able to supplement her living by growing plants at home. She never stopped being the sweetest, kindest woman on the planet, and Blue Heron never stopped loving everything about her, other than her disastrous taste in men.

PART THREE

THE HARVEST

CHAPTER SEVEN

When I woke up at six-thirty Friday morning, August 20, I realized two things. It was going to be a warm, sunny day; and it had been a week since Pete Thayer died. Or it would be by the end of the day. It seemed like a year. It seemed like only yesterday.

Every time I'd seen River during the past week she'd been focused on one minor detail after another, as if to take her mind off her grief; in moments of weakness the grief would leak out of her in spite of her brave effort to contain it.

In the past week I'd inherited a job, a Pandora's box that made me excited, irritable, nervous, and unable to sit still.

Carol, for some reason, was calm. But that was Carol. Always calm and sensible, and without her I'd be dead by now a couple of times.

She went off to the store after breakfast and I went out in the garden to weed. I don't know the first thing about gardening except for pulling weeds.

I sometimes think Carol married me because I'm built so low to the ground; I get down there and communicate with worms and bugs, slugs and snails. And weeds.

I was on my knees in my mud-stained working jeans, digging up roots and yanking out dock, clover, thistle, and the blackberry invaders that just wouldn't give up and let us alone, when I heard the garden gate open and close behind me. I stood up and turned around, and there he stood, the richest Rotarian in town, wearing a Jefferson County business suit: clean jeans, a golf shirt, and a Jefferson Sharks baseball cap.

"Morning, Guy," he said, smiling. "Forgive me for barging in like this, but nobody answered your doorbell, so I thought I'd come around back. Nice garden."

I pulled off my right glove and shook his hand. "Thanks. It's Carol's. Want a cup of coffee?"

"You bet," Seamus said.

We walked into the house through the garage. I filled Mr. Coffee with water and pulled the jar of beans out of the fridge. Seamus settled down at our kitchen table and said, "Didn't mean to put you to any trouble. I don't really need any more coffee this morning."

"I could use a cup," I said. Stalling for time. What was this about, this visit? "Want some toast, some, I don't know, cookies?"

"Guy, do me a favor and sit down. I want to talk to you."

"Okay." I turned off the coffeemaker and sat down at the table. I shifted my chair to look straight at my visitor. Folded my hands in my lap. "What can I do for you?"

He took a deep breath. Maybe this wasn't easy for him, either. "I got to say," he began, "that yesterday just wasn't a real Thursday for me without the *Jefferson Nickel*. Every Thursday for the past eleven years I've had something to laugh at, get mad at, downright hate, and thoroughly enjoy over my lunch at the Wildcat Saloon. Yesterday just wasn't the same. I'm going to miss that old rascal, you know?"

"Oh for Christ's sake," I said.

"Pardon?"

"Please don't remind me again that Pete was a Rotarian and a Giants fan. What is it you want, really? Sorry to be blunt, but shit."

He nodded, and his smile got a little sadder, but his voice was firm. "I meant that, you know. I want you to know I meant what I just said."

"Okay," I said. "I miss Pete too, and I'm not all that happy to have his job, but it looks like I do, and I expect that's the real reason you're here."

There was something almost human about his sad smile, a slight slanting squint to his right eye that reminded me of someone vulnerable. "Well, for one thing, I want to apologize for the way I charged into your bookstore, I mean your wife's bookstore, like a rhinoceros. I was on a tear that day."

"Pissed off at Pete, as I remember."

He chuckled. "Damn right. Look, Guy. I don't give a shit what your politics are. And I'm not trying to get you to join Rotary. I just want you and me to be friends. You think we can make that work? At least not be enemies?"

Huh? "Well. Uh, okay."

"See, thing is, Pete Thayer, bless his heart, went out of his way to needle my ass every week. I hope you're not going to do that, is all I'm saying. Liberal causes, great. Meals for the homeless, well, whatever. But there's a rumor going around that Pete was planning to run a huge spread in yesterday's *Nickel*, the one that never came out."

"I've heard that rumor."

"Well, it's a shame Pete was killed. I swear to God I mean that. But that story, well, that deserved to be killed. Whatever it was. I don't know what it was, but I've heard it was a personal attack on me and my family. That's all I'm asking, Guy. No personal attacks. I won't make any personal attacks in my paper, and you won't make any in yours. Deal?"

I stood up and paced around the kitchen. What the hell was this man talking about? "Are you telling me Pete Thayer was killed a week ago because his story exposing a link between marijuana growers and the fishing fleet was a personal attack on you?"

Seamus looked as surprised by my question as I was by his. "I despise the marijuana culture and the marijuana economy of Jefferson County, as everyone knows. I thought Pete was sympathetic to the growers and pushers, so why would he run a big story on how it's trafficked, especially since everybody knows about it anyway? And what's that got to do with me?"

"You tell me."

"Sounds like we're both in the dark," Seamus said. "I guess the rumors I heard were wrong. If that's all the story was about, by all means, print it. Give Pete Thayer the last word."

"No, I'm killing the story."

"River's orders, I bet. She grows the stuff, you know."

"Legally," I pointed out. Then the two of us sat there a couple of minutes saying nothing.

Seamus slapped his thighs. "Well. Glad we had this little talk. We ought to talk more often, Guy. Maybe I can get you to join Rotary. Anyway. Listen, I've got to be running along. Want me to drop you at your bookstore?"

"No," I said. "I've got a little more weeding to do, and then I have to get cleaned up before I walk into town."

"Well, enjoy this nice weather."

I saw Seamus to the front door and as we shook hands I looked up into the powerful face of his and had another look at that vulnerable squint in his right eye. It came to me: that squint reminded me of Freddy Webster. Made sense: Seamus was Freddy's uncle.

I thought about Freddy all the way to the bookstore, and there he was when I got there. The gangly teen stood at the front counter slouched forward onto his elbows, and Carol was smiling up from her desk. As I approached the counter, he turned his face up to look at me, then straightened up and looked down at me. He nodded. "Hey."

"Morning, Freddy. How are you doing?" I asked.

"Pretty good."

"How's your mom today?"

"I haven't seen her yet today. She was up late last night, listening to ancient music, like really loud."

"Do you think she's okay?" I asked.

"She's my mom," he answered. "You know my mom."

"How are you taking this? I mean you yourself?"

Freddy looked at me with zero on his face. "I'm okay. I got to go." He nodded at Carol, then at me, then walked past me and out of the store, the sleigh bells jingling goodbye.

"Nice kid," Carol remarked.

"He's a man of mystery. Was there something he wanted?"

"He just seemed to want to be friendly. He told me how he ran for student body president last year on a campaign of food, shelter, and clothing for the homeless. He lost by a landslide, but he's going to do it again this year, he says. He wondered if we had his great-great-grandfather's book in the store, and I told him we had four copies. He seemed pleased to hear that."

"That's all?"

"Seemed like a lot to me," Carol said. "For a teenage boy. Oh, and he apologized for screwing up the computer files from Pete Thayer's Zip disk. Said it was an accident."

"Which we both know is a lie."

"Why are you so angry with him, Guy? Seems like a nice kid. Okay, so he made a mistake. I think he was protecting his mother, or thought he was. I told him not to worry about it. No harm done. I told him Mickey over at Mac Mechanics was able to open the documents, we read them, and you decided not to run them. It's over."

"What did he say to that?"

"Nodded. Asked how I liked working in a bookstore. Wondered if we might want some help sometime. I told him we couldn't afford to hire anybody, but he was always welcome to come hang out and keep us company. That's about when you came in. What?"

"Nothing," I said. "I guess I'm just paranoid. When Mickey converted those documents to Word, how did he do it? Just curious."

"I already told you, Guy. He came over here with his laptop and a Zip drive. He copied the documents onto his laptop, opened them in Word Perfect, saved them in Word, then copied the Word versions onto the Zip disk. Did it for free, because we're good customers, and I gave him a free book. He likes Elmore Leonard. Okay?"

"Okay, okay."

"Anything else?"

"Yeah. I'm going upstairs to trash those Pete Thayer files. They've caused enough trouble, and we don't want to use them anyway."

"You're letting somebody or some imaginary threat push you around, Guy. I read the pieces, and Pete didn't name any names. River wasn't implicated, and I told her that. Blue told us it's common knowledge that weed goes out of here on boats. So what's the big deal?"

"Well, I told Seamus Connolly I was going to kill the story, and that's what I'm going to do. I'm going to kill it dead."

"Suit yourself," Carol said. "It's your paper."

"Yeah."

"Wait a minute…you told *who?*"

It was Friday evening, so we headed off to the Redwood Door after shutting down the store at six. We hadn't said much to each other all afternoon, but the chill had thawed and we held hands on the walk to the tavern.

When we got to the town square I looked across the street at the seedy denizens gathered under Thomas Jefferson's statue. The afternoon was still warm, and they were stripped down to T-shirts and shorts and even less than that in a couple of cases. Throwing Frisbees, sharing smokes, passing around brown paper bags, and banging on drums. The town square of Jefferson City was a daily be-in, reminding me of my fuzzy, freaky days in the San Francisco Bay Area, back in the sixties and seventies, when my hair reached my shoulders, I wore shirts long enough to be called dresses, and we all danced outdoors whenever there was the slightest excuse for a party or a protest. Whatever happened to those days? I wouldn't want to repeat them, but I will never forget them or regret them.

Now as I looked at these people, young and old, gently enjoying the late-day sunshine as I had done thirty years before, I tried to see them as Seamus Connolly saw them. To my surprise, I had to admit I saw his point. I didn't belong in their company. I would feel uncomfortable walking across the square, through the gathering, for fear I'd be hit on for cigarettes, spare change, or a laugh at my expense. I knew they had a right to be there, but I knew it was wise for a square to stay on the outside of the square.

Seamus's family had built that square, so perhaps he felt it was his. He was also a control freak, and this square of his was now beyond his control.

The side of the square we were on was the home of the bars; there were three of them in addition to the Redwood Door. One for loggers, we'd been told, one for fishermen, another for tourists and professionals. The Redwood Door was for anyone, and that's where we'd felt at home on Friday nights for three years.

We slipped inside and sat down at the bar. The TV was showing a ball game that nobody was watching, and the jukebox was silent. There was a couple in one of the booths and a single man at one of the tables, but no other customers. Carol and I were the only ones sitting at the bar.

Gloria sauntered over and placed our drinks in front of us, Bombay and Jim Beam. "Welcome to the morgue," she said. "Sorry, bad joke."

"I see the regulars aren't here tonight. The fishermen at the end of the bar?"

"Haven't been here all week. Nobody has."

Carol laid her hand on Gloria's. "Do you think it's slow because…of the, uh…" She let it trail off.

Gloria cleared her throat. "Let's put it this way. If you're going to throw a murder out back of your tavern, don't hold it on Friday the thirteenth. Bad luck. How are you guys doing? I understand you're taking over Pete's paper."

"We're taking over the name," I said.

"Somebody has to print the truth in the news," Gloria said. "That's the main thing."

"Well, don't expect the *Nickel* to keep raking the muck," I said. "I don't have the nose for that kind of news. Or the spine, I guess."

"We're going to be publishing local history instead of current news," Carol explained. "We have some old books in our store that we can dig stories out of."

Gloria said, "Local history. Okay. We could use somebody telling the truth about that for a change, too."

She walked off and we sipped our drinks. Drank our drinks. Gulped them, and Gloria brought refills. We ordered our oysters, our burger and fries, and our Cobb salad.

"I'm sorry I scolded you about whatever it was this morning," Carol said. "You were right to destroy those documents."

"You were right too, telling me I was overreacting. I'm getting tired of being so defensive. I wish we didn't have this paper now. We could just publish a book. I know about books."

"Well, we're stuck with it for now. I think we owe it to River to keep her paper alive."

"I guess I got us into a tangle of nettles," I said.

Carol shook her head. "It was my idea, remember? River and I hatched the plan at our house, the night of the murder, before you got home. My God, was that just a week ago?"

Gloria brought us our dinner. "I been thinking, you guys. How about we have a wake or something, right here in the bar? A memorial gathering? What do you think? Maybe Sunday night of Labor Day weekend?"

"Labor Day weekend would be appropriate," I said. "For Pete."

"I love it," Carol said. "For Pete." She lifted her glass of gin.

Gloria said, "Yeah. I miss that old son of a bitch. Besides which, I could use a little business in here for a change."

There was still a bit of light in the sky when we came out of the tavern. The statue had turned into a silhouette, and the people milling about in the center of the square were like moving shadows, but we could still see royal blue overhead. The streetlights had come on at the four corners of the square, and on our side neon shone from the signs and windows of all the bars. We threaded our way through the cluster of smokers on the sidewalk, who for the past year had not been allowed to smoke inside the bars. Carol and I were full and buzzing, sleepy and ready for bed.

Before we reached the corner I saw a shadow emerge from behind a wax myrtle bush across the street. The shadow left the square and crossed the street, growing clear in the neon light. Big guy in a black leather jacket, approaching with purpose till he stood right in front of us on the sidewalk. He opened his mouth in a large grin. Gray crew cut.

"Spare change?" he asked.

"No," I said. I gripped Carol's arm and tried to direct her around him, but he was a roadblock.

"Cigarette?" the man said.

"No," I repeated.

"We don't have any," Carol explained.

He turned his wide grin to her, reached into his jacket pocket, and pulled out a pack of Marlboros. "You can have one of mine, sweetheart."

"We don't smoke," I said. "Do you mind?"

He popped a cigarette into his mouth and lit it with a Bic. "I don't mind. I don't care whether you smoke or not. I don't mind anything but my own business, right?" He turned and began to walk back across the street.

"Wait!" Carol called after him. She fished a dollar bill out of her jeans pocket and walked it halfway across the street to him.

He took it, grinned again, blew my wife a kiss, and disappeared into the same dark bush from which he'd come.

"What was that about?" I asked her when she rejoined me under the neon light.

"Handsomest panhandler I've ever seen," she said.

"Oh, great."

"There was something familiar about his face. Something in the smile. Did you see something familiar in that man's smile?"

"Yup," I said. "I never forget a steel tooth."

CHAPTER EIGHT

"**S**hit!" Carol screamed. "You shit-head, dogshit piece of *shit!*"

Fortunately there were no customers in the store that Monday morning. Carol doesn't usually talk like that—I'm the one with the foul mouth—but there are times, and this was one of those times. I knew exactly what was wrong.

"Computer down again?" I called up the stairs. I was on the first floor, dusting my poetry collection. She was up in what we now called the publishing office, where we had moved the iMac.

She stomped halfway down the stairs and yelled over the banister, "That piece of shit! I wish we still had our little toy computer. We never had trouble like this with the MacPlus."

"The whole machine crap out, or just some of the files?"

"None of the files that we got from Pete Thayer's Zip disk work anymore. Blank screens. They must have some kind of tropical disease."

"Virus?"

"The clap, more likely. Call Mickey, would you? His card's on the front counter, next to the phone."

I shelved the book I was reading and went to the phone. I called the number and a voice answered, "Mac Mechanics. Can I help you?"

"Hi. May I speak to Mickey please?"

"He hasn't come in yet." The man did not sound happy about it.

"Do you know when to expect him?" I asked.

"I expected him two hours ago. Can I take a message, or is there something I can help you with?"

By this time, Carol was standing by my side. She handed me a scribbled note: "See if they have his laptop there."

"By any chance is Mickey's laptop there in the shop?"

"Look. I don't know who you are or what you're after, but I'm tired of answering that question. Mickey Chan's laptop is Mickey Chan's property. Not mine, not yours. Like I said, I have no idea where it is, or where he is, or who you are, or what you want. When you see Mickey, tell him he owes me a full day's work. Damn flake." The man hung up on me.

"It appears our friend Mickey is much in demand," I told Carol. "So how much do we really need Pete's documents anyway? I already dumped the editorial content, and Artie's taken over the production end. You need the circulation lists? The ad contracts? What?"

Carol sighed. "Oh hell," she said. "No big deal, I guess. I have a paper backup on everything that matters. Cheese it."

"Cheese it? What do you mean, cheese it?"

"The cops," she said. "Look behind you."

I turned around and looked out through the window. A city police car was parked in a red zone, and a tall, bald man in a tan business suit was crossing the sidewalk to our front door. He stepped inside, jingling the strap of sleigh bells.

"Mister Mallon?" he said. "Guy Mallon?"

I held out my hand and he shook it without smiling. "Wayne Marvin, Jefferson City Police Department," he said.

"I'm pleased to meet you, Chief. How's the inves—"

"I'd like to ask you a few questions if you got a minute," Chief Marvin said. "Is there someplace we can sit down and talk?"

I turned to Carol. "Do you mind if we go upstairs?" I asked. "I know you're in the middle of a computer crisis, but—"

"I'm happy to give it a rest. I'll mind the store. Or do you need to talk to me too, Chief Marvin?"

The Chief scratched his forehead and rubbed his eyes. "One at a time," he answered. He was chewing gum. He added, "Is how I work."

Carol and I exchanged a glance. Cops.

I led Chief Marvin up the stairs to our publishing office, where we both sat down on metal folding chairs. He handed me a business card, which I pocketed without reading it. He pulled a small steno pad out of the side pocket of his jacket, tapped it with a fancy ballpoint pen, and cleared his throat, his jaw grinding away on his gum.

"I gather you were a close friend of Peter Thayer," he said.

"No, not a close friend. We met only a few times."

"He was associated with the *Jefferson Nickel,*" Marvin said, flipping through his pad, checking his notes. "Which you now own?"

"No. I don't own it. I'm the editor."

"And it is owned by whom?"

"River Webster," I answered.

"Also known as Dorothy Webster, I believe."

"I believe you're right."

"And how well do you know Miss Webster?"

"Some," I said. "Not much. We're on a first-name basis. She owns the paper I edit, so we're business associates. That's it."

"I see."

"See what?" I asked.

"I see," he repeated. "Is it true you were the last person to see Peter Thayer alive?"

"No."

"You're sure about that?"

"Unless he put a kitchen knife in his own throat," I said.

Marvin actually copied that down. He looked up from his pad and said, "Were you the first person to see Mister Thayer dead?"

"No. And I'm sure of that, too."

"How are you sure of that?"

"River Webster discovered the body. She announced it to the whole bar."

"Dorothy Webster? So she was the first person to see Mister Thayer dead?"

"I doubt it," I said.

"Then who was?"

"I don't know."

"So what you're saying is Dorothy Webster was the first person to see Mister Thayer dead *as far as you know.*"

"I'm not saying that at all."

"Then who was?"

"Was what, the first person to see Pete dead? Well, my guess it's the same person who was the last to see him alive. And I doubt it was Dorothy Webster."

"Why do you say that?"

"Do you know River Webster?" I asked.

"That's not relevant to this investigation," Wayne Marvin said. "What I do know is that the two of them were fighting. Lovers' quarrel-type thing. Am I right about that?"

"I don't think they were fighting," I said.

"And that when Peter Thayer died Dorothy Webster wasted no time making you her editor."

"Are you saying—"

"I'm not saying a thing, Mister Mallon. I'm asking the questions."

We continued this pleasant conversation for another fifteen minutes or so, during which he got me to agree that I considered River Webster a progressive, brainy woman who cared deeply about her community. "But I'm new to this community," I pointed out. "I don't know much about the issues that concern her."

Marvin looked up from his pad and stopped chewing. "Never mind about that. I know plenty."

I pointed out that I observed other things that night in the parking lot behind the Redwood Door.

"Such as?"

"Such as a midnight blue BMW with two flat tires."

"Mister Mallon," Chief Marvin said, "I am not investigating a parking violation. I am investigating a murder." He snapped his steno pad closed, handed me another business card, and said, "Come to my office at the police station this afternoon at three o'clock p.m. I'll have a statement prepared for you to sign."

"Do you want to speak to my wife, as long as you're here?" I offered. "I think she would second my opinion that River Webster would never—"

"That won't be necessary." Chief Marvin stood up. "Three o'clock, then. Please be on time. I have a busy schedule."

Unlike the county sheriff's office, which was a grungy concrete block structure that looked more like a muffler shop than a civic building, the Jefferson City Police Department was a clean, bright facility as boring as a cake of soap. I walked in and gave my name to the receptionist, who smiled and handed me a clipboard with a typed statement on it. "Please read that over carefully," she instructed, "and when you're ready I'll witness and notarize your signature."

I sat in one of the waiting room chairs and read:

I was inside the Redwood Door tavern on the evening of Friday, August 13. I was seated at the bar beside Dorothy Webster, a.k.a. River Webster. Miss Webster was visibly inebriated, and I heard her make loud disparaging remarks about Peter Thayer, a man with whom she had been romantically and financially involved. I specifically heard her say, "Here's to Pete Thayer, darn him. Damn him. God damn him" and "I don't know whether to fire him or kill him."

While I was present Mr. Thayer entered the establishment and touched Miss Webster, who flinched as if highly annoyed. Mr. Thayer then went to the other end of the bar and subsequently exited the establishment through the back door.

I saw Miss Webster leave her seat at the bar and go out of the establishment using the same exit Mr. Thayer had used. She reentered the establishment a few minutes later and announced that Mr. Thayer was deceased. I walked out of the establishment, through the same exit, and confirmed that Mr. Thayer was indeed deceased. He appeared to have sustained a fatal puncture wound in the throat.

I cannot make a positive statement regarding who might have done this act. I can and do affirm that Miss Webster appeared that evening to be angry with the deceased, as well as inebriated. It is also my understanding that Miss Webster and Mr. Thayer were involved in a dispute about the editorial content of the newspaper that she owned, and that they were also at that time estranged from a long-term romantic involvement.

I affirm that this is a true statement by me, and I am making this statement of my own free will, on the afternoon of August 23, 1999.

I clipped the pen to the clipboard clasp and walked up to the receptionist's desk. I laid the clipboard on the desk and said, "I'm not signing that. Sorry."

She gave me a big smile and said, "Please have a seat."

"I'm out of here."

"Please have a seat, sir. I'll notify Chief Marvin."

"I'm out of here."

"Please have a seat." She lifted the receiver of her phone, punched a button, and said, "Mister Mallon is here to see you, sir."

He was through the door before I could reach the front door. "Come this way, please," he said, holding open a door to the offices behind the lobby.

In his office he said, "You have a problem with this statement? You haven't signed it." He sat down behind his desk and motioned for me to sit in the facing chair.

"I didn't make that statement," I said. "You did." I didn't sit down.

"Do you deny that it's true?"

"Those aren't my words. I don't called dead people 'the deceased.' I don't say 'establishment.' I don't say 'inebriated,' and I didn't tell you River was drunk. Where did you get this information?"

"You agree that it *is* information, then? That it's true?"

"One part of it is certainly not true. The last part, that I'm making the statement of my own free will. That's bullshit. I'm not the one making this statement."

"One more time, Mister Mallon. Do you deny that these assertions are true? Look at it this way. It's this or a subpoena. This is easier. Sign the statement and go back to your bookstore and have a nice day."

"You're trying to frame somebody, and I'm feeling coerced."

"Well," Chief Marvin said. He unwrapped a stick of Juicy Fruit and slid it slowly into his massaging jaws. "Maybe you should write an editorial in your little newspaper about police brutality. Tell everyone you were coerced into telling the truth." He stood up and handed me the statement and his fancy ball-point pen, which had JCPD inscribed on the side.

I pocketed the pen. I wadded up the statement and pitched it to him underhand. He snatched in the air and missed the paper ball.

"Be my guest," I said. "Subpoena my ass." I turned and walked out of the clean white building and into the afternoon fog.

Carol spent all day Monday and most of Tuesday on the phone, trying to get commitments from the businesses that had advertised in the *Jefferson Nickel* over the years. For the most part they agreed to stick with us through the month of August, but probably no further. So far nobody had renewed an advertising contract for the fall season or even for the month of September.

"Face it, Guy," my wife said. "The paper may die. It turns out you need money to put out a newspaper. Who'da thought?"

Mid-afternoon, while I was upstairs in the bookstore poring through old tomes, learning about the history of the Jefferson County dairy industry and the Jefferson County Quilting club, the phone rang. I let Carol pick up. Figured it was business, some advertiser getting back to her.

I heard the receiver slam and Carol stamp up the stairs. The look on her face...

"What?" I asked. "Did we lose another account?"

"River's been arrested," she said. "Charged with Pete's murder. She was allowed one phone call. She called here. Her bail's a hundred thousand dollars."

"Oh fuck."

"What are we going to do, Guy?"

"We're going into battle," I said. "With the biggest asshole in town." I looked at my watch. Four-thirty. "I'll be back soon."

"Sit down, Guy. What can I do for you?"

Seamus stood up behind his desk as I entered his office, which was rich with plush, dark furniture. The desk was a giant slab of polished redwood burl. The walls were hung with blown-up historic photos of loggers in the forest and ships in the harbor. The second-story windows overlooked the Steelhead River on one side and the Steelhead Mall on the other.

Seamus offered me his hand and a smile, and I took both as graciously as I could, given my fury. I sat down. Seamus walked around his desk and sat in another chair, so that we faced each other across a coffee table, also made of redwood burl.

"Can I get you a drink or something?" he said.

"Nope."

"So. What's up?"

"Are you aware that River Webster is in jail?" I asked.

He lost his smile and nodded. "I keep up with the news on a daily basis. That's my job."

"You put her there, I assume?"

The smile was back, but different. The squint was there. "I report the news, I don't make it. I don't make the laws, either, and I don't enforce them. You know that."

"I know only this: River did not commit that murder. You know that too. I want to know why she's in jail. Don't you want to know that, or do you already know why she's in jail? Come on, Seamus. Don't be a fucking tyrant here. What's going on?"

"I do know one thing," he replied. "I've known Dorothy Webster longer than you have, buddy, a lot longer. Long enough to know that woman is out of her tree. She's a dope-smoking paranoid schizoid. She thinks I murdered her boyfriend, and she wants to use her piddly-ass little newspaper to send me up to Pelican Bay Prison. Listen, kiddo, I didn't slap that woman behind bars, but don't ask me to be sorry it happened."

"From what I hear, Wayne Marvin is your right-hand monkey," I said. "I'm accusing you of waging war on poor River because you're afraid of what she has to say. Watch who you call paranoid. And she doesn't write the editorial content of the *Jefferson Nickel*, Seamus. I do. Are you going to throw me in jail too? Why don't you just move to some banana republic and get a job as a dictator?"

Seamus puffed out his scarlet cheeks, then slumped his shoulders a bit. "This is getting embarrassing for both of us," he said, and I nodded. "Now tell me, my friend. What is the *Nickel* going to make of all this? I know River wants to accuse me in print, and although nobody will believe that, it will be an embarrassment and I can't let the threat go unanswered. I'll fight back, and neither one of us wants that. So I want you to tell me, right now, that the *Jefferson Nickel* is not going to do this."

"So you're trying to tell me what I can put in my paper, right? Seamus, newspaperman to newspaperman, is that a good idea?"

"Kid, grow up."

I'm fifty-seven years old and I still haven't learned how not to resent being treated like a child. "I'll make a deal with you," I said.

"Show me your cards."

"I'll never mention your name in my paper. Not ever. River owns the paper, but she has given me complete editorial control. I will stay entirely away from this murder case, and I will not publish anything that adds fuel to the Webster-Connolly feud."

"I like those cards."

"If." I looked at my watch. It was already after five o'clock.

"If what?"

"River Webster walks out of that jail by noon tomorrow."

Seamus nodded. His squinty eye twitched. "I'll arrange for her bail first thing in the morning."

"No. You'll have the bullshit murder charge dropped. Oh, and one more thing. I want you to run an announcement of a party we're throwing. A memorial celebration of Pete Thayer, the man you liked so much. It will be at three in the afternoon, Sunday, September fifth. I want you to run the announcement in the *Jefferson Republican* every day next week. In Section A."

Seamus Connolly raised his eyebrows and scratched his cheek. He grunted. "You strike a hard bargain, my friend," he told me. Then he smiled, leaned forward, and stretched a hand out across the lacquered burl. "But I guess you won that round. It's a deal."

CHAPTER NINE

I got to the office at six o'clock Wednesday morning and rewrote my front-page editorial, stating emphatically that under its new management, the *Jefferson Nickel* would remain entirely out of current events and controversy. It would feature announcements of entertainment events, it would have a crossword puzzle and a few other syndicated features, it would have a classified ad section where legal announcements could be posted, a weather report, and a few other routine ingredients; but beyond that the paper would be devoted to rediscovering the rich past of our cherished North Coast city and county. I would be excerpting chapters from books off the local history shelf at Scarecrow Books, and the rest of the paper would be made up of stories submitted by local citizens, stories about their pasts and their families' histories. I encouraged people to contribute.

One more thing. I told my readers that the newspaper needed financial support. Specifically, I implored the local businesses that had advertised in the *Jefferson Nickel* in the past to keep those ads running into the future. I implored all my readers to encourage businesses to keep those ads in print by shopping at stores that supported the *Nickel*. Against all hope, I was hoping for the best.

By eight o'clock I had the editorial copy for the whole issue written, edited, proofread, and copied onto a Zip disk. Artie Miller showed up at eight-thirty, right on time. I handed him the disk. Carol had given him all the graphic elements—books containing historical photos and drawings, photos of the contributors, and a folder of ad art—the day before. "Cool," Artie said. "I'll have the whole issue locked in place by mid-afternoon, and I'll take it over it to Jefferson Printing. You can pick the papers up tomorrow morning and start delivering them. You got a truck?"

"Just Carol's station wagon," I said.

"That'll do. You might have to make two trips. Pete used to do all the deliveries himself, using his VW Bug. Six trips, took him all day. Okay, amigo. You get to take the rest of the day off."

"Make it look pretty," I said.

"No worries."

After Artie left, I walked down to the town square and dropped into the Steelhead River Café for breakfast. Blue Heron was occupying most of a booth, with a massive breakfast spread out before him. He waved me into the other side of his booth and said, "You're welcome to eat some of my food, but you'll have to get your own coffee."

Bea, the waitress, appeared beside the booth and stroked Blue's head. "You want something to eat, hon?" she asked me. "Or you going to mooch off the lawman?"

"Bring me a Danish, please," I answered. "And a cup of coffee."

"You better bring me a Danish too," Blue said.

"Sure thing, doll. Goes good with French toast."

When Blue could bring himself to set down his fork for a minute, he said, "So I guess you know that River Webster was in the slammer overnight. She's getting out this morning. That asshole Seamus was playing another practical joke, looks like."

"You mean he would have had Wayne Marvin drop the charges anyway?"

"Oh hell, of course. Everybody knows River didn't kill nobody. Seamus was just jerking her chain."

"The laugh's on me, then, I guess." I told him about the deal Seamus and I had struck the afternoon before: that he would get the charges dropped if I would promise not to mention the murder case in the paper and also to be nice to him and his family. "Looks like I gave him all that for free, if he was going to spring River anyway."

"He's a smart cookie," Blue said.

"Thing is, I was going to be nice to him anyway, and I had no plans to touch that murder in any way. See, I thought I was getting something for free."

Blue said, "You're a smart cookie too. Win-win situation. 'Cept nobody ever wins when they play against Seamus. See, he still got to harass River Webster, which always gives him a thrill." Blue chuckled, then attacked his sausage and scrambled. Bea filled our coffee cups, grinned at the sheriff, and winked at me.

"You know, Guy, you really need to watch your step as far as that Seamus Connolly is concerned. He's pretty touchy."

"About what?"

"You don't want to know."

"That's not fair."

"Neither is Seamus."

"Whatever happened to Seamus's wife?" I asked.

"Wife?"

"Chunky's mother? Did she and Seamus get divorced?"

"She died. We think."

"What—"

"Guy, believe me. The less you know about Seamus Connolly and his family, the safer you'll be."

I knew Blue Heron was too smart to think that would stifle my curiosity. In fact, I expect he was egging me on intentionally, not very subtly, and quite successfully. I didn't go back to the bookstore after breakfast. Instead, I went to the public library.

I looked over the local history shelves and reconfirmed the impression that I'd formed earlier, that there was nothing on those shelves that we didn't also have at Scarecrow Books. They didn't even have a copy of *A Long, Long Crime Ago*, no doubt because the Connolly family had expressed themselves on the subject.

I walked up to the reference desk and said hello to Candy, the librarian. I asked her if the library had back issues of the *Jefferson Republican*.

"On microfiche," she answered. "All the way back to 1972. And the *Democrat* before then, back to 1940."

"The *Democrat?*"

"Same paper," she explained. "Used to be the *Jefferson Democrat*, but when Seamus Connolly inherited the paper, he changed the name to the *Republican*. Of course."

Candy opened a cabinet behind her and gave me a box full of microfiche canisters. "The viewer's in the back room. Do you know how to use one?"

"I do. Thanks."

She led the way back to a clean storeroom and sat me at a table and turned on the microfiche machine. "Have fun," she said. "Do you know what you're looking for?"

"Sort of," I said. "By the way, do you happen to know what year Seamus Connolly was born?"

"Nineteen-forty-eight. April tenth."

"And the year he was married?"

"That would be nineteen-eighty-two. In April."

"You're amazing. Do you know everything?" I asked.

Candy grinned. "Of course. I'm a librarian."

"Okay, for the grand prize, when did Seamus's wife die?"

Candy disposed of the grin. "That I can't tell you."

"She did die, didn't she?"

"So they say. Don't forget to turn off the machine when you're finished."

Candy left the room, closing the door behind her.

I zeroed in on the month of April, 1982. I found it easily. The wedding, which took place Saturday afternoon, April 12, occupied the entire front page of the Lifestyles section for Monday, the 14th. I tried to read it, but wedding write-ups put me to sleep, and I didn't know any of the players except Seamus. The wedding took place in the Episcopal church, and the reception was held at the County Gun Club. The bride's maiden name was Audrey Coggins. She came from Yuba City, and that was all that was said about her. Her family was not mentioned.

There were pictures. The happy bride and groom. Seamus, at thirty-four, was a big, handsome fellow with a crew cut and a shit-eating grin. He wore a tuxedo with a white dinner jacket. His bride wore a white dress, cut low at the bosom and reaching down only as far as her knees. She sported a bountiful blond bouffant and a defiant smile. In the photos of the bridal party, the bridesmaids were more traditionally dressed, all alike with skirts from a 1950s junior prom. The ushers looked like Rotarians who had all played football together; one name I recognized was Wayne Marvin. Then there was the best man, William Connolly, brother of the groom, the only member of the party with hair bigger than the bride's. Billy was taller and brawnier than Seamus, and his grin more challenging. His white tuxedo jacket looked too small. The room looked too small for Billy Connolly. He stared out of the microfiche reader right at me, and I felt ice-cold. I turned the machine off.

When I finally got back to the bookstore, Carol beckoned me to the front counter and told me, quietly and firmly, that we had a problem I needed to take care of.

"What happened?"

"There's a raging River in the poetry section," she said.

"Is there any damage? Are the books all right?"

"The books are fine, Guy. Go."

I hurried to the poetry aisle, which was in the back of the store, my favorite part of the store, even though it never brought in any business. I had furnished it with a couple of armchairs and reading lamps, and I dusted the shelves and swept the floors every chance I got.

There, in one of the chairs, River Webster sat weeping into a bright purple bandanna. I sat down in the other chair, reached out, and put my hand on her shoulder. She shuddered, lifted her face out of the bandanna, and gave me what started as a frown and then turned into a battered smile.

"I'm sorry," I said. "How did they treat you?"

She shook her head, hiccupped, and said, "Jail wasn't so bad. That I can take. But I've never been accused of murder before. Murder! Wayne Marvin accused me of murder, Guy!" She dabbed her eyes, but there was no damming the flow of tears. "Murder? Me, murder Pete Thayer?"

"Everybody knows you didn't murder Pete Thayer," I told her.

"Then why did Marvin say that? What's going on?"

"Well, you're out now. Charges have been dropped."

"Seamus Connolly's behind this," River said. "I know he is. He's behind everything rotten in this county, everything bad. He pushes people around. He always has. Lord knows I've tried to tolerate that man. I've meditated, I've chanted, I've prayed, I've done my very best to love him like a brother even if he is fucked up, but Guy, I can't take this."

"It's over. You're out."

"Yeah, right." River stood up, a changed woman. This was not the gentle, loving River I knew, the spirit of the peaceful forest. This River was suddenly tall and fierce. She had stopped crying. "Guy, the gloves are coming off, and I want your support." She began to pace the poetry aisle.

"How do you mean?" I asked.

"I know I said we'd play it nice with the newspaper, but we can't let Seamus Connolly and his policeman puppet get away with something like this. Who does he think he is, King of the County? We have to speak up, Guy. We have to. Carol tells me this week's issue has gone to bed, but next week, I promise you, we're going on the offensive."

"River, hold on. Sit down, please. I have two things to discuss with you."

She sat. "What?"

"Do you want some coffee or a Coke or something? I'm afraid I don't have any wine in the shop."

"I'm okay. What? Two things, you said." She drummed the arm of her chair with her fingers, and looked at me with wide, waiting eyes.

"Okay. Look, River, we can't go on the attack. I gave Seamus my word we would not mention him in the paper. Ever. We would not say anything about Pete's death or any other controversial news or anything that attacks the Connolly family in any way. Just the entertainment news, the stringers, the historical articles, and that's it, the way you and I planned it."

"What do you mean, gave him your word?" Her eyebrows came together and her eyes narrowed. "What are you talking about? I love you, Guy, but what on earth are you talking about?"

"I made that promise to get you out of jail. To get all the charges dropped."

The weeping began again. "Oh, Guy. Don't you know I'd rather be in jail than have Seamus Connolly tell me what I can print in my own paper? What's happened to free speech? What's happened to *you*, Guy Mallon?"

"I thought we both agreed that revenge is not the business we want to be in."

"What's the other thing you wanted to say to me?" she asked. Her voice was smaller now. Fragile, like a Cellophane dam holding back a torrent of tears. "Two things, you said."

I took a deep breath, held it, then let it out through my fluttering lips. "River, what we want to print in the *Jefferson Nickel* may be a moot point anyway. We don't have enough ad revenue to support the paper. Our clients aren't renewing their contracts. They're dropping like flies. Carol says we can afford to publish two more issues, and that's it. Tomorrow and next week. Unless a lot of clients renew, and they're all backing away."

"I bet Seamus is leaning on them."

"Maybe he is. Or maybe they feel advertising in a history journal is a waste of time and money. But it takes money to put out a paper, and if we can't sell ads we can't stay in business."

River collapsed into her own lap, whimpering. I reached out and put a hand on her shoulder but she pushed it away. We remained silent in our armchairs for what must have been fifteen minutes.

Then I heard her mumble, "Okay. You win." She straightened up and dried her tears. "We don't go on the attack. Bygones be bygones. I feel better already. You were right. I guess I just overreacted to being thrown in jail and being accused of murdering my best friend, my lover, and my business associate. But I'm over it now. On with the show." She smiled, and I could see it was phony, but I could also see it was a genuine effort not to be phony.

"Good," I said. "But we still have the other problem."

"I'll raise the money," she told me.

"How?"

"Don't ask. How much do you need?"

That evening, Carol and I sipped our cocktails on our back porch and watched the full moon rise and light up our garden. "I'll take the papers around town and distribute them tomorrow," she said. "I might as well learn the drop-off spots in case we do another issue." The air was warm and clear for a change, and we held hands, gently propelling the glider back and forth and listening to insects and tree frogs. A skunk slinked across the grass, under the fence, and into our neighbor's yard. A dog barked somewhere. Carol squeezed my hand. "I hope you aren't terribly disappointed."

"About the *Nickel*? You know what? I'm relieved. How do you feel?"

"It would have been fun," she said, "but when I got on the phone to sell ads, I realized I was not made for telephone sales. How do you think River's taking it?"

"She doesn't want to give up," I said. "But I guess she'll get over it. I hope so. Actually, I'm just as glad I won't be working with her, much as I like her."

"How come?"

"She's a can of worms. Even Freddy says so."

"She's a good-hearted person. And she says she can raise the money."

"It seems to me I've heard that song before," I said.

"Isn't that moon gorgeous? After dinner, let's take a stroll through the garden. In the moonlight."

"Okay. It could be the start of something big."

"I've heard that song before," she said. "Let's have dinner."

The next morning, Thursday, I took care of the store while Carol delivered the newspapers to the drop-off points. We didn't have customers that morning, so I had plenty of time to make coffee, count the change in the register, sweep all the aisles, and sort the mail before I gave in to temptation. I picked a copy of the *Jefferson Nickel* off the stack on the front counter and walked it back to the poetry section, where I settled down in a comfortable chair with a cup of coffee and reread the first newspaper I had ever edited, cover to cover.

I saved the best for last: my editorial. My declaration of peace.

I was proud of it, and knowing that this might be the last issue of the only newspaper I'd ever edit, I was glad to have ended on a note of reconciliation. The county could thank me.

Yeah. Right. Well, somewhere else in the county somebody was reading this editorial and not getting it. Or not believing it. Or not trusting me. Somebody still did not want me digging into the past. Wanted me to mind my own business.

Which is what I thought I was doing.

Friday morning when we arrived at the store we found the front door unlocked. "You didn't lock up last night?" Carol asked me.

"I thought you did."

She nodded. "As a matter of fact, I did."

We tiptoed into the store, half-expecting to find a smarmy gang of weasels in zoot suits riffling through our rare books. But a quick check assured us that all was in order. Our rare books, including my poetry collection and Carol's illustrated first editions, were still in their bookcases, with the glass panels still locked and intact. The cash drawer of the register was open, but that's the way we always left it at night, with nineteen dollars and forty-two cents, the year I was born.

"It's a mystery, but one of us didn't lock up last night."

"Both of us," Carol said. "How about you sweep the aisles while I go upstairs and check email."

I was just starting down the fiction aisle with the dry mop when I heard her holler "Shit!" and once again I knew we had computer troubles. I ran up the stairs and found her with her elbows on the desk, her face in her hands. She looked up at me like a frightened child and said, "When are they going to leave us alone, Guy?"

"What's up?"

"What's down, you mean. This computer is screwed."

"What's it doing now?"

"Not a God damned thing," Carol said. "Somebody's out to get us, Guy. Why?"

"Well, it could be just a computer glitch," I said. I didn't believe it, but that's what I said, wishing I could believe it.

"I don't know who did this or what it is they did," Carol insisted, "but somebody did something to this machine, which is now majorly screwed."

"Sounds like paranoia to me," I said.

Her jaw dropped. "You're calling me paranoid?"

"No. I'm saying there's a paranoid loose in the world, and he or she is determined to prevent us from saying or even knowing I don't know what. What more can we do? We've made a public statement we aren't investigating pot growers or fishermen. We have promised to stay away from the investigation of Pete Thayer's murder. I have publicly stated I'm not interested in any family feuds in this county. What more do they want, or are they just pathologically paranoid and enjoy dicking with other people's machinery? So what's the problem exactly?"

Carol turned the computer off and stood up. "Go ahead. You boot it up. I'm ready to boot it out the window." She marched to the stairs and clumped down to finish my sweeping for me.

I sat down at the desk and hit the switch. The screen lit up. So far so good. I folded my arms across my chest and waited. I waited for fifteen minutes, staring at a white screen. I tapped the iMac on the sides. I jiggled the mouse till I thought I heard it squeak. I called the computer a bunch of foul names, then coaxed it with sugar. I gave up.

I called Mac Mechanics. I'm sorry to say I knew the number by heart.

"Thank you for calling Mac Mechanics this is Leon how may I help you," the voice told me.

"Hi, Leon, this is Guy Mallon."

"You again."

"Has Mickey come back to work?"

"Mickey Chan does not work for me anymore. What do you need?"

"My computer has a problem."

"Such as?"

"It doesn't compute. The lights are on but nobody's home. That something you can fix?"

"Of course," Leon said. "But I'm all alone here and I don't do house calls. You'll have to bring it in."

Leon looked like Santa's evil twin on a bad hair day. His head was bald on top, with a thicket of white that covered his ears and descended into massive curly white beard. The belly barely contained by his tie-dyed T-shirt was round and jiggly, but Leon did not support the myth that round people are jolly. He stared at the white screen and then looked up at me over his half-spectacles and told me my iMac had no business acting like a spoiled brat. "These are good little machines," he said. "They've been out a year now, and this is the first one I've had in the shop."

"What's wrong with it?" I asked.

"Let's have a look inside." He tipped the machine onto its screen and then searched his cluttered workbench for the right screw driver. "Just so you know," he said, "soon as I open this baby up, you already owe me fifty-five dollars."

"Don't stop now."

When he had the back off the computer he said, "Hard drive. That's your problem."

"Something's wrong with my hard drive?"

"Probably not," he said. "But it's not in your computer."

"Come to think of it, I thought it felt lighter than usual."

"I hope you backed this baby up," Leon said. "Because if you don't find your hard drive laying around somewhere, we're talking square one."

"Everything's on Zip disks," I said. "I assure you my hard drive is not just lying around. I didn't remove it."

"I know that," Leon replied. "Whoever removed the hard drive knew exactly what he was doing. Knew computers. You obviously don't know diddly."

So I drove back to the store and told Carol the news. "Looks like we're buying a new hard drive, maybe even a new computer. Good thing we have the back-up disks."

She gave me smile that wasn't a smile and said the obvious: "Do we?"

We walked up the stairs together, slowly. I sat down at my desk and looked into the box where we kept our collection of back-up disks. "Zip," I said. "Carol, this day just got a whole lot worse."

"Too bad we don't keep backup disks at home, like grown-up business people," she said.

"That's probably just as well," I said. "If we did keep backups at home like grownup business people, they'd probably hit our house next. What?"

Carol shook her head. "Whoever hates us probably thinks we do keep backups at home. Guy, I'm scared. I don't want people trashing our house."

"I'll call the police," I said.

"They're not going to do us any favors. Call Blue Heron."

So I called the sheriff and told him the latest.

"Huh buoy," he said. "You're a lot of trouble, you know that, Guy?"

"I know, I know," I sighed. "So what do I do?"

"First thing, get a security alarm system rigged up at your house."

"I hate those things."

"I hate a lot of things," Blue said. "Crime being number one. Do it, Guy."

"Okay."

"You can have it programmed to alert the police. Or me. Or your cell phone, which you don't own. Or your store. Or all of the above. It sounds like you'd better move on this right away. And if I were you, I'd stay at home this evening, with every light in the house turned on."

After we hung up I looked at Carol and smiled sadly. "Durn," I said. I let my gaze drift away from her face and travel across the bookshelf beside her.

"What?"

"It's Friday, and we don't get to have dinner at the Redwood Door. Oh, my God!"

"What?"

I stood up and walked over to the local history shelf, which had a gaping absence. All four copies of Donald Webster's *A Long, Long Crime Ago: A History of Jefferson County* were missing.

That evening I hung two signs on the front door of our house, signs made with a Magic Marker on shirt cardboard:

THIS HOUSE CONTAINS NO COMPUTER EQUIPMENT OR DATA STORAGE MATERIALS, and:

REWARD! FOR THE RETURN OF OUR HARD DRIVE AND BACKUP DISKS. NO QUESTIONS ASKED. CONTACT US AT OUR STORE. YOU KNOW THE ADDRESS.

Also prominently displayed on the glass pane of our front door was a butt-ugly decal proclaiming that our home was protected by Jefferson Security Systems, Inc. Howdy, neighbors! Welcome to the new millennium.

Carol and I spent the evening at home, doing our best to relax and enjoy cocktails, pizza, and cribbage, with the MJQ providing the sound track. It would have been a lot more romantic if every light in the house hadn't been on. And when we climbed the stairs and turned off the bedroom light, we were both still too nervous to take advantage of the dark.

We stayed home all weekend long. We gardened together on Saturday, and on Sunday we stayed inside, out of the rain. We didn't talk much. Neither one of us wanted to say anything about the problem we weren't facing, and neither of us could think of anything else to talk about.

Monday morning we went to the bookstore, as usual, and our first visitor of the day was Leon, the Mac Mechanic. He was on foot. He wheezed into the store, closing his umbrella. He stood the umbrella in the stand by the door and shuffled up to the counter, where Carol and I were drinking coffee. He set a grocery sack on the counter and said, "You heard?" He had a tic in his lower lip.

"Heard what?"

"You don't read the God damn paper?"

"Haven't read today's," I said. "What's up?"

Leon reached into the sack and pulled out that morning's *Jefferson Republican*. He opened it up with trembling hands and ironed it flat on the counter with his beefy hands.

The lead headline read, LOCAL COMPUTER TECHNICIAN FOUND DEAD IN WASTEWATER TREATMENT POND. There was a photograph of Mickey Chan, probably an old school photo, showing a smiling young man wearing a necktie. The article took up two columns of Page 1 and continued on to Page 4. Carol read aloud.

"…The body, which was discovered in a thicket of reeds at the northernmost end of the pool, was bloated and appeared to have been in the water for several days, according to Police Chief Wayne Marvin. 'It's not a matter for public concern,' Chief Marvin stated. 'The victim's body did not contaminate the water in any significant way. This particular pond is the first one in the treatment process, pretty

much contaminated to start with anyhow. By the time it reenters the city's water supply, it will be good as new. We have contacted the victim's family in San Jose. The cause of death appears to be accidental,' the chief added. The victim was positively identified on Sunday morning by his employer, Leon Epstein, owner of Mac Mechanics, where Michael Chan worked as a technician. Arrangements have been made to have the body transported to San Jose, where a funeral will be held...."

"Accidental my fat ass," Leon muttered. "So you didn't know about this?"

I could hardly speak. I felt as if I'd been rammed in the chest by a rhino. I took a deep breath and squeaked, "Not until now."

"You guys were the ones always kept asking for Mickey is why I asked, is all," Leon said.

"We had computer problems. Mickey did house calls."

A sob escaped Leon's lips and his hand flew to his eyes to wipe the tears away. "He was such a sweet guy, that little fart," he said. "Who would have done this? Mickey was the sweetest guy I ever met, wouldn't hurt a frickin fly." He yanked a bandanna from his back pocket and mopped his cheeks and honked his nose.

Carol put her hand on his arm. "It could have been an accident," she said. "That's what the paper said."

"Accident my fat ass. Jesus. You know? Too bad Mickey couldn't even live to see Y2K. He was looking forward to it so much."

Leon walked out of the store, into the rain, leaving his newspaper and his umbrella behind.

Carol turned to me and said, "That poor man."

"Leon or Mickey?"

She shook her head as if the question were irrelevant. I guess it was. She said, "Guy, I want to get out of town. My nerves are twitching. God, I can't stand this! Can we go away for a few days? Please? Just close the store and lock up the house and go?"

"We have a paper to bring out this Thursday," I reminded her. "The final issue of the *Jefferson Nickel.*"

"How important is that to you? Really?" she asked. There were tears in this strong, sane woman's eyes.

"Not important at all," I answered. "Where do you want to go?"

"I don't really care. How about we go down to Humboldt County? Southern Humboldt. The Lost Coast. I want to get lost."

CHAPTER TEN

"Tell me something, Guy." We sat beside the Mattole River in southern Humboldt County. High hills rose all around us, some of them covered with forests, others open fields of golden grass. The river was low and lazy this late in the summer, and dragonflies danced across the surface. A hawk wandered in the sky high over our heads, crying, crying. The riverbank was a small field of cobblestones, and that's where we sat eating the sandwiches we'd bought in the one-store town of Honeydew, just a few miles back. Turkey sandwiches, Fritos, and cold local beer on a hot, still afternoon, with no pressing agenda except to get back to Shelter Cove in time for dinner. I hadn't felt this relaxed in weeks. "Tell me something," Carol repeated.

"Hmmm?"

"Why is life with you such a dangerous road?"

"What are you talking about? We haven't seen a single other car since we left 101, and here it is Friday afternoon, the beginning of Labor Day weekend."

"There's one now," she said. I looked behind us and saw a black Jeep Cherokee parking behind our station wagon on the road. Two young men in jeans, sleeveless sweatshirts, and baseball caps got out of the Cherokee, retrieved rifles from the back seat, and started down the path to the cobblestone beach. "I'm serious, Guy. When did you decide on a life of spine-tingling adventure?"

I laughed. "All I want out of life is books, bourbon, and you. I don't court trouble."

The young men turned right when they reached the river and walked about fifty yards from us. I saw one of them point at the hawk still circling in the sky.

"Well, call it a coincidence, then," she said, "but since we've been together you've locked horns with swindlers, pornographers, arsonists, murderers, and the cab driver from hell. Were you always this much trouble?"

"I want you to know I've never picked a fight," I said. "I'm too short to pick fights. I don't even know how to make a fist. I tried once, and my fingers just don't curl up."

The crack of a rifle echoed in the valley. Then another. The echoes blended, and the hawk on high flew away from his circle and off into the distance. Two more shots followed him.

Carol rose quickly to her feet. "Jerks!" she said. "I'm going to beat the crap out of them. What is it about men?"

"Carol, sit down."

"Bullshit. They have no right to kill hawks."

"They didn't."

"They just missed, that's all. They tried to kill that hawk." She turned and walked away from me, toward the men with guns. "Hey!" she shouted.

I rose to my feet and caught up with her. "Don't try to stop me, Guy. I'm not going to put up with this."

"It's their territory, Carol."

"It's the hawk's territory."

By the time we reached the young men they had pointed their weapons at the ground and were facing us with dark, unsmiling faces. They were both trying to grow beards and having a hard time of it. They spoke together: "Tsup."

"Tell me," Carol said. "Is this open season on hawks?"

One of the men, the shorter one, probably six-one, smiled and said, "We're chicken farmers. Hawk raided our yard last night and carried off our rooster. Damn near overslept this morning."

The other one, the taller one who didn't smile, said, "Can I help you folks?" Ever notice that when somebody says "Can I help you," what they often mean is "Who the hell are you and what do you think you're doing, asshole?"

"We're on vacation," I said, before Carol could get us into any more trouble. "Staying in Shelter Cove. Been there for three days. Heading on home tomorrow, back to Jefferson County. Have a nice day."

"So how do you like the Lost Coast?" the smiler said. "Done any exploring?"

"We went to Petrolia this morning. Now we thought we'd go back to Shelter Cove on Kings Peak Road."

The taller man nodded. "Good road. Real pretty this time of year."

Carol said, "Well, I guess we'll be going. Are you two done shooting at wild animals and birds?"

The two men looked at each other and nodded. "Guess we taught that hawk a lesson," the taller one said.

The shorter one grinned and said, "Guess we'll get on back to our chicken farm. Farm some chickens."

When we got to the car Carol opened up the Thomas Brothers map. "We should be back to the motel soon. The return trip's a shorter route."

"Glad to hear it," I said. "I could use a nap before dinner. By the way, you handled those guys well. Fought to a draw, which is better than I usually do."

"What is it with men?" she asked again. "Present company excepted. No offense."

"None taken. Actually, it's not all men, just tall men. Tall people in general, present company excepted."

"Thank you." We laughed together and Carol put the station wagon in gear. "Buckle your seat belt."

"Dangerous driver?"

"Rough road."

Rough road indeed. And a long road. Kings Peak Road between Wilder Ridge Road and Shelter Cove is the longest shortcut in the world. I'm not exaggerating, by the way; you can look it up in Guinness. It was after five o'clock by the time we reached Saddle Mountain, which was a little more than half the distance, a distance during which we had to get out and roll boulders out of the road, move stones into streambeds to build roads for fording. We had to hug a cliff, scraping the right side of our car and holding our breath to keep from tilting over the left side and down into a fifty-foot ditch where what was left of a pickup truck lay rusting on its side. We averaged nine miles an hour. Our station wagon turned from faded red to solid dusty brown. Signs along the road told us POSTED, KEEP OUT, and NO TRESPASSING.

"Well, at least we're not snarled in any traffic," Carol said.

"Nope. Haven't even seen a Jeep Cherokee."

"Those assholes. They must have known this road was from hell. Why do you think they did this to us? We never did anything to them."

"Neither did that hawk they were trying to kill. God, I hate Jeep Cherokees."

"Why is that?"

"That's what Chunky Connolly drives."

Carol stopped the car. "I want you to take the wheel the rest of the way. I'm getting a headache from concentrating on all the gorgeous scenery."

"How's our gas?"

"We still have a quarter of a tank. We had a half a tank in Honeydew. So if we're halfway there, we'll pull into the Chevron station on fumes. But it appears we're now at the summit of our drive, which means the rest of it's downhill and we can coast. Be grateful."

We switched seats and I got us going downhill on a curvy wild ride at breakneck fifteen miles per hour. Carol put her hand on my thigh and said, "I don't mind a little adventure, you know. I'm having a wonderful time. I want you to know that. And I love you."

"At least we don't have Seamus Connolly sitting in the back seat, giving us directions," I said.

Carol said, "I'll thank you to leave him out of this. This vacation has been beautiful because there are no Connollys in the Lost Coast."

It was after seven when we rolled into the Chevron station and filled up for the next day's drive home. We drove to our motel, which had filled up during our absence. "No Vacancy" on the marquee, and a parking lot full of SUVs, trucks, and off-road toys. We took the last parking spot, right next to a black Jeep Cherokee. "I hope that's not our friends from the Mattole River," Carol said.

"If it is, you'll have another chance to beat the crap out of them. And another reason."

We dragged our weary selves up the two flights of stairs to the top floor of the only motel in town. We stripped off our clothes and got into the stall shower together. A sign on the bathroom mirror asked guests to conserve water, and we'd been showering together for three days to oblige. That was probably counter-productive because we'd taken our time soaping up each other's bodies. Not this evening, though. We were tired, dirty, hungry, and most of all thirsty, so we got the job done in a hurry, and a few minutes later we were dressed in jeans and sweaters.

It was a short walk across a park to the only restaurant and bar in town. Shelter Cove's a small community, part golf course, part air strip, part marina, part trailer park, and a convenience store in the middle, the only place in town to buy anything at all. There's a grocery store next to the Chevron, but that's five miles out of town, uphill on Shelter Cove Road.

The restaurant parking lot was full, too, and I noticed a couple of black Cherokees, but I was too worn out to be paranoid. We walked into the tavern half of the restaurant and found the last two seats at the bar. The seats weren't together, but a tall redhead smiled at us and moved over so we could sit next to each other. I sat between the two tall handsome women and felt halfway relaxed. The bartender brought us our drinks without asking, and I relaxed the rest of the way.

I turned to the woman on my left and said, "Thanks for making room for us."

"No problem," she said. "Seemed the neighborly thing to do."

"Is this your neighborhood? Do you live here in Shelter Cove?"

She shook her head. "Port Silva. I'm just up for a couple of days."

"Holiday?"

"Sort of."

"Port Silva's just down the road a ways, right?" Carol asked.

The woman laughed. "Not any road you'd want to drive. Even the crows don't fly that way. You want to stick to the main roads in the Lost Coast. For a lot of reasons."

Carol and I looked at each other, grinned, and clinked our bourbon and gin in agreement. We downed our first cocktails, then sipped our second slowly. Carol hummed along with Patsy Cline on the jukebox, and I turned again to the woman on my left. "So what do you do in Port Silva?" I asked.

She smiled. "Drink beer and play darts. My mother and I are in business together, but I've come here to get away from it for a few days, so…what do you folks do?"

"Carol owns a used bookstore in Jefferson City. I sweep the aisles. For a while there I was a newspaper editor, but I found that to be hazardous to my health. Come to think of it, we're here to be away from there, too."

The redhead stood up from her bar stool. "Well, I'm worn out. I'm going back to the motel. Cheers."

"Cheers."

She walked away and I turned back to Carol just as our third round of drinks appeared, like magic.

Carol sipped her drink, smiled at me dreamily, and said, "I'm going to kick Seamus Connolly's ass."

"I thought we agreed to leave him in Jefferson City."

"Who do you think did it, Guy? Huh?"

"Did what?"

"Shoot, all of it. Killed Pete Thayer, killed Mickey Chan, stole our hard drive, stole books off our shelves, trashed River's newspaper and Pete's house, broke into our damn store, let the air out of Seamus's tires, stripped Freddy naked and left him at the marsh, threw you in the harbor, yada yada jing jing jing. Boy, somebody must have put gin in my gin. Huh? Who do you think did all that? Whom? No, who. Who did it, Guy?"

"We'd better get some food in our bellies," I said.

"I'm mad."

I placed the palm of my hand over the top of her drink and forced her to look at me. "Carol, you're older and wiser than I, and you're also bigger and braver. But right now you're also drunker. Let's eat something before we both pass out."

She nodded. We had steaks brought to the bar, and by the time we'd finished the last French fry, Carol was talking sense again. We ordered a slice of blackberry pie à la mode to split and coffee, and Carol said, "I still want to know who's behind all this mishegoss."

"Me too," I said. "But mostly I want to know why."

"Oh, well that's obvious. Somebody thinks we know something that we don't know and we don't even know what it is we don't know, but they don't know that. Question is, who's they?"

"Are you as tired as I am?"

"Are you trying to get me into bed again?"

Nine hours later we walked back to the same restaurant for breakfast. The place was packed with Labor Day tourists, so we gave the hostess our name and waited outside on the terrace. The air was damp and chilly, as it had been every morning we'd been in Shelter Cove, but there was no fog and we had a clear view of the marina down to our left and the rocks down to our right, covered with lazily flopping seals.

There were other customers on the terrace also waiting for breakfast. I recognized the tall handsome redhead, who was focused on what was happening in the marina. She held binoculars to her face and seemed to be watching a particular boat in the harbor. I looked and saw that her gaze was trained on a group of four men standing on the deck of a fishing boat that looked familiar to me. And some of the men looked familiar to me.

"Excuse me," I said to the woman.

She lowered her binoculars and smiled. "Oh, hello."

"Could I have a look?"

She hesitated, then handed me her binoculars. "Do you know those guys?" she asked.

"I don't know," I said. I took a look, then another. Adjusted the left lens. The right.

"Guy, what do you see?" Carol asked.

I handed her the binoculars. "Holy shit," she said.

And the woman from Port Silva said, "You're going to have to give me those binoculars. I'd also like to know who it is you think you know."

"That fishing boat," I said, as Carol gave the redhead her binoculars. "The *Little Mermaid.* It's from our home town, that's all. Jefferson City."

She nodded and peered again at the gathering below us. "They're fishermen?" she asked. "I recognize one of them, the one in the hunting jacket. He's from Port Silva. He's…well, he's not a fisherman."

"Two of the others are fishermen. The big one and the little one."

"What about the other guy, the one in the black jacket? Looks like Burt Lancaster or somebody."

"Yes," I answered. "Or somebody."

The hostess called us in to breakfast.

We ate in frightened silence, and when we got back to the motel, we found that the black Cherokee was gone, and our station wagon had two flat tires in the rear. We went into the motel office and I called Triple A. I told the dispatcher our problem and she said, "I can put you down for four this afternoon."

"That's the soonest you can be here?"

"If you're lucky," she told me. "You're not exactly on the main drag, and this is a holiday weekend besides. If we have emergencies down around Confusion Hill, we may not be able to see you till tomorrow morning."

"Okay, put me down." I told her the address and hung up.

"You might try the Chevron," the motel manager said. He dialed the number for me.

"Hyyyello, Shelter Cove Chevron."

"Listen, I got a couple of flat tires. Can you tow my car in and fix them for me?"

"We don't have a tow truck, but if you like I can get Triple A to tow you in here. Might take a while, holiday weekend."

"Thanks, I'll get back to you on that," I said, and I hung up. I told the motel manager, "Might as well sign us up for another night. We'll try to get the car fixed this afternoon, but it may not happen till tomorrow morning."

"Can't help you, sorry," the manager said. "Full house."

Carol put both hands on the counter and said, "What do you suggest we do? Our car's been vandalized in your parking lot. Do you have a suggestion?"

The man scratched his cheek. "There's a campground on the edge of town. You have any camping equipment?"

"We have a couple of sleeping bags," I admitted.

"There you go," the motel manager said. "Tell you what. I'll put you down as an alternate tonight. Somebody cancels, you get the room. I'll make you a reservation at the campground just in case. You can leave your car here in my lot overnight if you want. You can stay in your room till noon, just in case there's any good news from Triple A. You got a cell phone so I can call you if—?"

"No."

"You really should get a cell phone. Be ready for the new millennium."

"I already hate the new millennium," Carol said.

"You and me both," the motel manager said. "This used to be a sweet little town. It's those video games the kids play these days is what's doing it. They got those machines up at the market. Godawful racket. Good luck."

"One more question," Carol said. "There was a Jeep Cherokee parked beside us in the parking lot last night."

"The world's full of Cherokees," I said.

She gave me the shut-up look. "Whose car was that?" she asked.

"Uh, I don't really think I can—"

"We have a friend in Jefferson City who drives a car just like that one. I was thinking maybe he could help us out, if it's the same guy. Did you have any other guests from Jefferson City last night? Somebody with a black Cherokee?"

The manager nodded and swallowed. He looked into his computer screen and punched a few keys. "That was room two-sixteen. Charles Connolly. Young fella. But he already checked out. He's long gone."

CHAPTER ELEVEN

On Sunday, September 5, we pulled open the redwood door of the Redwood Door and walked out of the bright afternoon sunlight, into the neon glow. The place was about half-full, and we recognized several of the regulars, including Nails and Louie Luau, who owned the far end of the bar as usual. In the center of the room was a life-size cardboard cutout photo of the late Pete Thayer, grinning through his thicket of gray beard, holding up a copy of the *Jefferson Nickel* with the headline: DEWEY DEFEATS TRUMAN!

Gloria looked gorgeous. I had never seen her in anything but a black T-shirt and well-worn jeans, but for Pete Thayer's wake on Sunday afternoon she wore a low-cut wine-red dress of slinky satin, which clung to her hips and gave us a glimpse of shapely leg through a slit up the side.

She hugged Carol, then me, then took a hand in each of hers and pulled us through the tavern to the back, where three tables had been shoved together and covered with a smorgasbord of salads, fruits, cheeses, meats, and desserts.

"Yum," Carol said. "You do all this in the kitchen?"

"Nope," Gloria answered. She plucked a Concord grape and popped it into her mouth. "Kitchen's closed today. This is all courtesy of the Jefferson City Rotarians. Nice, huh?"

"You gotta be kidding," I said. "Rotary did this?"

Gloria grinned, then lost her grin as she looked over my head with widening eyes.

"We take care of our own," answered the voice behind me.

I turned around and looked up into the big smile. He patted my shoulder with his paw and said, "Hiya dune, my friend?"

"Holy shit, Seamus," Gloria said. "Now I see what it takes to get you to come to my bar. I didn't expect you to show up in person."

"Hey, Gloria. How long has it been?"

"It's a small town. I see you around," Gloria answered. "But you haven't been in the Redwood Door since that night—"

"Don't remind me."

"Me either."

Clearly the subject needed a quick change as far as both of them were concerned. Seamus turned to Carol and held out a friendly hand. "You must be the famous and lovely Missus Mallon. Hi. Seamus Connolly."

Carol shook his hand and smiled. "Pleased to meet you. Thanks for all the treats."

Seamus chuckled and picked up a slice of rye bread, which he loaded with a disk of salami and a slice of hard, white cheese. "Like I say, we Rotarians take care of our own. What?"

Gloria said, "Oh boy. Seamus, are you ready for this?"

"Ready for what?"

Carol and I turned to see where Gloria was looking. And here she came, walking through the door in her granny dress and floppy purple hat, toting her straw bag. She waved, smiled, and strolled toward us until she was close enough to see all of us, including Seamus Connolly, who had just turned her way. Her wave dropped to her side and her stroll turned into a march. By the time she reached us her smile had gone south.

"I didn't expect to see you here," she told the big man.

"Hey, Pete was a very good friend of mine," Seamus insisted. "How're you doing, Dorothy?"

River ignored the question and the man who had asked it. She hugged Gloria, then Carol, then me. When her lips were next to my ear she whispered, "Save a few minutes this afternoon for me, Guy. I need to talk some business with you."

Gloria said, "Well, I'd better get back behind the bar. Draft beer's on the house, by the way. Logger Lager on tap, donated by Jefferson Brewery." She patted my cheek, then turned and swung her hips to the bar.

"That's one classy old broad," Seamus said.

"You're quite the phrase-maker, Seamus," River said. "Always were."

He shrugged. "I love Gloria. Always have. Back when I was a bar-hopper she had the heaviest pour in town."

"Still a generous lady," Carol said.

"Pours a mean cup of coffee," River said. "After she cuts me off. I'm going out behind for a smoke. You coming, Guy?"

"In a minute," I said. "Look, here come the staff of the *Nickel.*"

Artie Miller, Lydia Sweet, Jackie Haas, and Elizabeth Butler walked in together, waved in our direction, then piled into a booth. Gloria brought them four glasses and a pitcher of beer.

"Good people," Seamus said. "They've all been by my shop over the past week, applying for jobs with the *Republican.*"

River muttered, "That's loyalty for you."

"Oh hush," Carol told her. "They loved Pete. We all did. But they're newspaper people, and the *Jefferson Republican* is the only game in town now."

River's cheeks turned crimson and she put fingers to her eyelids, her shoulders trembling. I didn't know whether she was mourning her lover, her newspaper, or both. I handed her a napkin from the buffet and she blotted her eyes. "I need a cigarette," she said softly. "Guy come out back with me, keep me company. Please?"

I looked at Carol and she nodded. "Do it, Guy. I'm going to take my new friend Seamus over to the bar and buy him a glass of Logger Lager."

"That's generous of you," Seamus said.

Carol treated him to a special smile she uses when she's encouraging a horse's ass to appreciate himself. "Today, Seamus, I'll buy you all the Logger Lager you can drink."

I followed River through the dark hall, past the kitchen, past the rest rooms, and out the back door to the parking lot. I hadn't been in this scene since the night of Friday, August thirteenth. It looked different in the September afternoon sunlight, but two fixtures reminded me of that drizzly evening when the parking lot was dimly lit by an orange floodlight.

The Dumpster was still there, dingier by daylight, rust erupting where blue paint had chipped away. The asphalt where Pete had sat in a puddle of blood was scrubbed clean, a brighter gray than the rest of the parking lot.

Parked on the other side of the back door of the tavern was a midnight blue BMW. Exactly where it had been parked that night.

River lit up and dropped her Bic back into her straw bag. She looked around, flicking her cigarette with her thumb, even though it wasn't old enough to wear an ash. "This place gives me the willies," she said.

Me too, I thought. "Want to go back inside?"

"In a minute."

"Seamus seems to like this parking spot," I observed.

"He parks wherever he wants to. He owns every building on the town square. Guy, I need to talk to you about a publishing project."

"I can't go on with the paper, River. I'm sorry."

"I know," she said. "I'm willing to let go of that. It was Pete's baby anyway, and if we're not going to do it his way, we might as well drop it. This is something different."

"What is?"

"I'm thinking about a book. Local history thing. What do you think?"

I looked her straight in the eye. "Are you still hoping to stick it to the Connolly family? Because if so—"

She shook her head and smiled at me. "The hell with the Connollys, God bless them," she said. "There aren't that many Connollys left anyway. No, this is something I want to do for my great-grandfather."

"Donald Webster?"

"I want to republish his book, *A Long, Long Crime Ago.* I want us to republish his book. You and me. How much would that cost?"

"Well, in the first place, I don't think that's such a good idea, River."

"Why not? It's a wonderful book."

"It's also partisan."

"Guy, every history book is partisan. Come on!"

"But I happen to know that at least one person in this county doesn't want that book to exist. Doesn't want it read. Kept it off the shelves of the public library, and more recently, stole four copies of it off the shelf of Scarecrow Books. Can of worms, River. Can of worms."

She returned my gaze, eye to eye. "And you think because of this one person, who is either a bully or a thief or both, it's all right to suppress books?"

"No."

"Have you read the book?"

"As a matter of fact, I have read it. Or a lot of it. Yes, it's a good book."

"A wonderful book," she repeated. "Let's republish it. You and me. How much would that cost us? Not you, I'll pay for it."

"A lot," I said. I hoped that by making the price out of her range we could drop this notion. "A fortune."

She nodded and took another drag. "My great-grandfather paid a fortune to get his book published, and I'm willing to do the same. How much are we talking?"

"Well, if it's a straight reprint, and we can just photograph the existing pages—"

"No. I want a whole new edition. I want to update it, and I want to put in a bunch of sepia-tone photos. I have hundreds of photos, going way back. How much do you think it would cost to publish a book like that? Any idea?" She took a deep drag and held it, waiting for an answer.

"Have you got an extra forty thousand dollars to spend?" That ought to do it. End of nonsense.

"No problem," she said. "I don't have it now, but I can raise it by the end of the week."

"How?"

"You don't want to know."

"Then I don't want to publish."

She dropped her cigarette to the asphalt and stepped on it. "Okay, I'll show you."

The back door of the tavern burst open and Seamus strode out into the parking lot. "Dorothy, I have to talk with you," he said. "Guy, will you excuse us?"

River told me, "Don't leave." She turned to Seamus. "Whatever you want to say Seamus, you can say in front of Guy. From what I hear, the two of you have talked about me behind my back, right?"

Seamus looked at me and I shrugged back. I had never seen River behave with so much spine, but I found I liked it.

"Okay," he said. "Listen, Dorothy—"

"Call me River. Please, Seamus, you're the only person in the county who still—"

"Have you seen Charles?" he asked.

"Charles? You mean Chunky?"

"Have you seen my son, River? I'm asking you parent-to-parent. Have you seen my son, Charles? Call him Chunky, whatever. Do you know where he is?"

"He's missing?"

"He's been gone all week. School starts Tuesday, and he's nowhere to be found. I thought maybe you knew something, because he likes to spend time with Freddy."

"I have no idea," River said. "Sorry."

"Could you ask Freddy? I hate to say this, but I'm worried. The kid's been acting weird."

River turned away from both of us. Her shoulders shook. "River?" I said. I put a hand on her shoulder and she shrugged it off. She turned back and looked into Seamus's eyes.

"Freddy's been missing all week, too."

"Shit."

"It figures. They're probably together. Where's Chunky's car, that Cherokee?"

"Gone too."

"I'd like to wring your son's neck," River said. "That kid is a terrible influence. He'd better get Freddy back here in time for school, that's all I can say."

"How do you know this was Charles's idea?" Seamus challenged, leaning toward her like a tower about to fall.

"Because it's his damn car, Seamus. And Freddy doesn't even know how to drive. And Freddy likes school. And Freddy's polite, and he doesn't do hare-brained, stupid things. I'm sorry to insult your son and heir, Seamus, but Charles is rotten to the core. And he's behind the wheel, with my son in the passenger seat. I'm holding that son of yours responsible if they're not both at Jefferson High first thing Tuesday morning."

Seamus straightened up and shook his head. "Damn," he muttered. He patted my shoulder, gave River a smile he must have bought from the Dollar Store, and strode over to his BMW. He unlocked the car, folded himself into it, and backed out into the alley, then sped away.

"He makes a grand exit," I observed. "Good thing his tires aren't flat."

"What a dork," River said. "In high school kids were always letting the air out of his tires. Nobody liked him back then. Shall we go back in and join the party?"

"River, I think I ought to tell you. Carol and I saw Chunky's Cherokee down in Shelter Cove on Friday."

She frowned. "How come you didn't tell Seamus that?"

"I'm trying to keep my nose clean. There's more to the story, and I don't know the details."

"You're hiding something from me, too, right? Was Freddy down in Shelter Cove too?"

"I didn't see him," I said.

"God, I wish Freddy didn't hang out with that Connolly kid. They'll be back, though. Freddy won't miss the first day of school. He loves school. So, what else do you have to tell me?"

"That's all I know," I said. Not exactly true, but the rest was too vague and worrisome to speculate about. "Let's go back in and join the party."

She nodded. "Right you are. This day is about Pete Thayer, not a couple of bratty teenagers." We both glanced at the place we'd last seen Pete Thayer, then she shuddered and I followed her back into the Redwood Door.

The party was cooking. Elvis on the jukebox, *"Are You Lonely Tonight?"* Gloria singing along with the King, gliding from booth to booth, table to noisy table, carrying pitchers and smiling like a movie star. I found Carol at the bar, swigging a Logger Lager next to Sheriff Blue Heron, who was drinking coffee. Carol planted a kiss on my forehead, and Blue shook my hand. "He was a great guy," Blue said. "Pete." In case I thought he was talking about the bulldozer out back.

Tell me dear, are you lonely tonight?

"That he was," Carol said. She drained her glass and held it out for Gloria to take back to the tap. Gloria refilled the glass and shoved it back to Carol.

River joined us and linked her arm through Blue's. She finished her glass too, and Gloria brought her another. "I've been making the rounds, mending fences with my former staff. Turns out they don't hate me." She smiled. "Blue, you don't hate me, do you?" She chugged half her beer.

"You know damn well I don't hate you, River," Blue said.

"Then how come you're drinking coffee at my party? Do I bore you?"

Blue kissed her gently on the lips, like a two-hundred-pound butterfly with courtly manners. "You know how I feel about you, Miss Webster. How I always have."

River grinned, drank the rest of her beer, and kissed him back. "Blue, will you go down to Shelter Cove and arrest Freddy and Chunky if they're not in school on Tuesday morning?"

Blue chuckled. "No ma'am. I'm not allowed to arrest people outside Jefferson County."

"You're no fun. Well, I'd better mosey, Sheriff. I have an empty glass and I see a table with a full pitcher. I'm going to go over there and propose another toast to Pete."

"River, are you driving? You plan on driving home after this?"

"Oh, Blue, sweet Blue," she crooned. "Yes, I'm driving, and this is only my second glass of beer. One more and that's it. You know I can handle that much." She squeezed Blue's arm, then sashayed across the tavern, stopping on her way to plant a kiss on the cheek of the cardboard Pete.

Jess wanna be yo' te-huddy bear....

"You drinking, Guy?" Blue asked.

"I'll have a Coke," I said. "I can't do alcohol in the afternoon. I'm too short."

Carol rammed an elbow into my ribs. "Guy's all-purpose excuse."

"Do me a favor, will you?" Blue asked me. "Follow River home, make sure she gets there okay? I have to meet some of my cousins at five o'clock. Besides, she won't let me take care of her."

"Is she safe to drive?"

"If she knows somebody's watching her. Then she gets self-conscious and proves she's in control."

"Whatever works," Carol said.

Baby it's just you I'm a-'hinkin' of....

River drove carefully all the way home; maybe it was because she knew I was right behind her, ready to tell the Sheriff if she blew it. The afternoon was dry and hot as we climbed the mountainside on Bear Gulch Road, and it was a relief to turn into the shady redwood grove on the private road that led to River's gravel driveway.

I parked right behind River's car. River had parked right behind Chunky Connolly's black Jeep Cherokee, which was still dusty from the Lost Coast. River and I got out of our cars and smiled at each other. "Well, that's one less thing I have to worry about. Want to come in?"

"Well—"

"Come on. Help me give these teenagers a hard time for being bad boys."

I followed River into the house. I was curious to hear how the boys explained where they'd been. What they'd been up to in Shelter Cove. What was going on with Nails, Louie Luau, and the mysterious Jefferson Thomas.

Inside the house, River hollered, "Freddy? Freddy, you home? Boys?"

No answer.

"Freddy?"

The house was silent except for the echo of her voice in my ears, and a tinnitus of insects buzzing around the flowers outside. "They've probably gone for a walk," River said. "Want something to drink?"

"No thanks. I guess I'd better get back home. I'm glad the boys are back from their adventure."

"Before you go…"

"What?"

"I want to show you something. Come for a walk with me, Guy." She smiled, a twitch at the corners of her eyes.

Freddy had summed her up perfectly the day I met him: *My mom's a can of worms.* I would have looked at my watch, but I don't wear a watch. No excuse, and what harm would it do me? "Okay," I said. "What do you want to show me?"

"I'm going to show you where the money's coming from. My investment in the book. Come on."

I followed her from the front hallway through the living room and back to the kitchen. We went out the back door, where once again I admired the climbing rose that adorned the south-facing wall of the house.

"This way."

We walked across the back garden and through the hedge of marijuana plants to a trail that led into the woods. We walked along the trail, which was cool, dry, dappled with light through the trees, and singing with afternoon bugs. We came to a clearing, and on the other side of the clearing was a small barn. It was old and weathered, and it listed to one side. "That yours?" I asked.

"My grandpa built it. He kept a horse here, and also a Model T. It's falling down, and I should probably get rid of it, but it came in handy this summer."

"Oh?"

"Come on, I'll show you."

The closer we got to the barn, the clearer it became what River was talking about. Either she was raising skunks or she was drying pot, and who raises skunks these days? "You had a good harvest, I gather?" I asked her.

She grinned at me. "Oh honey, you have no idea."

"What's the street value of what you can pick from thirty-four plants?"

"Thirty-four?"

"That's what you have, right? That's what you told me."

She chuckled. We had reached the side of the barn. Whoo. The scent was enough to lift a small man up a couple of inches. River said, "I haven't even clipped the buds from those thirty-four legal plants. Get real. This is from the plantation. Freddy and I have been farming all spring and summer. Now it's dry, cured, and manicured, hanging like happy bats and ready to be bagged for market. Come on in."

We walked around to the front of the barn, which faced south. In front of the barn was a dirt road with deep tire ruts. "Where does this lead?" I asked.

"Out to Bear Gulch Road. Our property goes that far. The plantation is down that trail on the far side of the meadow." She reached under a loose board to the right of the padlocked barn door. "Wait," she said. "Where's the key?"

"That's okay," I told her. "I don't really need to see this."

"Yes, you do. Damn it, where's that key? Okay, here it is." She pulled a key ring out of the crack between the warping boards and worried the padlock open. She removed the lock, pulled back the hinge, and yanked on the door.

The door opened slowly, and we walked into the dim, dry, stinky cavern.

River gripped my hand and gasped. "Where is it? Jesus, *where is it? Guy, it's, Jesus Christ, it's gone!*"

As my eyes adjusted to the dim light, her face came into focus, a face of horror and betrayal and panic.

"I've been ripped off!"

"When was the last time you were in the barn?" I asked her.

"It's been a couple of weeks," she said. "I helped with the harvest and helped hang the plants, but the drying and curing operation was Freddy's department."

"Maybe he took it to market," I said. "Maybe he's come home from Shelter Cove with a great big ten-pound box of money."

"But I had made arrangements. I told him I didn't want him involved with the selling part. Too dangerous, I told him. He wouldn't have done that. He wouldn't have ripped me off, would he?" She began to whimper. "Would he?" She held her hands out to me.

I held her hands in mine. They were ice-cold. "Let's go back to the house," I told her. "Maybe he's back there by now and you can ask him some questions. He probably has a good answer, right?"

I drew her out of the barn. Her hands were shaking too badly for her to manage the padlock, so I offered to help. She shook her head and threw the padlock across the dirt road and into the ferns. "Nothing to hide anymore," she mumbled. "What are you looking at?"

I was squatting on the road, looking at a set of tire tracks. "When was the last time it rained around here?" I asked her.

"Last Monday it rained some," she said. "Dried out on Tuesday, hasn't rained since. Why?"

"Whoever made these tracks came in after the rain but while the ground was still pretty wet. I'm going to bet these marks match the tread on that Cherokee in your driveway."

"You're saying Chunky and Freddy—"

"Let's go," I said. "We don't want to miss seeing them. That must have been really strong weed," I added. "It's been gone for days, and the barn still smells like cloud nine."

On the trail back to her house I told her about the rest of what I'd seen in Shelter Cove on Friday. The *Little Mermaid* in the harbor. Nails and Louie Luau. The man who called himself Jefferson Thomas, and the man in a hunting jacket from Port Silva. A black Jeep Cherokee and the motel manager who confirmed that it belonged to Charles Connolly. "I don't know what it means," I said, "but it looked like a deal was happening."

When we reached the house, we walked around to the front. The Cherokee was still there, and the back was open. So was the front door of the house. River stormed up the steps and nearly crashed into her son, who was coming out the door, carrying a suitcase.

She placed her hand on his chest and said, "Just where do you think you're going, mister?"

"Mom." He didn't look at her.

"Don't Mom me. What's going on? And where in the world have you been?"

"I'm leaving, Mom," Freddy said. "Hey, Guy."

"You're what?"

"I'm moving out. Sorry, but I'm moving out." He didn't look at me, either.

"Don't make me laugh," River said. "You think I'm going to give you permission to leave this house?"

"Mom, I don't need your permission," Freddy said. "Now please step aside so I can take my suitcase down the steps."

"Don't need your permission? What is this? Kiddo, you're fifteen years old."

"He has my permission," said a voice from the open door. "Freedom's coming with me."

There he stood. Gray crew cut. Black leather jacket. Mean grin with a steel eyetooth. Jefferson Thomas.

River said, *"Billy?"*

"Hey, Dodo," the man said. "Long time no see."

"You're out of jail?"

"So it would appear," Billy answered. "How you been, babe?"

"Billy? Billy Connolly?" she stammered.

"I'm going to take Freddy with me for a while," he told her. "Hope that's all right."

"Where are you living now, Billy?" River asked in a small, timid voice.

"Here and there," he answered. Then he turned to me. "You. That newspaper guy, right?"

I nodded, then found my voice. "I'm out of that business now," I said.

"Safer that way," he said, with a grin and a wink.

Freddy walked back up the steps and into the house. He still had not looked once at his mother.

"Some news is best kept to yourself, know what I mean? Like I think it would be a very bad idea if you told anybody you'd seen me. Dorothy, that goes for you, too. We have an understanding?"

Freddy came out of the house again, another suitcase in one hand and a laptop computer in the other. The top of the laptop wore a decal of a black skull with glowing red eyes. He walked past the three of us and loaded his stuff into the back of Chunky's Cherokee.

"Billy?"

"Yes, Dodo. Yes. I'm Billy. Get used to it. Me and Freedom are going to travel together for a little while. I'll bring him back. Relax, baby." He walked down the steps and held her shoulders in his massive, gnarled hands. "I'll take good care of him."

"That's it, Dad," Freddy told him. "All packed."

"Ready to hit the road, hot shot?" Billy asked.

"Ready."

"Wait a minute, Billy," River begged. "You can't stay for dinner or something?"

"Long drive ahead of us," he said. He opened his arms wide. "Give us a hug."

River studied the big man in front of her, then shook her head as if it were full of fleas. "Shit, Billy. You're the one who ripped me off! You ripped off my dope!"

"Your dope?" Billy said with a kindly smile. "Not yours, not legally. It was up for grabs."

"What do you mean, not legally mine? I grew it, I—"

"It's not legal, so how can it be legally yours? You still have your legal plants. That should hold you. No hug?"

River didn't answer. She sat down on the third step up to her porch and buried her face in her hands.

Billy turned to Freddy. "All set, sport? Ready to roll?"

"Ready to roll. Bye, Mom."

Freddy climbed into the passenger seat of the Cherokee and Billy Connolly walked around to the driver's side. Over the hood he called back, "I'll take good care of him, Dorothy. I'll bring him back in one piece. Just be sure you keep quiet about seeing me. And that goes for both of you."

He opened the door of the vehicle and climbed aboard. In the passenger seat, Freddy looked straight ahead with zero expression on his face. The Cherokee roared alive, then sprayed gravel as it turned and drove away.

I sat down on the step next to River and put my arm around her shaking shoulders.

She squeezed my knee and whimpered, "There go the only two people I've ever truly loved."

Fog had rolled in off the coast by the time I got home. Carol and I sat in the living room and I told her what had happened out on Bear Gulch Road. As I spoke, her face went from curious to amazed to aghast.

"She let her son drive off with that thug?" she cried. "Guy, how could you?"

"How could I? Could I what?"

"Let that happen? You should have stopped it."

"That thug, as you call him, can be pretty persuasive. If I had tried to stop him, I'd probably be at the bottom of some canyon in the Jefferson Alps right now, serving dinner to coyotes."

"Jesus, this is awful," Carol said. "So where was Chunky during all this? I mean, it was his car, so where was he?"

I held out empty hands.

"Tell me something, Guy. How long have you known Jefferson Thomas was Billy Connolly?"

"Well, when I saw those old newspaper photos of Seamus's wedding, I realized that today's thug resembled yesterday's best man. But I figured it was a coincidence, since for all I knew, Billy was in prison. Then when I saw him through the binoculars, down in Shelter Cove—"

"So you think he broke out of jail?" Carol asked.

"Doubt it. If he'd broken out, the state police would be swarming all over Jefferson County, since this was where he might try to hide. And the guy's been around a long time, going back to the night Pete was killed. He's out on good behavior, or maybe a loose parole."

"So you think Billy Connolly killed Pete Thayer."

"And Mickey Chan. I just don't know why. Also trashed the office of the *Jefferson Nickel*, trashed Pete's house, stole our hard drive and four copies of *A Long, Long Crime Ago*. I just don't know why."

"So what are we going to do about this? Go make us a drink and then tell me what we're going to do about this. Jesus! Poor River!"

I walked out to the kitchen and thought hard while I dropped ice cubes into tumblers and drowned them in alcohol. When I got back to the living room I handed Carol her drink and sat down.

"Well?"

"I'm going to go see Blue Heron first thing tomorrow morning. I tried calling him from River's house and got no answer. Called his house, called his cell phone, no answer. There was an answering machine at the sheriff's office, but the place is obviously closed till tomorrow. So I'll go over there first thing in the morning."

"Don't bother," Carol told me. "Blue won't be there tomorrow. He and his cousins have gone on a fishing trip to the upper Steelhead River. Tomorrow's Labor Day, remember?"

"Well, then first thing Tuesday, I guess."

Carol sipped her drink. "By which time, if we're lucky, Freddy and Chunky will be in school, all in their places with bright, shiny faces."

"One can hope," I said. But I didn't believe it.

I got to Sheriff Blue Heron's office at ten o'clock Tuesday morning. He poured me a cup of French roast from the electric pot on his filing cabinet, and we faced each other across his cluttered desk. "How was your fishing trip?" I asked. "Catch anything?"

Blue laughed. "My cousins caught a hangover and a sunburn. I caught up on my sleep and my reading. How was your Labor Day?"

"Okay." I put my coffee cup down. "So much for small talk. Do you happen to know if Charles Connolly and Freddy Webster showed up for school this morning?"

Blue narrowed his eyes. "What do you think I am, Guy? A truant officer?"

"I want you to find out."

"What's going on?" he asked.

"Who do you think killed Pete Thayer, Blue?" I answered.

"Guy, settle down."

"Blue, call the high school." I stood up, found a place among the piles of paper on his desk to plant my fists, and leaned over so my face was close enough to smell the sheriff's after-shave. "Go on. Find out if Freddy and Chunky are all in their places."

"Are you on something? How much coffee have you had this morning?"

"Those two kids are in trouble, Sheriff. I mean serious trouble."

"Okay, okay, easy now. Sit down. Sit down and spill the beans. Start at the beginning and talk slowly. Go."

I sat and spoke. "I've been thinking about who killed Pete Thayer. We've ruled out all the possible suspects, meaning everybody we know who was there at the Redwood Door or had some motive for killing Pete. That means it had to be somebody we don't know, or didn't know at the time. Somebody who had access to Seamus Connolly's car, somebody with wet boots, who climbed out the men's room window after he was finished washing the blood off his hands. Escaped into the side alley and disappeared into the crowd in the town square."

"Okay. I'm with you so far. An outsider. But who? And why? And what does this have to do with the high school?"

"I know who that someone was," I said. "I don't know why, but I do know who."

Blue nodded for me to take another turn.

I inhaled then spoke. "Jefferson Thomas."

"The man who threw you in the harbor?"

I nodded. "But his name isn't really Jefferson Thomas."

"Go on. Do you want some more coffee?"

"No thanks. See—"

"Guy, would you please quit waving your hands all over the room? You're driving me nuts. Okay, settle down and tell me. This person, this Jefferson Thomas or whatever his name was, he had access to Seamus's car keys?"

"I believe he did. I believe Chunky let him have the keys. Call the high school."

"Guy, slow down."

I folded my hands in my lap and took a deep breath. Carol had told me the same thing over and over the day before: "For God's sake, Guy, it's Labor Day. You're supposed to relax." I couldn't then, and I couldn't now.

"Billy Connolly," I said. "That's who."

"Who what? Killed Pete Thayer?"

"Yeah, and Mickey Chan, and robbed Carol's bookstore. Trashed the *Jefferson Nickel* and Pete's house. For starters."

"Billy Connolly's in prison, last I heard," Blue said.

I said, "I beg to differ." I went on to tell the sheriff all I'd seen on Sunday at River's house. And the Friday before that, down at Shelter Cove. "I'm sorry to inform you, sheriff, but Big Bad Bill is in your county now. And he's got those two kids with him, which you might call kidnapping at the worst, or contributing to the delinquency of a couple of minors at best. Unless Freddy and Chunky are at the high school, in which case all we're dealing with is a simple double murder, plus some vandalism and theft."

Blue stared at me with no expression on his large, flat face. When I was done talking, or maybe just taking a breather (I couldn't be sure), he lifted the phone and asked his front-office assistant to get Bud Bailey, the principal of the high school, on the line. While we were waiting with his ear to the receiver, he asked me, "Sure you won't have some more coffee?"

"No. It'll keep me awake."

"Pour me some, okay?" He placed his empty cup on a stack of papers in front of me. I got up and carried his cup to the filing cabinet, where what was left of the coffee had turned to tar. I poured it into the cup and turned off the machine. By the time I got back to Blue's desk, he was connected.

"Yeah, Bud. This is Blue Heron....Yeah, good, and you?...Listen, I need to have a talk with a couple of your students....I don't know yet, that's why I need to talk to them....Freddy Webster and Charles Connolly, a junior and a senior....Right. Can you have them in your office by eleven o'clock?...Good, I'll be there....Listen, I don't have time to chat just now. We'll catch up after I've had my chat with those kids, okay?...Good. See you in..." he checked his watch "...twenty minutes. Bye."

He cradled the receiver and then said, "You hungry at all?"

"No."

He picked up the phone again and asked his assistant to call the Redwood

Door. The call went through. "Gloria, this is Blue....Fine, babe. Listen, I'm sending Guy Mallon over there to talk to you, okay? You got a few minutes to talk?...Very good."

He hung up again and said, "Gloria's waiting for you. I want you to get her to tell you about the night Billy decked Seamus at the Redwood Door. I gotta go over to the high school. Meet me back here, okay? We'll do lunch."

I was on foot, so it took me fifteen minutes to get to the Redwood Door, by which time my body was hot from the exercise and my face was damp with chilly mist. I walked in and let my eyes adjust to the dim lighting. Gloria was behind the bar washing glasses. There were no other customers in the place. I suppose it was too late for the breakfast drinkers, too early for the lunch drinkers.

"Hi, there, Mister Mallon," Gloria said. "Sheriff told me to expect you. Want something to eat? Drink? Cup of coffee?"

I walked over to the bar and said, "Good morning, Gloria. I, uh—"

"Whatcha need, Guy? Blue says you want to talk. Lots of people want to talk to their bartender, just not so early in the day. You're all right, aren't you? You and Carol? Everything's okay?"

I waved those questions away like flies. "I'm fine," I said. "Blue says I should ask you about what happened one night here in the bar. Billy Connolly decked Seamus, he said. What was that all about?"

Gloria's eyebrows lifted an inch. "He wants me to talk about that? Nobody's supposed to talk about that night."

"Says who?"

"Who makes the rules in this town? Go take a seat in the booth back in the corner. I'll join you in a sec. I just have to wipe down the counter."

I went back to the darkest corner of the tavern and crawled into the booth. I folded my hands on the table and worked at controlling my breathing. I was calmed down some by the time Gloria slid into the booth, placing a glass of beer in front of each of us.

"You really want to hear this, huh?" she said.

"So I'm told." I took a sip of beer.

"Well, okay. This goes way back. You know who Billy Connolly was, right?"

"Is, as far as I know. Yeah, Seamus's little brother."

"Little as in younger. Not little as in—"

"As in me?"

Gloria laughed and put her hand on my cheek. "Right."

INTERLUDE
The Connolly Brothers

A nyway [Gloria began], Billy was a good deal bigger than Seamus. Big and mean and he could charm the pants off any female in this county. I ought to know, but that's another story. I'll start over.

Okay. Those two Connolly brothers hated each other from day one. Day one of Billy's life, that is, because Billy was the younger, the baby, the invader, the monster who killed their mother. They say even as little kids those two boys were like the two sides of their father, Norman Connolly, the only Connolly to amount to a hill of beans in half a century. Norman the businessman, Norman the playboy. Seamus got the business side. Billy got the other. And just as the two sides of Norman Connolly made war with each other inside his gut and sent him to an early grave at the age of sixty-two, his two sons warred with each other nonstop too, and it's a wonder one or both of them aren't dead. God knows they both came close more than once, with all that fighting.

They're the only Connollys left now. Them and Chunky. Or Charles. At least the only Connollys named Connolly.

Like I said, their mother died giving birth to Billy. He was always a wildcat and he probably shredded that poor woman's insides on his way out. So Norman raised those boys by himself, with the help of a series of mistresses. He pinned his hopes on Seamus because Seamus was the smart one. President of the Jefferson High student body, editor of the school paper. But the one he loved more, the one who made him laugh, was Billy. Norman gave Billy a weekend with his current mistress when Billy turned fourteen, drove the two of them up to the family lodge in the Jefferson Alps and left them there for three days and two nights; in fact it was a birthday present for both of them, because the mistress turned thirty-six that same weekend. From that day on, Billy enjoyed giving women the times of their life as much as he enjoyed giving Seamus a pain in the ass.

Norman Connolly ran the town until he died. Seamus runs it now.

History lesson. You've probably heard Seamus claim, or read it in one of his editorials, that he's descended from the original sea captain that brought the

Connolly family to the Jefferson Coast? That Brian Boru, named after the famous king of Ireland? Don't believe it. Brian Connolly was a bachelor until he left California late in his life, and if he had any descendants they're down in Mexico somewhere. Norman wasn't descended from Brian's brother Patrick either; that brother's four sons were all worthless fuckups who never married as far as anybody knows. Kevin was still a boy when he died, and Dennis never married. Bill and Bob had daughters. That's all the original Connolly brothers. The whole gang. The clan nearly died out, along with the Websters, except for one branch who barely held on through the influenza and the Depression, held onto the Connolly business enterprises and the Connolly name.

So who are Seamus and Billy descended from, and why do they get to call themselves Connollys? Think again. There was another Connolly on that first ship: Katie, the halfwit sister. She never married, but she had a good time, had several children, all of them by different anonymous men, some of whom might even have been close relatives of hers, brothers even. Whatever, it was thanks to Katie that the Connolly name survived halfway into the twentieth century. How do I know all this? My mom told me. She was descended from Katie Connolly too, which means I have Connolly blood in me, which makes me and Billy cousins a bunch of degrees away and several times removed. I guess that adds incest to the catalog of his mortal sins, his crimes and misdemeanors. Mine too, but who cares. All I have to say about that is, oh lord. Oh sweet lord.

Anyways, back to their childhood. I've heard these stories from both sides, because both brothers have spent a lot of time in this bar. Seamus, back when he was a drinker, used to come in and run a tab, because he was my landlord. He owned the building. Still does, but he doesn't own my business. Billy, he'd come in a lot looking for action. So like I said, I heard it from both sides, and it amounted to what was obvious anyway: Billy was a bully. He was always a bully, right from the get-go. Seamus griped about it, Billy was proud of it.

He would shove Seamus's face in the sandbox when they were both little guys. He threw stones at Seamus's head when Seamus was trying to learn to ride a bicycle. Once when they were eight and ten years old, their father took them up to the family lodge to let them camp there overnight, be men. Left them and promised to return for them in the morning. Well, the two of them discovered an abandoned mining camp on their property, back in the woods, and Billy locked Seamus in a bunkhouse and left him there in the dark all night long. Only way out was a sheer drop to the Damfool River, two hundred feet below. Stuff like that.

As soon as Seamus turned sixteen, he got his driver's license and his father bought him a car, one of the very first Ford Mustangs. The day after Seamus's birthday, that Mustang was the very first car Billy ever stole. Norman whipped Billy's ass for that one, and I mean that literally, and so he never stole the Mustang again. Instead, he contented himself with letting the air out of Seamus's tires. He never did it in plain sight, and never admitted it to anybody except the buddies he bragged about it to.

How do I know all this stuff? I was in high school with both boys, and I got around, is how. I was head cheerleader my senior year, same year Seamus was editor of the newspaper, same year Billy was captain of the football team in his sophomore year. Still rubbing Seamus's nose in the sand, one way or another. By that time he had lost his cherry, thanks to his dad, and Seamus had not. Rubbed his nose in that, too. Me and Billy—well, let's just say the team captain has his privileges, and so does the head cheerleader.

So Seamus graduated from high school in 1965. Glad to get away from his brother, for sure, he went down to Stanford where he learned about journalism and business. After that, with a couple of degrees, he worked as a junior editor for the business section of the *San Francisco Chronicle*.

Billy didn't bother to graduate from high school. Without his brother to beat up on, he decided to team up with his friend Nails in the fishing business, where he learned about fishing and crime. Those two would come in here drinking, sometimes together, sometimes alone. I liked it better when Billy came in alone. Nothing against Nails, you understand.

Norman Connolly died in 1972, and Seamus came back to town to take over the family businesses: Jefferson Lumber, the *Jefferson Democrat,* Jefferson Construction, and Connolly Enterprises, which amounted to a ton of real estate. None of the other old historical Connolly ventures were still around. Bill and Bob's Ice House was long gone, and Denny's Saloon is still there, but it's a rotgut dive on the other side of the tracks, and it's not a Connolly business. Dennis lost it to a fisherman in a fair fight. But most of the commercial real estate in this town is owned by Connolly Enterprises, which makes Seamus my damn landlord. I'm glad I got my lease on the property back when Norman was in charge. He gave me a good deal. He was sweet on me, to tell the truth, but that's a whole nother story.

Anyway, Seamus came back to Jefferson like gangbusters, and it wasn't long before he was running the whole town. He joined Rotary, established the Chamber of Commerce, got his cronies into office and into uniform and on the planning commission, and changed the name of his newspaper to the

Jefferson Republican. Running this town. Running it like nobody had since Brian Boru Connolly, back in the eighteen-hundreds.

All except for his brother Billy and his buds. That element Seamus never could run. By this time Billy had a bushy beard and monster hair, which just made him all the sexier, and he was in the export business. He was living up in the hunting lodge, and during harvest season he would take his truck around to all the pot plantations in the Jefferson Alps and carry crop to the harbor, where he'd turn it over to Nails. What Nails did with the stuff or where he took it in that boat of his, I never wanted to know. A lot of money changed hands is all I can tell you, and a lot of that money ended up in my till, so I wasn't asking questions. Whatever Billy and Nails and all their suppliers and all their customers were doing, it was good for the economy.

Seamus took a public stand against marijuana in his newspaper, but everybody in town knew he was just taking a stand against his brother out of principle, and nobody paid much attention to it. It wasn't till Billy moved out onto the Steelhead Rancheria and actually started growing the stuff that Seamus wanted to bust his ass, and then he couldn't do much because River Webster had gone and given that land to the Steelhead Tribe. It was sovereign Indian land.

So it was pretty much of a standoff between those two big brothers. I didn't see much of Seamus for a while, because he started doing most of his drinking over at the Wildcat Saloon, where the Rotary gang hangs out. Every now and then Billy would come in, when he'd get restless out on the rancheria. Sometimes he came in with Nails, and sometimes with some of his Indian friends, but of course I liked it best when he came in on his own. When that happened he'd be looking for action, and he'd leave with some lady or other, always somebody different; but when I was lucky he'd stay till the place closed down, and then he'd walk me home and whatever. Mostly, though, he stayed out on that rancheria with lucky River Webster. I guess River was lucky. Who knows when it comes to somebody like Billy.

And that's how it remained, season after season, until the fall of 1981, when Audrey Coggins flounced into town, and all hell broke loose.

Boy oh boy. Audrey. Now there was a piece of work.

II

Seamus Connolly had met Audrey Coggins that summer in San Francisco at a national convention of small-town newspaper owners and editors. She was from Yuba City, doing some kind of entertainment thing for the convention, is what I heard. That's all I know for sure, but there was a lot of talk here in the tavern late at night after customers had had a few drinks. Entertainment? Like a stripper for a private party? As in busting topless out of a great big cake? Who knows. Maybe she was just an escort, but whatever that means could mean whatever you want it to mean.

Whatever it meant or whatever she did, she did it to Seamus. She caught him in her net, if you want to call it that, and pretty soon he was finding excuse after excuse to take business trips to Yuba City for more of the same. I heard some of his cronies grumbling, wondering if he was planning to invest Jefferson City and County money outside the city and county, but that turned out to be a false alarm, because just in time for Halloween, Seamus brought this bombshell back in a rented U-Haul truck. Her and all her stuff, most of which was probably make-up and tacky silk-fringe pillows. Oh stop it, Gloria. She wasn't that bad. Well, she was, but it was none of my business.

Got to admit. She was a tasty morsel. She didn't dress like any other woman in this rainy county I can tell you that, but wet or dry, she was a bombshell. Those pouty lips? Big brown eyes? She had a blond bouffant hairdo when she first came to town, but the style and color seemed to change from time to time. Legs to die for, and the less said about her shape the better. The better for me, that is. She was a live one, Audrey.

Seamus gave her a job as a clerk in the classified ads department, which meant moving the existing classified clerk to real ad sales, which made everybody happy. Pretty soon Seamus and Audrey were a regular couple for Saturday night dances out at the County Gun Club, which is the closest thing we have to classy in these parts. She started out living in a little bungalow two blocks from the town square, but by the end of the year Seamus had gone public and moved her in with him in the big Connolly house on Connolly Avenue, and Audrey had quit her job at the paper.

They announced their engagement at the annual Connolly New Year's Eve party, right here in the Redwood Door. What an evening that was. That was the first time Audrey met Billy. That was the night she made up her mind Billy was going to be her husband's best man. Announced it to the crowd, then kissed Billy on the lips. Then kissed Seamus on the lips too, to show it was just family. Said, "Shake hands." The two brothers squinted at each other. Billy held out his hand. Seamus reached across the distance. They shook, and the champagne popped and flowed. Audrey turned around and found somebody else to kiss, because it was New Year's Eve.

I'll never forget that damn wedding. I mean, shit. For one thing, the whole affair stretched over two weeks, one before, one after. Seamus rented the entire Jefferson City Travelodge, the biggest motel on 101, to take care of the out-of-towners: a couple of his fraternity brothers from Stanford who were on his team of ushers along with the local Rotarians, plus a whole bevy of trashy chicks from Marysville and Yuba City who came to town to stand up with Audrey in the church and mainly to boogie for two weeks solid, all expenses paid.

For example. They rented the dining room of the Wildcat Saloon for the bridal shower, which I had to go to. "I have to work that evening, Audrey," I told her.

"Oh bullshit, Gloria," she said. "Are you my girlfriend, or what?"

What, I thought, but I traded hours with the day-shift bartender and went to her damn shower, which consisted of about twenty presents to open: dildos, skimpy nightwear, cayenne-based massage oil, anatomically correct Ken dolls and G.I. Joes, candles in various shapes I don't even like to think about, stuff like that. There was a chocolate cake in the shape of a you know what. One of the cocktail waiters was dressed up like Charlie Chaplin, you know, bowler hat, tramp suit, cane, but every time he came out of the kitchen he had less of the costume on, until by the end all he had on was the bowler, the mustache, and a gold lamé jewel pouch. Smiled shyly and never said a word. All the while these women are screeching and doing tequila slammers, until it's time to settle up and wander on over to my base, the Redwood Door, where the male members of the wedding party were waiting for the real party to begin. Billy was there. Seamus was not. The whole gang drank and hollered for about an hour, then paid up and screeched out, and I'm told they went on back to the Travelodge, and I can only guess what happened out there.

I didn't have anything to do with the bachelor party. Those guys all took it out of town, down to some whorehouse in Eureka is what I heard, but I also heard that Seamus just went along for the ride, stayed sober and drove the school bus. I heard that from Billy. Maybe it was just a strip club, but I'm told a number of the boys got laid, not including Seamus, and not including Billy either, according to Billy. Yeah, right. All expenses paid.

The rehearsal dinner Friday evening was at the Connolly mansion, and Seamus hired me to tend bar. I had never been in that house before, driven by it a million times, but never was in it. What a nice place. One of those real classic Victorians, kept up perfectly. At least Seamus had that much class. Wainscoting, Oriental carpets, hardwood floors, a curving staircase with an oak banister, chandelier in the dining room, stone fireplace, the whole nine yards, and what's more, people behaved themselves, even after I'd poured enough free liquor to drown a village. I guess they'd already partied hard for almost a week and it was time to give it a rest, to get rested up for the bash the following night.

I poured the wine for the dinner too, so I got to hear the toasts. The only one I remember was Billy's toast to the happy couple. "Seamus," he said, "Brother of mine, I thought you'd never get laid." The room erupted in laughter, but Billy signaled for attention. "But I got to hand it to you, bro, you done good. Way to go, my man. You've got yourself a handful, and she's a lot prettier than the handful you've had up till now." He turned to his future sister-in-law, dug his fingers deep into that big beard of his, gave his chin a leisurely scratch, and said, "Audrey, you princess you, you're a prize, a peach, a gem, a honeybunch, and I want you to tell that husband of yours, by God he better treat you good. Cause if he doesn't, tell him I know someone who will let the air out of his tires!" Billy then turned his grin on and showed it around the dining room, allowing them all to whoop and laugh and applaud, even Seamus, who was a better sport than I expected him to be. But why shouldn't he be? He was marrying a princess, and the two of them had a secret.

The wedding ceremony was at the Episcopal church, and the reception was at the Jefferson County Gun Club. The wedding was polite and the reception was lavish, and everybody smiled a lot. It was a rainy day, so the whole reception took place in the ballroom, not out on the garden as planned. That didn't seem to bother anybody except the photographer, who made the most of the moment. He told me, "I wish I could just do head shots. I mean, my gawd. A white miniskirt wedding dress? What is this world coming to?"

She looked radiant. Well face it: she was a woman of questionable background marrying the richest man in an entire county, even if it was the smallest, poorest county in the state. She was a cat who landed in a pot of cream.

We met up in the ladies' room and she hugged me. She grinned. She told me, "This is the biggest moment of my life."

I could believe it. I could even see it. I looked down at her scoop-necked white dress and saw that her goodies had grown a cup size since the last time I'd checked them out.

"Me and Seamus, we're going to Cancún on our honeymoon," she said. "Gonna do slammers and ball for a solid week!"

I said, "Audrey, hon, maybe you ought to think about laying off the sauce, under the circumstances."

She frowned. "You think?"

"That's what they say."

"Old wives' tale, is what I heard."

I shrugged. "Maybe. But still."

She pouted. "What about sex? It's my damn honeymoon, Gloria."

I smiled. "Go for it, honey."

III

Charles Brendan Connolly was born October first, 1982. Premature, everyone said and nobody believed.

Then, talk about strange. For one thing, Audrey never took to being a mother, which didn't surprise a lot of us. Seamus was still Seamus, and not much of a father. But what really surprised us: Billy decided to take being an uncle seriously. He started spending time in town, staying in that big Webster house on the corner of Webster and Connolly, the one Seamus had bought from River back when her grandparents died. He would babysit the kid when Seamus and Audrey went out on the town. Sometimes he even came along when they took the baby out to dinner, and if the baby hollered, why Billy would be the one to pick him up and take him out for a walk around the town square, let the parents eat in peace.

Some people said Billy was probably having an affair with Audrey, but I don't believe it. For one thing, he would of told me. No, I think he just happened to like that little monster. The kid was just like him.

Some people said Billy was Chunky's real father, but don't you believe it. Not a chance. Those first few months when Audrey came to town, her and Seamus were together every minute, practically, and Billy had nothing to do with either one of them except at the wedding, by which time the chicken was already in the oven.

But the strangest thing of all? Billy and Seamus Connolly got to be friends that year. Friends for the first time in their whole life. You'd see those two together at the Jefferson High baseball games. You'd see the whole family in the park. Out to dinner. That friendship lasted almost a year, which blew everyone's mind. Who would have believed it? And who would have thought something good would have come out of the birth of that horrible child, the one who threw salt shakers, scattered full plates of French fries (with ketchup) all over my floor?

Sometimes, late at night, after the parents got home from painting the town and Billy's babysitting shift was over, he'd drop by the Redwood Door, and I was always glad to see him. See him so mellow, not like the old Billy. But he wasn't even looking for action. Wouldn't leave with other women, wouldn't stick around till closing time, either, which was just as well for me. I guess.

But did you expect that nice family feeling to last? Me neither. None of us did.

For one thing, Audrey may have been bummed about being a mom, but she sure didn't waste any time with the post-partum blues, let me tell you. She was back on the town in no time, dragging Seamus along for the ride of his life, while Billy stayed home with the baby. They used to come in here every Friday night, just like you and Carol do now, and Jesus, those two could drink. He could anyway. She could drink but she couldn't hold it very well. She would laugh like a jackass and cuss like a pissed-off parrot.

Every now and then Seamus had to work late. She'd come in here to wait for him, except she didn't wait for anybody when it came to drinking. Sometimes by the time he got here she was already stewed and acting up. He put up with it, though, God knows why. Guess he figured that's what he should do for the mother of his son. But if he didn't show up, she got nasty. I guess she didn't like to be kept waiting. Piece of work, that Audrey.

Well, so anyway, one night she comes in here and it's this hot September night outside, and she's wearing a skimpy polka-dot dress cut way down, and she had a lot to show off in that department, and she plops right down at the bar and gets started on the Wild Turkey, knocking back shots as fast as I could pour them. Her voice got louder and louder, and people started moving away from her at the bar. Probably some of the guys were just moving away for safety, because everybody in town knew that Seamus Connolly was a jealous and possessive son of a bitch.

The place was crowded that night, I remember. Old Nails—he was Old Nails even when he was younger—was down there in his usual place. Louie wasn't around back then. A different crowd, but you know, crowds in bars are pretty much all the same. Everybody was ready to look at Audrey Connolly, because she was something to look at. But nobody wanted to talk to her, much, because she had the brains of a washcloth and the mouth of a Dumpster, and besides, who wants some big bulldozer tearing their arms off?

So Audrey's whooping it up and following guys around the place, hopping from stool to stool, and guys keep moving away, and she keeps asking me what time it is, and I'm like, Seamus'll be here any minute, sure hoping he'll show up and take this foul-mouth polka-dot bombshell out before she blows the windows out or cracks my mirror with her voice.

Jesus. So that's when old Audrey climbs up on the table right in the center of the room. The jukebox is playing Patsy Cline. "Crazy." Talk about timing. And as soon as the song ends, and there's silence, and it's real, real quiet, because everyone in the bar is staring at this, I got to admit it, beautiful nutcase standing on the table, who's grinning ear to ear, she pulls up her polka-dot skirt as high as it will go, and let's put it this way: I pour more Vermouth into a very dry martini than she was wearing in the underpants department that night. She yells, top of her lungs, "IS THERE A CONNOLLY IN THE HOUSE?"

Well, as a matter of fact, there was. Cause, right out of this very booth we're sitting in climbs Billy Connolly, who's taking a night off from the commune and partying with his buds. Made me wonder who was babysitting Chunky, but it was probably one of Billy's friends. Girlfriends. Anyway, everybody in the place all start applauding and cheering for Billy, and Billy grins and bows this way, then that, then walks over to where Audrey is still on her pedestal, on parade. He holds out his arms and she falls into them like he's a comfortable armchair, and he carries her towards the front door of the bar.

But before he can reach the front door, the back door of the bar opens, and people gasp, so Billy turns around to see what's up. And in from the back struts Seamus, smiling like a big shot till he sees his wife in his brother's arms. Hears her whooping. Watches the two of them kiss real nasty. Billy tears his face away from Audrey's and goes, "Hey, bro."

Seamus walks right up to the pair of them, goes, "Put her down." Quiet, but everybody in the bar could hear, because the jukebox was silent, nobody was talking, and I wasn't even washing glasses. "Put my wife down, Billy."

Billy, I got to hand it to him, tries to set Audrey on her feet, but she won't have any of it. She wraps her arms around his neck and her legs around his waist, and plants another one right on his lips. Billy finally pries her off his big, strong body and gently sits her down on a bar stool. He turns around, and smiles at his brother, but his brother isn't smiling back. Seamus has picked up a cocktail, I forget what, maybe an old fashioned, from somebody's table, and he pitches the contents into Billy's face, ice cubes, fruit, liquor, it was a mess. Seamus sets the glass down on the table and looks up, just in time to watch Billy's fist crash into his face. Seamus did a back flip over the same table, just like in the movies. Audrey shouted, "Whooee!" Billy picked her up again and marched out the back of the bar, into the night.

It felt like an hour, but it was probably three minutes before anybody said a thing. Nobody helped Seamus to his feet. He eventually pulled himself up, using the table for leverage. The table fell over, more drinks on the floor. Seamus turned all the way around, glaring at everyone in the place, showing them all his bloody nose and busted mouth. He pulled a handkerchief out of his pocket and spat two teeth into it. He blotted the mess as best he could, then roared. "Anybody says one word about this night to me, or I hear about anybody talking about this night behind my back, and I'll run him out of town. You understand me?"

Well, nobody said a word, from that day forward, far as I know. Oh. One other thing. When Seamus finally got himself cleaned up and ready to leave, he gave me a wad of money to cover damages and then went out back to the parking lot, where he had left his car. The car was there all right, but the tires in back were flat. I had to call the police.

Okay. Well, Audrey never came home to Seamus. Her and Billy went up into the Jefferson Alps and shacked up together in a cabin the Connolly boys used as a hunting lodge. It's like a two-hour drive from here, straight uphill. According to Billy, Audrey was afraid of Seamus, said he was a violent man, begged Billy to protect her. Billy always swore he never, you know, got, you know, intimate with her, but I have my doubts about that. Billy could of had any woman he wanted, and Audrey wasn't what you'd call choosy, so they probably did it like bunnies, but it's none of my business. It didn't last long anyway. According to Billy, Audrey split. Left her husband, left all that money, left her little boy forever.

Pretty soon Billy was back on the commune and back in town, spreading this story around that Audrey had moved on. He had no idea where, he said. Probably hitchhiked back to Yuba City, or on to Las Vegas, or maybe she was hooking in the Tenderloin in San Francisco for all he knew.

Seamus didn't believe him. Went up to the cabin to see for himself and found the cabin burned to the ground. I mean burned to…the…ground. Nothing left but a pile of ashes.

Nobody knows why that place burned down. Some people think maybe Audrey burned it down because by that time she'd had her fill of Connolly men. Some people said Billy burned the place down, with her in it. Some folks think Seamus went up there and tried to burn it down with the both of them inside.

My guess is Seamus went up there and burned the hunting lodge down because he was so all-fire pissed off at his brother, who liked that place so much. Most people just kept their mouths shut. Anyway, we never saw Audrey again, and as far as the Redwood Door was concerned, good riddance. Too bad for Chunky, though. Probably didn't help his disposition one bit to be raised by that bulldozer of a father.

A year later, Billy and River had a child of their own, sweet little Freedom. You know, Freddy. And a couple of years after that, Seamus got his hands on the commune ranch in some business deal and kicked everybody off the land so he could build his mall. That's how he finally got back at his brother. Brought a whole army in to take over the place, and things got ugly and Billy almost killed a guy. Maybe on purpose, maybe an accident, or maybe that's just the way Billy was. Whatever. They threw the book at him, called him menace to society. Well maybe he was. Sent him to jail down in San Luis Obispo County, where he'll rot till he rots in hell, they said. Menace to society, they said. Well, maybe he was.

But gawd, I have to admit I miss that boy. He was the handsomest man that ever walked into this or any other bar, had all the ladies slipping off their bar stools one way or another. Including me, but that's another story.

Guy, honey, do me a favor, will you? Don't talk to River about all that stuff I've said about Billy and me. River's my good friend. She's like a little sister. Of course she knew about Billy and me all along, me and all his other occasional screws, because that boy never even tried to keep anything a secret. But it's ancient history by now.

PART FOUR
THE JEFFERSON ALPS

CHAPTER TWELVE

"That's quite a tale," I said. I finished the beer that I'd been sipping through the whole story.

The telephone rang. Gloria got up from the booth and walked across the room to answer it. "Guy," she called, "it's for you."

I went over to the bar and she handed me the receiver. "Yo."

"Guy, this is Sheriff Heron. I'm calling from Seamus Connolly's office. I'd like you to come over here. Right away."

"I'm on foot," I said.

"Get Gloria to give you a ride. I need you here. Now."

I thanked Gloria for the ride and for the story. She patted my knee and told me, "Stay out of trouble, big guy."

"Thanks for that, too," I said. I got out of the car and walked into the *Jefferson Republican* building, where I was shown down the hall and into the office of the publisher.

Seamus Connolly was there. So was Blue Heron. So was River Webster. Seamus smiled at me. River smiled at me. Then they looked at each other and stopped smiling. They were seated around Seamus's desk, and there was one empty chair.

"Four of us," I said. "Anyone for tennis?"

Nobody laughed. I asked Seamus, "What brings you here?"

"This is my office," he answered. "What brings you here, is what I want to know."

Blue said, "I bumped into Seamus at the high school fifteen minutes ago. He was there for the same reason I was."

"So was I," River added. "Hi, Guy."

Blue said, "Sit down, Guy. I said I'd tell this story only once, so you're all hearing it for the first time." He whapped a yellow pad against his thigh.

I sat and we all waited while Blue Heron stretched his neck and cracked his knuckles. "Okay," he said. "Before I went over to the high school I called a colleague of mine down in San Luis Obispo County, law enforcement, department of corrections. Here's the deal." He consulted the pad and continued, "William Connolly was released from the men's penal colony two years ago, on parole."

I looked at Seamus. I looked at River. Neither of them looked as surprised as I thought they'd look. Seamus said, "Go on."

"His supervision ended six months ago. Apparently he was a good prisoner, released early for good behavior, and since getting out he's been a model citizen. He's been gainfully employed on the crew of a fishing boat out of Port San Luis. He is a member of the Baptist church and he does volunteer service at a senior center."

Seamus said, "Billy? Volunteers?"

River said, "Baptist?"

Blue nodded. Then he said to me, "Guy, River has already told Seamus about the scene out at her house on Sunday afternoon. And for your information, neither Freddy nor Charles showed up at school this morning. They haven't been seen for a week, either one of them."

"They're with my brother," Seamus said. "That asshole."

"Nice way to talk about your brother," River muttered. "Honestly, Seamus."

Blue said, "Stop that right now, you two. Everybody in this room wants those kids back safely. Am I right?"

Suddenly everybody was looking at me. I wondered if I really cared about the safety of two teenagers who had caused me nothing but trouble, and I concluded that yes, I did want those kids back safely. I nodded.

"Also," Blue continued, "everybody in this room has expressed an interest in finding out who killed Pete Thayer. Right again?"

We all nodded.

"Well, I'm interested in that too," Blue said. "I happen to believe that Billy Connolly knows something we would like to know. That's all I'm willing to say at this time. I happen to believe that right now that man is outside the City of Jefferson but there's a chance he's still inside the County of Jefferson. If so, that would put him in my bailiwick. I intend to find William Connolly if he's still in the county and bring him into town, then turn him over to the police department for questioning. That's all. And I could use some help."

"What kind of help?" River asked.

"Information. Seamus, do you have any idea where your brother might be hiding out?"

"The Connolly mining camp," Seamus said. "That's where we used to hide when we were kids. There's a bunkhouse about a mile back into the woods, back from our hunting lodge. But I haven't been out to the camp since we were kids, and I haven't been up to the property at all since the old hunting lodge burned down, back in the early eighties."

"Billy always said he wanted to mine gold," River added. "Said he knew there was gold in those old mines."

Blue said, "Okay. Well, as it happens, my colleague in SLO County had some more information to give me. He said that Billy once told him, this was back when my friend was a guard at the penal colony, that Billy wanted to mine gold if he ever got out of prison. Of course all prisoners have crazy dreams. But I think we may have struck pay dirt, friends."

Seamus and River and I all exchanged frowns.

"Oh. And one more thing," Blue said. "I asked my colleague if there had been any unsolved crimes lately in San Luis Obispo County. He told me there was one. A reporter for the San Luis Obispo *New Times* was found floating in the harbor at Port San Luis. This was in early August, and there have been no leads on who might have put him there. Of course, that's just a coincidence. The question now is: what do we do? Any ideas?"

Seamus stood up and stretched. "I'm going up to the mining camp. Right now. I'm going to grab a sandwich in the mall food court and hit the road."

"No you're not," the sheriff said.

"I'm going with you," River said. She stood up and hefted her straw bag.

"No you're not," Seamus told her.

"My son's up there too, Seamus. We're going up there together."

"Shit."

Blue Heron said, "Neither one of you are going up to that hornets' nest. Now sit down and let's come up with something practical."

Neither of them sat down. "It's my property," Seamus reminded the sheriff. "I have every right to go see my property."

River said, "I'm going too. Don't anybody try and stop me. I'm Mother Tiger, and I'm dangerous. I'll go down and buy sandwiches for the road. Vegetarian okay, Seamus?"

Seamus shook his head. "Roast beef."

"Carnivore. Okay, okay. Guy, are you coming?"

"Me?"

"People, stop it," Blue shouted. "Don't get any wild ideas. This is a matter for the sheriff's department. I don't want a bunch of civilians getting killed in the field. Leave it to the sheriff's department. Me and a couple of deputies can handle this, and we don't need amateurs along for the ride. Anybody who goes up there and interferes will be charged with obstruction of justice, and that's a promise."

"Shit," Seamus reasoned. "Look. I'm the only one who knows how to find the bunkhouse where they're probably staying. And I could use some help. I'll be honest. I can push Charles around and Freddy's a featherweight, but I could use your help against Billy, if it gets ugly. So call your office and—"

"Listen to me, Seamus Connolly," Blue Heron ordered. "For once you're not in charge. The three of you sit tight. Seamus, I want you to draw me a map, showing how to find that fucking bunkhouse. Excuse me, River."

"Excuse me, Blue," I said. "You said you wanted to see me. Would you please tell me why I'm sitting in this chair?"

"I plan to charge William Connolly with assault. I need a reason to bring him to town for further questioning, because I don't have enough evidence to link him to Pete Thayer's death. But I do have a case for an assault charge, if you're willing to back me up."

I thought about that. About that cold water. Falling. Scraping my hands on those barnacles. God, that water was cold. "Count me in," I said.

Blue nodded. "Good. Something else. You told me some books were stolen from your shop a few days ago."

"One book, actually. Four copies of the same book."

"What book?"

"*A Long, Long Crime Ago,* by Donald Webster. Why?"

Blue said, "You tell me. Why would Billy Connolly steal that book? Those books? Sounds like there was something in that book he didn't want you or anybody else to know about."

"That was my great-grandfather's book," River said. "He had no right to steal it."

"Nobody has a right to steal any book," I said. "The book was a history of the county, and it was also a diatribe against the Connolly family, but I can't imagine—"

"Gold mine," Blue prompted. "Think. Any clues?"

"I didn't read that part very carefully," I said. "River?"

"Hold on a minute," Seamus said. He stood up and walked to a bookcase, where he found a copy of *A Long, Long Crime Ago.* He blew dust off the top, opened the book to a map, and set it on his desk for all of us to see. "Map to the Connolly mines. Donald Webster had no right to publish this information, but it didn't matter all that much, since the Connolly family gave up mining a long time ago. This road leading back from the highway isn't there anymore. You need to go through the woods. But there's the site of the mine, right there on the edge of that ravine, and that's where the bunkhouse is. Or was." He shut the book and sat back down.

"Can you make me a copy of that map?" Blue asked.

Seamus opened the book and found the map again. He picked it up and carried it to the copy machine on the other side of the room. He hit a few buttons, and in a minute we were all holding copies of the map to the Connolly mines, enlarged to 120 percent.

"You still don't know how to get from the highway to the bunkhouse," Seamus reminded the sheriff. "You still need me with you."

Blue handed his copy of the map across the desk. "Draw me the path."

Seamus shook his head. "I can't remember exactly. Besides, the path's probably all grown over by now."

"Then there's no need to have you along for the ride," Blue said. "Give me back that map."

"Shit," Seamus said. His favorite word. He picked up a blue pencil and drew a line, winding east from the highway. "There's a creek that goes from the lodge to the bunkhouse, where it connects with the Damfool River. The path was beside the creek. The creek bed's dry this time of year, so if the path isn't there, we can just go right down the middle of the creek."

Blue snatched the map back. "Thanks. Not 'we,' Seamus. Let me tell you one more time. You're staying here, standing by. You'll have your chance to beat up your brother when I release him from questioning, if I ever do. Till then, cool your heels."

He took his cell phone out of his pocket and thumbed in a number. "Betty? Get the car ready. I'll need weapons, first aid, cuffs, all the usual party supplies, plus a thermos of coffee if there's any already made.…That's right. I'll be there in ten minutes. Call Eric and Toby and tell them to put on their badges, they get to play posse." He punched off the cell phone and slipped it back into his pocket. He stood up, folded his copy of the map, stuffed it into his pocket, nodded once at each of us, and strode out of the room.

I then saw something I never thought I'd see. Seamus and River were smiling at each other, giving each other thumbs-up. River turned to me and said, "What kind of sandwich do you want, Guy?"

"Me?"

"I want you to go up there with us, Guy," Seamus said. "I could use a little help."

"You have me," River said. "Guy, we need you. Both of us. Help us out here."

"Are you people nuts? Didn't you hear the sheriff say to stay out of it?"

Seamus nodded. "I just want to give Blue a little back-up, that's all. Billy and a couple of teenagers may not sound like much of an army, but I know Blue's deputies, and frankly, they're not much of a posse. They need us, whether they know it or not. It's a numbers game, big man. Their squad against ours."

Why? Why do I get stuck in situations like this? Do I really like danger? Do I think life's too long? Am I nuts?

And then I remembered again how cold that water felt when Jefferson Thomas tossed me into the harbor. How I'd cut my hands on barnacles pulling myself up so I could get my head out of the water so I could breathe. How the salt water stung my wounds. How fucking *cold* that water was.

And how that son of a bitch had stolen four books from me.

And the expression on my friend Pete Thayer's face last time I saw him, sitting on the asphalt and leaning against a Dumpster.

"I have to call Carol," I said.

"What?" Seamus asked. "Gotta ask your mom's permission?" But he shoved the phone across his desk. "Dial nine to get out."

Carol answered on the first ring. I said her name and she said, "Where are you, Guy? Are you all right?"

"I'm going for a drive," I told her. "River needs my help."

"Did those boys show up for school?"

"No. But we think we know where they are, and River's going to go talk some sense into Freddy. She wants some support."

"Guy."

"What?"

"Be careful."

"I'll be home by cocktail hour," I promised her.

I hung up.

"Make mine tuna fish," I told River. "On rye. No mayonnaise."

Seamus led River and me out of the Jefferson Mall food court with a paper sack full of sandwiches from the deli. I carried a six-pack of Pepsi and River carried a bag of potato chips in one hand and her straw bag in the other. She had argued for pasta salad, but Seamus told her, "For Christ's sake, Dorothy, keep it simple. We're going to eat this on the road."

When we reached the parking lot behind the *Jefferson Republican,* Seamus said, "We're traveling together. I don't want River here to get lost."

"Fine," she responded. "We'll take my truck."

"My car," Seamus said, and that was enough. Even River must have known her truck would die of exhaustion before we reached the summit of the Alps.

Mr. Bigshot unlocked all four doors of his midnight blue BMW, using the gadget on his key chain.

"Fancy schmantzy," I said.

"I never rode in a BMW before," River said. She crawled into the back, behind the driver's seat, clutching the potato chips.

"Welcome to the grown-up world," Seamus said.

I said, "I've never been inside a BMW either, come to think of it." I got into the passenger seat and River and I exchanged winks.

"Couple of losers," Seamus mumbled. He turned the ignition key and the machine growled *Jahwol.* "Buckle your seat belts."

"Why?" River asked. "Are you a dangerous driver, Seamus?"

"Because it's the God damned law." Seamus gunned the engine and roared out of the parking lot.

"Seamus, open the windows."

"Forget it. I have the air conditioner on."

Driving east on County Highway 7, we passed through dry, hot fields of late summer in the foothills of the Jefferson Alps. Grassy hills were watched over by families of California live oaks, and the grass was the color of pale gold. The narrow road had its potholes, but it was paved, and with Seamus at the wheel we made good time.

But when we reached the redwood forest and Highway 7 began its steep, winding ascent into the mountains, the pavement wore out and we were skidding on gravel.

"This road used to be paved all the way to Skyline Highway at the top," Seamus said. "But after the Connolly hunting lodge burned down, we let it go."

"Who's we?" I asked.

"The county."

"Which Seamus runs," River added. "You mean the county spent our tax dollars every year paving and maintaining a road that nobody ever used except you and your family?"

"Nobody else uses this road?" I asked.

"You see some trucks," Seamus said. "Pot farmers, probably. It's not smart to ask."

"And of course they don't deserve to have paved roads," River said.

"Oh shut up, Dorothy. Shut up and pass me my roast beef sandwich."

"You're not going to drive and eat at the same time, are you? On this road?"

"Why the hell not? Guy, crack me a Pepsi, would you?"

"Because it's the God damned law," River said.

"Give me my sandwich."

"Carnivore. Here. You want chips with that?"

Seamus continued to drive as fast as the switchback curves and gravely ruts would allow, his left hand on the wheel and his right wrapped around his sandwich. River tore open the bag of potato chips and placed it on the small counter surface of laminated artificial birds-eye maple between the front bucket seats. It was already almost two in the afternoon, and we were hungry. And it was a relief to have Seamus and River's mouths occupied by something other than vitriolic Ping-Pong.

River finished her sandwich first. "When we get up there, Seamus, I want you to let me do all the talking."

Seamus snorted a laugh through his nose, swallowed his mouthful of Pepsi, and said, "Are you out of your mind?"

"Because I know how to talk to Billy. He'll listen to me. He won't listen to you, Seamus. He never did listen to you, and you know it."

"I want you to keep your damn mouth shut. Do you understand me? This matter is between me and my brother, and you're just along for the ride."

River plucked a couple of chips from the bag and stuffed them into her mouth. She chewed like a machine. She said, "Bullshit." She swallowed. "Bullshit, Seamus. You're a pigheaded fool, and you always have been."

"I'm a fool?" Seamus shot back. *"I'm* a fool? What about—"

"CHILDREN!" I shouted. "Seamus, stop the car."

Amazingly, he did as he was told. He didn't pull over to the side of the road, because the road had no sides, and he didn't stop the engine; but he did stop the car. He rolled down his window and seethed, his foot on the brake and his fists gripping the steering wheel. He said, "What?" The BMW's engine and air conditioner purred so softly we could hear the gentle breeze brushing the tops of the redwood trees.

"I want you both to stop arguing. Right now."

The car was silent for a moment while I tried to figure out where that voice had come from.

"Okay," Seamus said. "Suits me."

"Fine for now," River said. "But when we get up there—"

"Hush," I said.

"Yeah, but—"

"Seamus, why are we making this trip?" I asked. "What do you really want out of this encounter with your brother?"

"All I want is my son back."

"River?"

"Same here."

"Good," I said. "Then let's concentrate on that, shall we? Freddy and Charles. And let your past history with Billy Connolly stay in the past. That goes for both of you. Okay?"

River smiled at me from the back seat. "Guy, I knew it was important for you to come with us."

Seamus took his foot off the brake and the car eased forward. He said, "Okay, so we have a common goal. Now what? How do we deal with that asshole brother of mine?"

"Listen to him," I said.

"Listen?"

"Listen. Did you ever try that?"

"Okay, troops, this is it." Seamus slowed down and turned left onto a narrow lane that cut through the forest. We drove over a short hill, then descended into a valley. A broad meadow stretched out before us, and in the center of it stood a lone stone chimney, all that remained of the Connolly family hunting lodge. The lane ended there. Seamus parked his BMW next to a rusty pickup truck. On the other side of the truck was Chunky Connolly's black Cherokee.

"Looks like we guessed right," Seamus said. He pulled his Jefferson Sharks baseball cap from under his seat and put it on. "Okay. All out."

We stretched in the warm, still afternoon air. "Whose truck is that?" I asked.

"Nels Andersen's," River said.

"You mean Nails?"

Seamus said, "Crazy little fucker. He used to be my brother's sidekick when they were in high school."

"He looks a lot older," I said.

"He always looked older."

River walked over to the chimney and ran her hand across the stones. "I used to love this place," she said.

Seamus said, "I didn't know you were ever here."

"Billy used to bring me here sometimes," she said. "Freedom was conceived in this lodge." She turned to Seamus and asked, "Did you burn this place down, Seamus?" Her voice sounded fragile and her face twitched. "Billy said you burned it down because you were so pissed off at him and Audrey."

"I didn't burn the lodge down," he answered. "Swear to God. Billy burned it down, with Audrey tied up inside. That's what happened."

"How do you know?" I asked. "For sure."

"I don't. Let's get going before the sheriff shows up."

He led us across the meadow to a dry creek bed on the other side. "We used to have a trail that went beside the creek," he said, "but I see it's all grown over. No matter, there's no water in the creek this time of year. Come on. Dorothy, are you going to lug that big handbag the whole way?"

"Of course."

"Why?"

"You never know."

"Never know what?"

"It's got my cigarettes, Seamus. And toilet paper."

Seamus shook his head. He clambered down into the creek and set off, stepping from stone to stone.

River was the only one of us with the right shoes for this walk. She wore clunky, fat-soled walking shoes, the ones she always wore. Seamus and I had on brown loafers, but he didn't seem to care, so I didn't either.

He set the pace. His legs were longer than River's and a lot longer than mine, so we had to struggle to keep up.

"How far is this place, the mining camp?" I asked.

"About another mile. Shit!"

"What?"

"I should have brought a flashlight."

"I've got one in my bag," River said. "Speaking of which, Seamus, any chance we could take a short break, have a cigarette? I'm getting a little winded here."

Seamus looked at his watch. "It's almost four. Well, okay. Tobacco, though. No dope."

River laughed. "Seamus, you're a stitch. Don't worry. Tobacco."

Seamus sat on a large boulder, and River and I found a dry, mossy log to share. River pulled her American Spirits out of her bag and fired one up with a Bic.

Seamus lit a Marlboro. "You don't smoke, Guy?"

"I'm afraid it will stunt my growth," I said.

Giant trees rose all around us, and the banks of the creek bed were thick with dusty ferns. Even in the splotchy shade the afternoon was warm, and sweat was plastering my shirt to my chest.

"So, Seamus," I said, "you didn't seem all that surprised to learn Billy was out of jail."

"No. I've known ever since he got out. I didn't know he got off parole, though."

"You knew?" River asked. "Why didn't you tell me?"

"I didn't tell anybody. It was a family matter. I knew Billy wasn't coming back to Jefferson, so what difference did it make?"

"Well, you got that one wrong," she said.

Seamus ignored her. He took his baseball cap off and wiped off his forehead. He tapped the visor of the cap against his knee and said, "When Billy got out, he contacted me and asked me to give him some money, twenty thousand dollars so he could buy into a fishing boat in Port San Luis. I said okay, but he had to stay the fuck out of Jefferson County. He laughed and told me he had no interest in seeing me or Jefferson County ever again. Ever. I believed him."

"He's your brother," River said. "You might have known."

"We stopped being brothers a long, long time ago." Seamus took a last drag from his cigarette, stubbed it out on the rock, rolled the coal between his fingers to be sure it was out, and flicked the dead butt into the ferns. He stood up and put his cap back on. "Let's go," he said.

A half-hour later we reached the end of the dry creek bed, where during the rainy season the water cascaded down a steep, rocky chute into the Damfool River two hundred feet below us.

The river this hot afternoon was brown and lazy. I'd never seen the Damfool before, but I imagined what it must be like in the winter and spring, in flood season, a fast, fat dragon of ice-cold fury.

"So where's the camp?" River asked.

Seamus pointed. "Up that trail, at the top. The bunkhouse sits on a cliff overlooking the river. There are a few smaller cabins, or there used to be. You guys ready?"

"Maybe we should wait till Blue and his boys get here," I said. "I mean if Billy's got Nails up there—"

"I can handle Nails," Seamus said.

"Maybe so, but if Nails is there it's a sure bet Louie Luau is there too. Can you handle him?"

Seamus laid an impatient sigh on me. "All we want to do is go up there, knock on the door politely, have a little chitchat, tell the damn teenagers to get their shit together and drive down the hill where they belong. I want them in school tomorrow morning, that's all. No big deal. Now come on. River?"

"I'm with you."

Seamus said, "Guy, if you want to wait here for the law, fine. River and I are going after our boys. Get them out of there before the sheriff shows up and things get ugly."

"Oh, all right," I said. "Jesus. Let's go."

The trail was steep and full of switchbacks. It was lush and green, even in late summer. We were out of the thick redwoods now, although we still passed occasional groves of giants reaching to the sky, their trunks covered with lichen and moss. Most of the trees we walked through now were sycamores and poplars, madrone, manzanita, and pungent bay laurel.

Seamus stopped. In a quiet voice he said, "It's just around the next bend. Keep your voices down. I want to surprise them."

"I thought we were going to knock on the door and—"

"Shut up. Come on."

CHAPTER THIRTEEN

The mining settlement looked like the poorest part of Dogpatch. The bunkhouse stretched about forty feet along the edge of the cliff. I could see it had been solidly built at one time, but weather and neglect had had their way with it. The roof sagged and the windows lining the front porch were all busted out. Next to the bunkhouse a small barn or tool shed was falling to ruins, its boards warping off and rotting. Four small cabins were lined up on the other side of the clearing, and they were in bad shape too.

"What a dump," River said softly.

"It looked just as bad when we were kids," Seamus replied. "They gave up on mining after the first couple of years, back in the eighteen hundreds, and nobody's done a thing with this place since."

He strode across the clearing, and River and I had to trot to keep up with him. When he reached the bunkhouse, he walked up the rickety steps and waited for us to join him on the porch.

He didn't knock. He shoved the door open with a painful creak and stepped into the large room. River and I meekly followed.

The three of us stood in a line.

The three of them looked up from their benches at the long redwood table and folded their cards. The table was littered with beer bottles and overflowing ashtrays. Billy Connolly gave us a big smile, flashing his steel eyetooth. "Visitors!" he said. "What do you know. Nice of you folks to drop up. Long time no see, Seamus, you old fart. You look older than shit. Hey, Dorothy. And you. Mallon, right? Still trying to figure out how to mind your own business?"

He never stopped smiling. Sitting at his right, Nails chuckled and bobbed his head. Louie Luau, at the head of the table, stared at us with the expression of a tombstone. All three wore camouflage hunting jackets, and Nails wore his watch cap. The room was messy and the floor was covered with dust and rot. Ancient tools decorated the back wall—picks, sledge hammers, a long two-handled cross-cut saw. An open door in the back wall gave us a view of the forest beyond the river canyon.

Seamus said, "This won't take long, Billy. We just—"

"We want our boys," River said. "Where are the kids?"

Seamus shook his head. "Dorothy, let me handle this."

Billy stood up. Still grinning. "Yeah, *Dorothy*," he said. "Let the big businessman take care of business. Business as usual, right bro?" He walked right up to us and stood in Seamus's face. I'd always considered Seamus a tall man, but there was no comparison.

"Billy, where's Freddy?" River insisted.

Billy dropped his smile on the floor. He turned to her and answered, "He's down at the corner store buying me some cigarettes, okay? Just shut up, Dodo, and let me talk to my brother here. In other words, *River*, shut the fuck up."

He turned to me and said, "That goes for you, too, peckerbreath."

"I didn't say—"

"Shut up and get out!" He put his fist against my chest and pushed so hard it knocked my breath out. The force of that shove hurled me backwards through the front door of the bunkhouse and right off the porch, into the air. I landed on my butt in the dust, facing the bunkhouse steps.

As I struggled to catch my breath I considered options. I could run down the trail and intercept Blue Heron and his men, tell him to go back and pick up a Howitzer. I could run off into the woods and hide for the rest of all time. But instead, I rose to my feet, slapped the dust off my sore butt, and walked back up the steps and into the bunkhouse.

Apparently I'd missed something while I was away. Billy was still a foot from Seamus's face, but Seamus's arms were behind him, pinned in the grip of Louie Luau. River stood at the end of the redwood table, hugging her straw bag and looking on in terror. Nails still sat behind the table. He was now cleaning his fingernails with a ten-inch fishing knife.

"Is that how it's going to be, Billy?" Seamus shouted. "Two on one?"

Billy chuckled. "You're a caution, big bro," he answered. "You and I both know I could whip your ass by myself. I always could. But my man Louie here needs the exercise. Tell you what. How about a tag team match. You and your midget against me and my giant?" He plucked the baseball cap off Seamus's head and sailed it across the room.

"Fuck you," Seamus muttered.

"No, I guess we don't have time for that. Me and my boys are taking off tonight, and I want to get back to our car before dark."

"Where are you going?" I asked.

"Didn't I tell you to shut the fuck up? Nels, take care of this little piece of shit."

Nails stood up and walked around the table, still scooping dirt out from under his fingernails. He was a small man, but as he approached me he seemed to grow, until he stood in front of me, with the fishing knife pressing my belly. He was breathing down on me through his rotten mouth, and I wanted to turn and run, just to escape the smell, not to mention the steel point in my gut. He hooked a gnarly finger in my shirt collar and pulled me like a puppy dog to the redwood table. He gestured with the knife for me to sit down on the bench. I did. He tossed the knife on the table and I started to stand up again, but he put his hands on both of my shoulders, close to my neck, and shoved me back where I belonged. He walked around the table, reached below it, then returned, holding a roll of silver duct tape. He taped my wrists together behind my back, then wrapped my ankles together. I was facing out into the room.

"Don't cover his mouth," Billy told him. "Yet. I have some questions to ask him after me and Seamus are done talking. Right, Shame?"

Seamus shook his head. "Billy, give it up. We're not here to give you any trouble. We just want to take our kids back. They've had their adventure, and now it's time to get back to real life."

"Real life! That's rich, Shame. Real life." Billy giggled. When a man that big giggles, it always means trouble, more trouble than we were in already. At that point I knew for sure that the man in charge was a man out of control. He may have looked like a man, a very big man, but he had the morals and the reasoning power of a rabid wolverine.

River took off her purple hat and laid it on the redwood table, on top of her straw bag. She said, "Please, Billy. Just give us Freddy and Chunky. Please! You're not going to get away with this, you know. Just give us our sons, and we'll be on our way and we'll tell Blue it's all taken care of. Billy?"

Billy spun toward her. "Blue?"

Seamus sighed. "Oh for Christ's sake, Dorothy."

Billy turned back to Seamus. "You got the sheriff coming? Is that it? Speak up, asshole. What's happening. Huh?"

"Blue Heron's coming out here later this afternoon," Seamus told him. "But not as the sheriff. Just as the truant officer. Dorothy and I reported our missing kids, and—"

"Since when are you and Dorothy so lovey-dovey?"

"We're not," River said. She walked over to Billy and put a hand on his arm. "We're not. We just both have kids who should be in school, Billy."

Billy shook her hand off his arm and said to Louie Luau, "Hold my brother down on the bench. Nels, you tape him to the bench, and then I want you to hike out the trail. If you see the sheriff, tell him I've already left. Tell him the boys will be home before dark. If you don't see him before you reach the parking lot, wait for us there. While you're waiting, let the air out of my brother's tires one last time, just for fun." He turned back to Louie Luau and said, "Go on. Tape him down."

Louie Luau shoved Seamus to the same bench where I was sitting. He forced Seamus to lie on his stomach while Nails wrapped his wrists behind his back. Seamus tried to kick while Nails was wrapping his ankles, but Louie Luau subdued him by jerking his bound wrists up into a high double hammer-lock. Seamus lay prone and docile while Nails wrapped the duct tape around his torso and under the bench.

Nails nodded at me, then River, then Billy, then left the bunkhouse. I heard his boots clump down the rotten steps.

River whimpered, and Billy scowled at her. "Shut up, Dorothy. For Christ's sake."

"What are you going to do with me, Billy?"

"Do with you?"

"Are you going to let Freddy come home with me?"

"Freedom's with me from now on, Dorothy. Get over it."

River faced me, tears streaming down her cheeks. She gave me a look of hopeless apology, then turned back to Billy. She put a hand on his arm again, and before he could shake her off, she whimpered, "Take me with you."

Billy laughed. "Take you with me?"

"Please, Billy."

"Do you still know how to do that thing with your—?"

"Of course. For you, of course."

"You kept in practice."

"No, Billy. No. Only with you—"

"You never wrote me while I was in prison. Not once."

"I couldn't."

"Why not?"

"I just couldn't. I don't know why. And you never let me know when you got out. I had no idea."

"Why bother, baby? By that time you were balling that newspaper guy. Fuck that. Fuck him. Fuck you."

"But I would have dropped Pete like a hot rock, baby. I would have run to you. And we could be a family. We still could—you, me, and Freddy."

Seamus shouted, "Dorothy, don't be crazy!"

Billy walked over to the bench, spat in my lap, then sat down on the small of his brother's back. Seamus yelped, and Billy thumped him on the back of the head, cracking his brother's forehead against the bench. "Come sit in my lap, Dodo," he said.

"Billy, this is crazy! Let's just get Freddy and let's—"

Billy turned to the giant and said, "Go get the boys." Then he turned to me. "What are you staring at?"

CHAPTER FOURTEEN

When Louie Luau marched the two teenagers into the bunkhouse, River screamed. "What have you done to him?" she cried. She ran to Freddy and put a hand on his bruised and swollen cheek. "Freddy, sweetheart, what have they done to you?"

"Nothing, Mom," he answered, turning his face away.

"Huh?"

"Nothing, I said."

Billy said, "Sit down, lads. You too, Dorothy. The fuckin meeting is coming to order. Sit down, I said. *Now.*"

River sat beside me at one end of the bench. Freddy and Chunky sat down at the other end, on the far side of Seamus's bound body. Louie Luau stood by the door, impassive as a Sherman tank.

Seamus called out, "Charles, are you okay?"

"Never better, Dad."

"Freddy, what's going on?" River cried. "What are they doing to you?"

"SHUT THE FUCK UP!" Billy paced back and forth in front of his captive audience. "Freedom has just been having a little old-fashioned discipline, which he needed. You don't know how to raise a kid, Dorothy. Shit, somebody had to teach this boy some manners, isn't that right, Freedom. Huh? Answer me."

"Yeah," Freddy said.

"Huh?"

"Yeah."

"And he appreciates a little tough love, don't you, Freedom."

"I guess."

"Huh?"

"Yes."

"Yes, what?"

"Dad."

"That's right. Dad. I'm the boy's father, and from now on we're doing things right. Little discipline. Little respect. See what I'm saying, Dorothy? You come with me, we're going to be real parents. No more loosey-goosey bullshit. Little discipline. You got that, River? Huh? Speak up, babe. Last chance."

"Okay, Billy," River whimpered.

"My way. Okay, people, listen up. Here's the deal. Me and Dorothy and the boys are leaving the county before dark. Little more business here, and then we're out of here. We got work to do, appointments to keep. Right, Chunkster?"

"You got it, dude."

"Huh?"

Chunky corrected himself. "Uncle Bill."

"What about Louie Luau?" I asked.

Billy looked at me as if I were dogshit on a white carpet. "Did I say you could talk?"

"Charles, I want you to tell me what's going on here!"

"Shut up, Dad."

Billy laughed. "Shame, old boy, you obviously didn't raise your son right. Telling his old man to shut up? That's rich." Then he turned to Chunky and said, "You ever use that tone of voice with me, you little fuck, and I'll wrap your tongue around your neck."

Chunky grinned.

"You think that's a joke? Funny?"

Chunky stopped grinning.

"Huh?"

"No. No, Uncle Bill."

"Okay. Just jerkin your chain. Okay. Listen up. To answer your question, you little editor, Louie and Nels, my main men, they're staying here in Jefferson, taking care of business. Me and the boys, and Dorothy too, we're going out on the road to raise some capital. That's all I'm saying, because we don't have a lot of time here. So Seamus, you make the decision."

He pulled a pistol from one of the pockets of his hunting jacket. "You and the little editor want to take a bullet, or would you rather die in the fire?"

"Holy Christ, Billy!" Seamus shouted. "Quit talking nonsense!"

Billy grinned. "Nonsense?"

River whimpered, "Billy, what happened to you? You used to be such a nice man, such—"

"Can it."

"Uncle Bill?"

"What, Chunkster? God. Pussy. Crybaby. What?"

"Couldn't we just go, just leave?" Chunky's face was twisted in horror. "I mean, do we have to kill anybody? I mean, my dad—"

"Sorry, kiddo. No witnesses. You don't know your dad like I do. He won't sleep till we're all in the can—you, me, Freddy, Dorothy—all locked up for life. That's what your dad does, kid. No more. Sorry. Just business. The building gets torched."

"Just like he killed your mother, Charles," Seamus said. "Burned her alive."

Billy tapped his brother on the head with the barrel of his pistol. "For your inforfuckingmation, asswipe, I didn't kill Audrey, and I didn't burn down the hunting lodge. She burned the building and split. She was pissed off at both of us. That's what she told that stupid reporter in San Luis. Reporters give me a pain in the ass, know what I mean? That includes you, Mallon, you little dipshit."

"You want to tell me what you're talking about?" I asked. Was I curious or just stalling for time? Or just dumb? You tell me.

"No I do not." Billy cracked the pistol across my face. My left cheekbone stung like a blinding, red-hot coal. My neck was twisted. My head throbbed and my ears wouldn't shut up. I gasped for breath and trembled, straining my raw wrists against the duct tape handcuffs. My undershorts and the crotch of my trousers were drenched with urine.

"Sorry, stud," Billy said. "Just business. It won't hurt long."

"Billy!"

"Shut up, Dorothy."

"Dad—"

"Freedom, shut up! Everybody just shut the fuck up!"

The room was silent except for the echo of pain still roaring in my ears. But even with my ears full of pain, I could hear, and so could everyone else, the heavy clump of boots on the steps outside the bunkhouse.

CHAPTER FIFTEEN

The two deputies rushed in first, holding their guns, one of them shouting, "Everybody freeze!"

"Aw, shit," Billy sighed. "I don't have time for this." He shot the first deputy in the chest, the second one in the face. The two uniformed men dropped together into a dead heap, oozing blood.

Then Sheriff Blue Heron appeared in the doorway, his pistol in both hands. "Drop your weapon, Billy," he shouted.

"Blue, my old comrade! Come on in!" Billy lifted his pistol but Blue shot first.

And missed.

Before he could fire again, Louie Luau's arms were wrapped around him from behind, pinning Blue's arms to his sides. His weapon clattered to the floor.

Billy calmly walked over and picked up the sheriff's gun, stepped back and said to the giant, "Let him go."

Blue shook his hands, then clenched his fists. "Listen, Billy," he said. "We—"

"No! You listen! I'd like to say it's nice to see you again, you fat-ass Indian, but I don't have time for lies." Billy held a gun in each hand, clicking their barrels together like rhythm sticks. "Thought you'd come up here and rescue your girlfriend, didn't you? Didn't you? Always been sweet on River, right, Blue? Well listen up, asshole, River's my girl, just like before, and she's going with me. Got that?"

Blue turned his gaze to River, who sat on the bench next to me, her face in her hands. "River?" Blue said.

She raised her wet face and said, "I have to, Blue. To take care of Freddy."

"And to be with me," Billy added. "Blue, I'll give you a choice." He held the guns up, one in each hand, and said, "Which hand do you like better?"

Blue Heron didn't answer that one. Growling like a cougar, he charged into the two bullets that hit him in the belly. He fell to the floor and rolled in the dust, clutching his gut.

"One each," Billy said. "Sorry to hit you in the flab, Blue, but I mean it was such a hard target to miss." He looked at me and said, "One more down. He ain't going nowhere, right, reporter?"

"Jesus!" Freddy shouted. He jumped up from the bench and ran to kneel down beside the sheriff.

"Leave him alone," Billy told him.

Freddy looked up at his father. "But he's hurt, Dad."

"That's the point. Go sit back on the bench."

Freddy did not. He put a hand on Blue Heron's cheek.

"Chunky, give the kid a little discipline."

Chunky stood up and walked toward his cousin. But before he could reach his cousin, Louie Luau stepped away from the door and caught Chunky in the face with his fist. Chunky dropped to the floor and crawled back, howling. Louie Luau picked Freddy up, threw him over his shoulder, and stamped out of the bunkhouse.

Billy shook with laughter. "My man Louie has a real crush on that boy. Jesus, where was I? Oh yes—"

"Christ's sake, Billy," Seamus pleaded. "Charles, are you okay?"

Chunky didn't answer, but I could see his face. He was not okay.

"Why do you have to take it out on the kids, Billy? Your beef's with me, not them."

Billy wiped his face. "God, this is getting messy. You know what, Shame? You old fart?" He pocketed the two pistols in his hunting jacket, then pulled a pill bottle out of another pocket and shook two capsules into his palm. He walked to the table, reached over Seamus's back and grabbed a half-empty beer bottle.

"What are you taking?" I asked.

He kicked my shin. "Nosy little fucker. They're little red mothers, and they make me strong, okay?" He popped the pills into his mouth and swallowed them with beer.

He paced in front of us. "Sorry bunch of dumb fucks. Okay. Time for sports. Dorothy, take that knife there and cut my big brother loose. Him and me, we're going to have a bit of fisticuffs. That okay with you, Shame, since you're the one I have a beef with? No holds barred?"

Seamus said, "No guns."

Billy said, "Bite me."

"Biting?"

"No holds barred. Dorothy, cut him loose."

River did as she was told, and Seamus rose from the bench, stretched his torso left and right, looked Billy in the eye, and said, "This is crazy."

Billy gave him back a steel-toothed grin. "You've always wished you could whip my ass, big bro. Now's your chance. Your *last* chance. You been staying in shape, by the way? Sitting on your ass real hard at your desk while I was training for ten fucking years in the best fight gym in California, thanks to you? Ten fucking years?"

River sat next to me, Nails's fishing knife still trembling like a feather in her hand.

Billy took off his hunting jacket and flung it into a far corner of the bunkhouse, where the metal in the pockets clattered on the floor. He wore a black T-shirt, stretched thin over his bulging muscles. He grinned at the teenager who was still crumpled and crying in the corner of the room. "Check this out, Chunkster. You're gonna love it.

"Okay, Shame. This is it, big fella. Super Bowl time." Billy stepped over the bodies of the two deputies and walked right up to Seamus, lifted a heavy work boot, and brought it down hard on Seamus's brown loafer.

Howling with pain, Seamus put a hand on Billy's chest and shoved. Billy reeled backwards, swinging his arms and laughing. "Ooooo, oooo, oooo, that *hurt*, Shame! Oh, my *goodness*. Oh *dear*. Well, I guess you hit first, didn't you? Well, fair's fair."

He slow-danced forward on his toes, his left fist jabbing the air between himself and his brother. Seamus backed away, his own fists up to guard his face. Billy backed him to a wall, then dropped his fists. Seamus took a poke at Billy's jaw, but Billy ducked and sprang back with an uppercut to Seamus's face that slammed Seamus's head against the wall behind him. And a left and a right to Seamus's gut. Seamus doubled forward into Billy's knee, which rose to meet Seamus in the nose. Billy grabbed Seamus by the shirt collar and hurled him into the center of the room, where he tripped on the sheriff's body and fell on the floor.

Billy laughed, the sound of manic joy.

I was mesmerized by the sight of this psychopath. And just as I was contemplating what an ugly death I was sure to meet before sundown, I felt River stick me in the arm with Nails's fishing knife. What the hell?

I turned to her and she gave me an anguished whisper. "Hold still, damn it." I looked down, and she had cut through the duct tape around my wrists. She gave me the knife and I freed my ankles. "Guy," she panted, "you've got to run for it. Your only chance. This fight won't last much longer!"

She was right about that one. Seamus lay on the floor, tucked up like a fetus, and Billy was attacking him with his boots, whooping like a warrior.

Run? How? Where? Billy was between me and the door.

At least he wasn't watching me right now. I stood up and moved quietly behind the long table to the back wall.

My back was turned on the action, and I was on my tiptoes, reaching for a pickax, when I heard Billy shout, "What the fuck?"

I grabbed the axe and spun around in time to see Billy slap River's purple hat and handbag across the room, yank her to her feet by her hair, and slap her face back and forth with his other hand. *"You fucking bitch! Whose side are you on?"*

"Let her go," I shouted.

He did. He let her go and she crumpled to the floor, sobbing. "Oh Jesus Christ," he sighed, as if he had one more fly to swat.

He stepped over River's body and took a step toward the end of the table. The pickax in my hands suddenly felt heavy as lead, but I was unable to drop it.

I did what any rat would do: I ran through the open door behind me, out onto the back porch.

CHAPTER SIXTEEN

I had no time to look around, but I could see it must have been a sleeping porch for the miners, and it was still serving that purpose. Billy and his gang had sleeping bags and packs spread out on the floor close to the wall. The porch was about fifteen feet wide, and the outside edge had no wall.

Escape?

No.

Beyond the porch was a sheer drop to the rocky floor of the Damfool riverbed.

"Okay, you little shit."

He stood in the doorway. He wasn't bothering to grin anymore. He seemed tired, even a little sad. And pissed. His face told me there would be no more games.

I held the axe like a cudgel. It grew heavier and heavier in my grasp. It was as useless as a Ping-Pong paddle against the tide of muscles that was coming at me in slow motion. I lifted it over my head, but by the time I was ready to swing Billy was right in front of me. He easily plucked the pickax out of my grasp and dropped it on the floor. "You're a pain in the ass, you know that, kid?"

I shook my head.

"You like being dropped from big heights, don't you? Relax. The water in the river isn't as deep as the harbor. Ready, squirt?" He grabbed the front of my shirt and lifted me up off the deck.

I watched his face. All business. Then it turned to pleasure, and he gave me one last shot of that gleaming silver tooth.

Then his eyes widened and his grin turned to a spastic snarl. Cords popped out on his neck, and his face and shoulders shook. He dropped me to the floor and spun around to face the little fisherman behind him.

There it was, sticking out of his back just below his ribcage. The wooden handle of Nails's ten-inch blade. A puddle soaking out across the black T-shirt.

Billy roared and groped for Nails's neck, but Nails stepped aside.

Trouble was: Billy wasn't dead yet.

I picked up the pickax and stepped up to the plate. "Jefferson Thomas?" I said.

He turned and pitched in my direction.

I closed my eyes and threw my whole tired body into the swing. I connected. It felt like slamming into an iron wall, and the pickax dropped out of my sweaty hands and clattered again on the floor.

Billy still wasn't down.

He lurched at me and I stepped out of the way. He stopped and teetered on the edge of the porch, as if trying to hold onto his balance.

I reached out to him with a trembling hand and gave him a gentle goodbye pat, just enough to send him on his way.

"*Fu-u-u-u-u-u—*"

Billy Connolly's last word on earth was finished by the crack of his skull hitting a granite boulder two hundred feet below.

I gazed down on the body of the first person I had ever killed.

I had, and I still have, no regrets. I'm glad I killed someone.

And I will never do it again. Ever.

When I turned back from the edge, there was Nails. Nels Andersen, once again holding his fishing knife. He must have pulled it out of Billy's back just before Billy lunged at me. No use wasting a good knife. He had wiped the blood off on his jeans and was once again cleaning his fingernails.

Nails wiggled the knife in his right hand and looked me square in the eye.

"You owe me a drink," he said.

CHAPTER SEVENTEEN

I remember almost nothing of the rescue. From what I've been able to piece together out of River's and Freddy's accounts, it was a pretty efficient operation. After Nails left me out on that sleeping porch to deal with my demons by myself, he hurried over to where Louie Luau was taking care of Freddy. When Freddy heard what had happened, he ran back to the bunkhouse and burst in on what looked like the last scene of Hamlet, just before the curtain falls: bodies all over the floor. He checked first with his mother, whose teeth were chattering so hard she couldn't talk. Then he knelt by Blue Heron, frisked him, and located his cell phone. Called 911.

Freddy came out onto the sleeping porch and found me staring down at the broken heap below.

"Hey," he said.

I'm told there were tears in my eyes when I turned around to face him. "Freddy, I'm sorry. I killed your father."

He nodded at me, the way teenagers nod, with no expression on his face. Finally he spoke. "Way to go."

We walked back into the main room. Seamus and Blue lay on the floor, unconscious and barely alive. The deputies, Eric and Toby, lay on the floor, not so lucky. The rest of us, River, Freddy, Chunky, and I, sat on the bench and waited in shivering silence. The two fishermen had left the scene, forever.

It didn't take long. In about twenty minutes, which felt like twenty hours, we heard the wopwopwopwop of two rescue helicopters. One was an ambulance helicopter from Saint Joseph's Hospital in Eureka; the other was a Huey from the California Department of Forestry, in Redding. Between the two of them, they were carrying two paramedics and three EMTs. They set down in the meadow, rushed into the bunkhouse, and got to work. Seamus, Blue, Chunky, and the dead deputies were placed in the CDF Huey—Seamus and Blue on gurneys, Chunky strapped to a bench, and the bodies in bags.

"The rest of you can ride in the ambulance," one of the paramedics said. "You okay to walk to the craft?"

I said, "There's one more victim."

"Alive or dead?"

"Dead."

"Where is the body?"

I led the paramedic out onto the porch and pointed down into the rocky river bed.

"We don't have time to get that one out now. We'll have to leave that for local authorities." He looked up at a pair of circling turkey vultures. "If they get here in time."

River told me later that it was a beautiful flight down the spine of the Jefferson Alps and then down the west side of the Trinity Alps to Eureka, where we were wheeled into the Emergency Room of Saint Joseph's Hospital. Seamus and Blue went straight into Intensive Care, and the rest of us were admitted for the night, River and Freddy in one room, Chunky and I in another. I don't know what River and Freddy talked about that night. Chunky and I did not say one word to each other, as far as I can remember.

River and the boys were all released the next day, and they were escorted home in the back of a California Highway Patrol car. The three of them had bruised faces, but they did not need surgery. Nor did I, but an MRI revealed a hairline fracture of my left cheekbone, so they kept me another day for observation.

Carol picked me up on Thursday afternoon and drove me home. It was a chilly three-hour drive. She gritted her teeth the whole way, asked me nothing about my adventure, and gave me only clipped answers to my questions about the bookstore, the garden, and a bunch of other subjects neither of us was thinking about.

When we finally got home, we walked into the house, where she poured herself a gin on the rocks. I took a Vicodin and toasted her with my water glass. We walked into the living room, sat down on the sofa and she began to cry. I tried to touch her shoulder and she shrugged me away with an angry glare.

"We have to talk, Carol," I said.

Carol answered, "We certainly do."

We fell into each other's clutching arms, trembling with relief, fear, anger, and most of all, love.

River gave the story to the *Jefferson Republican*, which ran it in the Sunday paper. It filled one short column on page four and had no photos.

Two sheriff's deputies, Eric Larson and Toby Jenkins, were shot to death Tuesday in an altercation involving a marijuana transaction in the Jefferson Alps. Sheriff Blue Heron was also critically injured, suffering bullet wounds to the abdomen. The suspected drug dealer was also killed. His name is being withheld pending further investigation of the case.

Also injured was Jefferson Republican publisher Seamus Connolly, on whose land the incident took place. He and Sheriff Heron cooperated in the effort to apprehend the suspect, and are both recovering well at Saint Joseph's Hospital in Eureka.

Obituaries and funeral announcements for the two fallen officers appear in today's Local Events section.

That was it. So far there has been no follow-up, and I doubt if there will be one. The case was dropped, and no one was charged.

Except for me, of course. Carol charged me with being an idiot.

Seamus was released from the hospital by Tuesday, September 14, one week after the incident. He walked back into his office, or so I'm told, as if nothing had happened. Nobody mentioned anything to him; no one even dared welcome him back. Business as usual.

Sheriff Blue Heron's recovery took longer. He had received severe abdominal injuries and had undergone two surgeries to get his insides straightened out.

I got a call from him Thursday, October 7, letting me know he was back in his office. He asked me to come see him the next morning.

When I told Carol, she said, "I'm coming with you."

"To wish Blue well?"

"To keep you out of trouble," she said. But I suspected it was to find out the latest gossip on the shootout. She wouldn't admit it, but she's always been every bit as curious as I am about what makes people turn into monsters.

"You look good, Blue," she said as we walked into his office. "You've lost some weight."

Blue returned her hug and shook my hand with a smile. "You got that right," he said. "Including one of my kidneys, a bunch of my stomach, and seventeen inches of my small intestine."

"How are you feeling?" I asked.

"Pretty good. Can't drink alcohol anymore, but that's okay. I never could drink alcohol. That's not the problem. Problem is, I have to cut down on the food and no coffee. *No coffee?* Shit. Sit down. Sit, sit."

"So, Blue, I guess I'd better turn myself in," I said, as Carol and I took the metal chairs facing him across the desk. "In case you want to charge me with murder. I don't know what you've heard from Freddy or River, but I'm the one who tipped Billy Connolly over the edge. Did you bring me in here to charge me with murder?"

Carol said, "He's making that up, you know. Guy, for God's sake. Shut up."

Blue laughed out loud. "If you had killed Billy Connolly I'd nominate you for a Nobel Prize," he said. "But that's not how it happened. I ought to know, because I was there."

"How did it happen, then?"

"Billy Connolly went nuts. Maybe it was the drugs, maybe it was just Billy, but he plain went nuts. Killed two men and then tried to kill three more, then freaked out and jumped to his death. End of story. End of case. Good riddance. Sorry, Guy, no medal for you."

Carol reached across the distance and squeezed my hand. I squeezed back.

"I thought you'd like to know the rest of the story about how this all happened," Blue continued. "I figure I better tell you all there is to know, just so you don't get curious and start poking around again. For your own good, is what I mean. Ready?"

Carol said, "Shoot."

Blue winced, then winked. "Okay." He reached under his desk and brought up a laptop computer, the one I'd seen Freddy carry out of River's house, the one with the skull decal on the top.

Carol drew in a sharp breath. "That's Mickey Chan's laptop!"

"So you know this can of worms?"

"What's in it?" I asked.

"Worms, like I said. Snakes, more like it. It's the whole story, folks. The reason Mickey Chan got killed, the reason Pete Thayer got killed."

"What did Mickey have to do with all this?" Carol asked. "He seemed like such a nice kid."

"Bad luck," Blue answered. "Pete had lost an email trail on his computer at the *Nickel* office, probably trashed it by mistake. Or maybe it was a crash, or a software issue, I don't know much about that stuff. Anyway, Pete told Freddy about it, and Freddy asked his friend Mickey to help Pete out. So Mickey did just that. Went over to the office, copied Pete's files onto his laptop, and took them back to his place to see what he could find. What he found out was a ticking bomb, an email correspondence between Pete Thayer and Stew Morris, that reporter I told you about at the San Luis Obispo *New Times*. This guy Morris was doing a story about a parolee from the men's colony down there. Parolee by the name of William Connolly. Stew was in contact with his old friend Pete Thayer to see if Pete knew any home-town gossip about this guy, Billy. Which of course Pete did. Plenty, in fact."

"So that's what got Pete killed?" I asked.

"I guess so. Billy found out Morris was nosing around in his private past, and he fed Morris to the sharks. When he read the email on Morris's computer, he knew he had to get rid of Pete Thayer, too."

"Wasn't that overreacting?" Carol asked. "I mean, Billy was never that secretive about his crimes and misdemeanors. It was all public record, right?"

"Not all of it. Anyway, Billy came north. First person he made contact with was his nephew, Charles. Chunky told Billy that Freddy knew about the email correspondence between Pete and Stew Morris, and also told him Freddy's friend Mickey Chan knew, and that put a death sentence on poor Mickey's head."

"How did Mickey die?" Carol asked.

"The details aren't clear, but Chunky assures me he knew nothing until he read about it in the newspaper. Same with Freddy. I believe them. Chunky's a rotten kid, but not that rotten, and Freddy wouldn't have hurt anybody, let alone his best friend. And now those kids are back in school, as if nothing ever happened."

"So you're saying Billy came back here to Jefferson City specifically to kill Pete Thayer."

Blue nodded. "Which is exactly what he did. But by then he was already going crazy and he started getting some other wild ideas. Gold mining. Stealing River's dope crop and shipping it out on Nails's boat. Kidnapping his son and his nephew. Who knows what else he had planned. Robbing banks? I don't know whether he had it in mind to kill Seamus too, but he sure tried when the opportunity arose. The guy was definitely going batshit. Doing some serious drugs."

"What kind?" Carol asked.

"Little red mothers," Blue answered. "Make you feel good. Bring out the best in you. In Billy's case, the best was the worst. In any case, they kill you, one way or another."

"So what happened that night Billy killed Pete?" I asked.

"Well, Billy comes roaring into town on his motorcycle, and like I said the first person he contacts is Chunky. Calls him from a pay phone downtown, and Chunky tells him come on over, because Seamus has taken the Cherokee and gone away for the weekend, over to Redding. Remember, by this time, Chunky already knew Billy was out of jail, already knew about that email exchange between Stew Morris and Pete Thayer. So Billy tools on over to the Connolly mansion. Chunky doesn't recognize him, but then he hasn't seen the guy since he was a little kid, and that was when Billy was a young man with big hair and a bushy beard. Now he's this practically bald, gray-headed, much older man. Nobody in town was going to recognize him; he couldn't have worn a better disguise. Anyway. Billy asks Chunky where he can find the Pete Thayer guy, and Chunky says what he learned from Freddy, that Pete and River are having dinner at the Redwood Door. So Billy and Chunky get into Seamus's BMW and Billy drops Chunky off at the mall for the evening, promises to come for him later, which never happened. As you know. Billy goes on down to the Redwood Door, parks in the parking lot out back. Puts on rubber gloves. Wipes down all the surfaces on that car, inside and out. Takes a kitchen knife out of his backpack, and waits.

"At this point, I'm making the story up, but it makes sense to me, so here it is. Pete Thayer comes out into the back to smoke a cigarette. So does Billy's old friend Nails, and Nails's new friend Louie. Louie and Nails leave and walk down the alley. Billy gets out of the BMW, walks up to Pete Thayer, asks him what his name is, and that's all she wrote. Does the deed, steals Pete's keychain, goes back to the BMW, lets the air out of the tires for some strange reason, hears traffic in the alley, ducks into the back door of the saloon, goes into the men's room and washes his hands, climbs out the window, and disappears into the rainy night."

"But he stuck around town," Carol said.

"He sure did. Next stop the *Jefferson Nickel* office. Smashes every computer in the place."

"And then he still didn't leave town."

"By then he knew he was in with both feet, might as well go the whole nine yards. Couple of nights later trashed Pete's house when he didn't find any computers there. And of course he had to deal with Mickey Chan. Learned the first night from Chunky that River had a plantation of dope, so it wasn't long before he got together with his old buddy Nails to move some merchandise. Nails didn't know whose dope it was, by the way, didn't want to know. All he knew was Billy had contacts in Port Silva and San Luis, and Nails wanted in on the connection."

"I gather you have no intention of charging Nels Andersen and Louie Luau with a crime?"

"What crime?" Blue answered. "Besides, they're gone, who knows where. And besides, Nails had no idea what he was getting into with Billy. Once he saw what was going on, up there in the Alps, he did what he had to do to get out on the trail so he could intercept me and the boys and warn us. As for Louie, he was just a beast of burden. Did as he was told, till he figured out Freddy was getting beat up. Then he got mad. He probably would have gone in there and kicked Billy all over that bunkhouse, but unfortunately for us we got there first."

"So nobody really got punished for all this slaughter," I said. "Oh, well."

Blue Heron chuckled. "Nobody but Billy. I really ought to charge you and River and Seamus for interfering with my arrest, but of course I won't. Without you I never would have known Billy was back in town, and you're the one who first guessed Billy was the one who killed Pete. You just didn't know why. Of course I'm not going to charge River. As for Seamus, well, we never would have caught up with Billy and the boys if we didn't have his map to the mining camp."

"That reminds me," I said. "Any idea why Billy stole four copies of that book, A Long, Long Crime Ago? Was that necessary?"

"My guess is he was thinking of setting up headquarters at that old mining camp. Nobody knew about that place, but there it was in the book, with maps."

"I told Freddy about those books," Carol said. "I guess Freddy told his father. I had no idea."

"Of course not," I said. "Who we were really dealing with."

"What a paranoid," Carol said. "I mean, as I said, all his past behavior was well known by everybody. Why did he feel he had to murder this Stew Morris person? Then Pete Thayer, of all people?"

"And don't forget Guy Mallon," Blue added. "Billy was planning to murder you, too, Guy. Didn't care much for investigative reporters. He would have whacked Tintin if he had half a chance."

Carol shivered.

Blue nodded. "Hold on. There's more. See, Stew Morris first heard about Billy Connolly last June from a woman who claimed she knew the dude from back before he was in the slammer. Woman named Audrey Coggins. Sound familiar? Right. This Audrey woman called Stew Morris out of the blue and told him a story that made his teeth curl. Carol, you know who Audrey Coggins was?"

"Seamus's wife, right?"

"Guy, Gloria told you that story?"

"The famous Audrey Coggins. I thought she was dead."

"So did most people, including Billy. According to Audrey, he got her drunk, beat her silly, and left her lying on the sofa, then poured kerosene all over the floors, lit the place and left in a hurry. Somehow, Audrey got out of the burning house and staggered uphill to the road, where she passed out. The next thing she remembered was waking up in a clinic in Yreka, where some kind soul had left her on the doorstep in the early hours of the morning. I don't know what happened to her after that, but her face and body were badly burned, because when Morris met with her fifteen years later she was grotesque, covered with scar tissue. She was also dying, last stages of lung cancer, she said. Stew promised to hold the story until after she died. She died in July and that's when Stew contacted Pete."

"So this whole story is locked up in Mickey Chan's laptop?" I pointed at the computer on Blue's desk.

"Was. I erased it this morning."

"One more question," I said. "Did anybody ever go back and retrieve Billy Connolly's body?"

"The CDF went out there, but there wasn't a whole lot to retrieve besides clothing and bones. Scavengers had done most of the cleanup."

CHAPTER EIGHTEEN

That night, because it was Friday after all, Carol and I went to the Redwood Door for our usual. And once again, we found ourselves in the company of River Webster and a gentleman friend. This time the gentleman friend was Blue Heron, the same person we'd spent the morning with. They asked us to join them in their booth, and as we sat down I could see that the two of them were holding hands.

"You're looking good, River," Carol said. "As usual, but better."

"I'm feeling heavenly," River said.

"She should," Blue said. "She's an angel."

River giggled. "Oh hush."

"She visited me nine times while I was in the hospital, down in Eureka," Blue said. "That was a long drive."

"Aw, Blue," she murmured. "You kept count." Then she turned to me and said, "Guess what, Guy. I've been mending fences with Seamus Connolly. Turns out he's a sweetheart. Really."

I scratched my head. *Hmmm.*

"And he wants to bankroll our newspaper."

"Which newspaper?" Carol asked.

"The *Jefferson Nickel.* And we can say anything we want in the paper, because he trusts us to be fair."

"There have to be some strings attached," I said.

"Well, yeah," she admitted. "Seamus convinced me that we don't want to republish my great-grandfather's book. He's right."

"Seamus? Right?" Carol asked.

"It was a good book, but it really was the story of a feud between the two families, is what it was, huh, Guy?"

"That's what it was," I agreed.

"Well, Seamus Connolly and I have agreed that it's high time the Connollys and the Websters stopped fighting. There's only the two of us left, except for our sons, and we don't want to pass this feud on to another generation."

Gloria brought us our drinks, our dinner.

Our dessert. "Coffee for you, Blue?"

"No. Thanks, babe, but no can do."

"Decaf?"

"Not even decaf," Blue lamented.

"What's this world coming to?" Gloria wondered.

"A happy ending," River answered. She kissed Blue's blushing cheek.

"Right," Carol agreed. "No more cliffhangers." She turned to me and added, "From now on. Period."

After Blue and River had left the Redwood Door, Carol and I paid up and strolled out into the chilly, misty October night. We held hands as we walked the two blocks back to Scarecrow Books, where our car was parked.

As we strolled, I wondered aloud, "I'll never understand what River Webster saw in Billy Connolly."

"You're not a woman," Carol answered. "I saw that man only once, and I was tempted to follow him across the street and into the town square."

"What? But—"

"Don't worry, my love. I didn't. I didn't and I wouldn't ever risk the best thing in my life. I don't take dumb chances. Unlike you, I might add." She squeezed my hand hard.

I stopped walking. She stopped too and faced me.

"Don't be angry with me," I pleaded.

"Oh, my darling—"

"Because I'll keep my nose clean from now on."

She smiled. Mist sparkled in the streetlight around her head. "I'm going to hold you to that."

"After all," I said. "I've had my kicks. Did I ever tell you about the night the Palo Alto Bookshop was bombed while I was painting the men's room walls after hours?"

"Oh please," Carol told me. "Just drive me home and put me to bed and tell me something else instead."

ACKNOWLEDGMENTS

I am grateful to a great many people for assistance and support throughout my journey with this book. They include the writing groups from whom I've learned so much: the Great Intenders of Arcata, California; my Pirate Workshops at the Santa Barbara Writers Conference; and my writing classes at Northern Humboldt County Adult Education. Thanks to Morgan Daniel, for information regarding helicopter rescue; to Janet LaPierre, for loaning me one of her wonderful characters for a cameo appearance; to Eric Larson for sacrificing his life for my plot; to Meredith Phillips, Janine Volkmar, and Susan Daniel, for wise and eagle-eyed reading of the manuscript; and to Barbara Peters for rescuing me from my first draft.

ABOUT THE AUTHOR

John M. Daniel is a freelance editor and writer. He has published dozens of stories in literary magazines and is the author of ten published books, including three mystery novels: *Play Melancholy Baby, The Poet's Funeral,* and *Vanity Fire.* He and his wife, Susan, own a small-press publishing company in Humboldt County, California, where they live with their wise cat companion, Warren.

M

CPSIA information can be obtained at www.ICGtesting.com
Printed in the USA
LVOW061751081111

254068LV00007B/79/P

9 781610 090230

mL   1-12